I dedicate this book to the Universe, for not only bringing people into my life, but also removing them. Without you, none of this would have been possible.

Killer Vibes

Julie Rose

Julie Rose

Paperback ISBN: 979-8-9985658-0-9

eBook ISBN: 979-8-9985658-1-6

PROLOGUE

THE RADIO TURNS ON. *Wake Me Up Before You Go-Go* by Wham! starts playing.

I swing my head back and forth, pumping my fists in sync with the beat, belting out the lyrics. I add a kick to my steps as I prance around the room.

Some people read, others take long hot baths, but what really gets me relaxed and in the zone is 80's music. Singing is good for the soul. I recommend everyone set aside some time to just sing and dance like no one is watching. You'll thank me afterwards.

I may not have been on this earth long, but in this short time I've learned a thing or two. Mainly, when you want something done right, you have to do it yourself. No one is going to save you, we all have to save ourselves.

Wait, that's not right. Every now and then, if we're lucky, someone comes along to be strong for us. To do the dirty work.

I clean the blood off my hands and knife, feeling thankful not only to be alive, but to be truly making a change in the world; helping others.

I'm not quite sure how I'll dispose of the body yet, but I'm sure I'll think of something.

CHAPTER ONE

"Hi. My name's Felicia and I'll be your server this evening. Can I start you off with something to drink?"

The restaurant crowd has dwindled down this evening. The bar stays open until two am, but food is only served until nine. The dimly lit restaurant is full of wooden tables with white tablecloths and tea candles in glass jars. The candles put off enough light to read the menus, but not enough to see the paths worn into the floors where the carpet is in need of replacement. Nor the cracks in the plaster walls that strategically placed framed photographs have attempted to hide.

"Thanks doll, we're actually ready to order food too. I'll have linguini with alfredo and a coke. The misses'll have a grilled chicken Caesar salad, dressing on the side, and a diet coke." An older man with greasy dark hair, who appears to never say no to an extra cannoli, sits across from a thin blonde woman who's age cannot be accurately determined. The many glittering gold necklaces in varying lengths do well to hide the telltale neck wrinkles that are helpful in assessing a woman's age.

"Great. I'll be right back with your drinks and your food will be out shortly after." Felicia takes their menus while successfully managing to hide the cringe she's feeling after being referred to as 'doll'.

Felicia couldn't be happier that this was her last table of the night. It's been a long week and she will finally have a weekend off. She grabs two glasses from the rack and starts filling the drink orders. *Why do couples order for one another? It puts off such a controlling vibe. Ugh, I hate this job.* Felicia is fed up with the fake smiles, the meaningless small talk, the subtle ogling that happens to all the female servers, and the less-than-subtle pet-names. Not to mention being trapped indoors all day. She wants to quit, but right now she needs to keep busy. And she needs the money. *I should have finished college, gotten a degree, made something of myself. But no, I met prince charming, fell in love, thought that was all I needed. Then my world crumbled. I'm still young, perhaps my fairytale could still come true. Maybe I just was duped by the wrong guy. He just wasn't the prince charming I originally thought him to be. Maybe he was never supposed to be. Maybe he was the evil fallen angel, sent on a mission from the underworld. Lucifer to do the bidding of all that is evil. I refuse to let myself believe I live in a world where love does not conquer all. There is just so much going against—*

"Shit!" Felicia says louder than she should have. She's spilled coke all over her hand. She has gotten distracted by her thoughts as usual.

She wipes her hand on her apron and begins to make her way back to the table. She first makes sure to pull down the back of her skirt before she leaves the kitchen area. No need to give more of a reason for the oglers to think their actions are warranted. The dress code for this job is ridiculous. Short black skirt and tight white button down shirt for the female servers. Black dress slacks and white button down tops for the males. And let's not even get started on what the hostesses are wearing. Isn't the whole 'sex sells' thing supposed to be *faux pas* in this post 'me too' world? Not in this restaurant. It's referred to as a classy place, if you think Scorcese movies are classy.

"Here you go. Your food will be out shortly," Felicia says, wearing her best customer service smile. This is her last table of the week. She can afford to give them her best. She makes her way back to the kitchen.

Felicia likes making people happy, but it's never come easily to her. That's part of the reason she took this job in the first place. Practice. She figured if she practiced making people happy when there wasn't much at stake, she would be able to get good at it and apply what she learned to situations in the real world—where it does matter. And it is nice to give people what they want, to make them smile, even if it is just because they didn't feel like cooking today. The real reason she likes making people happy is because there is so much beauty in it. Felicia can be quite sappy at times.

Most people don't often stop to appreciate the beauty of the mundane things in this world. A smile on someone's face. A perfectly assembled salad with the ideal ratio of lettuce to croutons. Most people spend their days trapped in their heads. Focusing on thoughts, with no regard for the content.

Felicia stands by the stacks of plates and flatware, waiting for the cooks to call her table order. She starts to prepare the salad so it will be ready when the chicken is done being grilled. There are so many sounds and smells here. Servers hustling around entering orders and filling drinks, cooks preparing the final meals of the night, dishwashers getting things cleaned for the following day. *I guess this job isn't so bad. I just need to focus more on the beauty of everything around me. The positive aspects. Be in the moment. Not let myself be distracted by the bad things. It's much easier when I'm outside, in nature. Easier to take in all the sights and the sounds. The aroma after rain once the sun comes out. The grass turning green in the springtime while everything else is still muted and bleak. The warmth of the sunshine through a window. The bright pop of color from the–*

"Felicia! Your order's done! It's already getting cold!" Jeff, the cook, yells from the flattop. "Seriously Felicia, hurry up, you always do this, we all want to go home!"

"Sorry." Felicia places the chicken into the salad, grabs the rest of the food and heads over to her table.

"Here you go," she places the plates down, "can I get you guys anything else?"

"Took you long enough sweet cheeks. Busy flirting with the chef?" This wannabe *capo* smirks at her. The woman sitting across from him gives him a look that could send Satan himself back to hell. He notices, and with a stutter, adds, "I'm just messing with you hun, we're all good." Italian men are always so powerful until an Italian woman decides she wants to be in charge. Then, God help the man who becomes her target.

Remembering most of her income comes from tips, Felicia smiles and says, "I am so sorry about the delay. The cooks were trying to close the grill and just got a bit sidetracked. I had to wait for the grilled chicken to be done. I am so very sorry about the wait." When you are getting tipped, it's always helpful to deflect and blame someone else. This was just one lesson Felicia learned during her time in the restaurant industry. The patron then feels sorry for the server. It quite often makes the tips better.

Felicia walks back to the kitchen to finish up her side work so she can get home at a decent hour. She checks back on the table a few times—always with her best smile—before giving them their check. She even decided to leave her skirt ridden up. It is her last table of the week after all, didn't she say she could afford to give them her best?

Once she sees the couple leave, she goes back to check her tip. 25 percent; they must've been pleased. These tricks she's accumulated do work. She inwardly smiles at her success. She finishes up, cashes out, grabs her coat, says good-night to everyone, and heads out the door.

She walks to the corner and waits for the traffic signal to change. It's a chilly evening. It always is at this time of year. The wind is much colder than the air and the temperature difference stings her bare legs. She's starting to shiver as the little white man lights up on the traffic signal allowing her to cross the street. She walks down a half a block careful not to trip on the raised portions of sidewalk that lost their battle against the mature roots of the nearby cherry trees. Felicia approaches the house and is met with the sight of candle lights flickering through the darkness. *I really need to get my own place*. Taking a breath, she quietly turns the key in the door and opens it. She is assaulted by the aroma of incense. She tiptoes through the foyer and has just started her fourth step on the stairs when she suddenly hears, "Felicia, why don't you join us?"

"Ugh, I'm caught," Felicia says under her breath. Then speaking at a volume loud enough to be heard she replies, "Not tonight, thanks. It's been a long day and I'm really tired." She realizes she's still hovering in mid stride and places her foot down on the tread.

Nicole's smiling face pops out from the doorway to the living room. "All the more reason to join us!" she says while still smiling. "Come on Felicia, we need to make the time to take care of our spiritual selves. I could feel your stress as soon as you walked through the door!" Nicole takes a few steps forward and gives puppy dog eyes, "pleeeeease?"

"Fine," answers Felicia, "but only for a few minutes...and only because you're my big sister and I love you."

"Yay!" Nicole smiles even more brightly and claps her hands together.

They enter the living room—the Zen room as it has become more commonly known—where Sean is sitting in lotus position with that subtle distant smile he continuously seems to have plastered on his face. *They both really buy into this crap*, Felicia thinks to herself while attempting to match their enthusiasm. It's difficult to conceal the eye roll that she feels coming on. She's had to do that enough times already during her shift at work.

"I'm so happy you're joining us. Your additional energy will really help strengthen our meditation session," says Sean.

Those words did it. The eye roll escaped. Felicia

couldn't help it.

"Your skepticism is understandable," Sean says in a voice that sounds eerily like a preacher. "But give it a chance. Meditation has turned my life around. And, you know, I was hesitant to 'drink the Kool Aid' at first as well. But I assure you...it is delicious." He drags out this last word like he's part of an infomercial.

Sean was once not so long ago—although it seems a different life—an alcoholic. After his alcoholism caused the loss of several jobs and destroyed countless relationships, he then nearly killed someone during one of his many drunk driving episodes. That was the straw that broke Sean and forced him to accept his reality. He had a problem. After several months of trying Alcoholics Anonymous meetings—court ordered—he managed to convince himself that it wasn't working and he'd always be an alcoholic. He readily accepted his fate. Both his mother and father had been alcoholics and they turned out just fine. Soon after this acceptance, he found himself in a liquor store one Tuesday night. He bought himself a bottle of Cognac; if he was going to be an alcoholic he might as well be a sophisticated one. He strolled from the liquor store towards his home on State Street. He was debating on whether or not to start drinking before he arrived home when he started to hear the sound of drums. He checked his bottle to make sure he wasn't already drunk. Nope, seal is still intact.

Where the hell is that noise coming from? His eyes were scanning the surrounding store fronts. He walked until the sound got louder and he noticed a sign:

ARE YOU SUFFERING FROM DEPRESSION, LONELINESS, ADDICTION, OR ANY OTHER HEALTH ISSUES????? JOIN OUR

HEALING DRUM CIRCLE!!!! FREE!!!!!!!!!! TUESDAY 8/13
8PM. <u>ALL</u> ARE WELCOME!!!!!!!!!!

Someone went a little trigger happy with the punctuation marks. He chuckled to himself. The drums had then stopped suddenly. Beyond the sign, there was a footpath leading between two buildings. A movie theater with string lights out front was on the left and a quaint store with crystals and wind chimes adorning the wrap around porch was on the right. The sign for the crystal store read Feeling & Healing. *They must be the weirdos hosting this drumming event.*

Just then, as he restarted his walk home, he looked up the street and saw the most beautiful woman he had ever laid eyes on. He could almost *feel* her beauty. She was practically sprinting towards him, her cheeks flushed, blond hair sticking to her sweating face, her hands grasping at her flowing skirt, holding it above her knees.

"Did I miss it?" the woman is pants to him, "did they start yet?"

For the first time in Sean's 28 years of life—subsequently the last time as well—he was without words. He tried to open his mouth to say something but the words just would not come. Just when he thought he had composed himself enough to speak, he was cut off by the drums starting up again.

"Oh sugar! We're missing it!" the woman grabbed his arm and pulled him down the footpath, "My name's Nicole. C'mon!"

Sean had no choice but to follow behind—not that he wanted to leave now—and the pair emerged into a backyard strung with the same lights as the theater.

Glints of light could be seen reflecting from the artfully crafted lawn ornaments covering every open inch of the yard. Mature oak trees caused a buffer between this and the adjacent yards. There were 8 people seated on pillows on the ground in a circle around a large bonfire. Small handmade drums of various colors and styles were positioned between each one of their legs.

The drumming ceased once again. A petite woman in a flowing white skirt and dark corseted top with long mousy hair stood up. "Welcome. We are just beginning. Please, grab a drum and join us." The woman motioned with her open hand over to the side of the circle. Sean now noticed the collection of drums. He and his guiding angel each grabbed a drum and took a seat on the remaining empty pillows on the lawn.

This was 6 years ago and was the beginning of not just Sean's new spiritual journey, but also the beginning of he and Nicole's relationship. Needless to say, he never did open that bottle of cognac.

"You're such a dork," Felicia says as she playfully sticks her tongue out. "I don't know why my sister loves you so much, but since you make her happy, I guess I'm happy to put up with you." She smiles and gives him a playful punch on the arm. Once you get past his oddities, deep down he really is a great guy, but Felicia will never ever let him know that.

"She opened my eyes to all the beauty in the world. She completes me," he threw a wink and air kiss to Nicole. This action once again elicits the all too familiar eye roll from Felicia.

"Thank you, hun," says Nicole while shooting a 'you're just jealous' look at her sister. "That's enough idle chit chat, you're disrupting the deep peaceful vibe."

Felicia exhales and gives what will hopefully be her last eyeroll of the evening. She then joins them on the floor.

Nicole & Sean may be quirky—and often disgustingly cute to a level of annoyance—but they took Felicia in when she was at her lowest, when she was desperate. And they did it with smiles on their faces and no questions asked. Well, there was one question: Are you willing to let us help you? And Felicia was. The least she could do now was humor them while they showed her what their definition of help looked like.

Nicole lights an incense cone. It is not the first one that was lit this evening. This household should buy stock in the stuff.

"Now, relaxing into a comfortable position, closing our eyes, we simply breathe."

Simple is not how Felicia would refer to these exercises. Meditating has never come easily to her. Her mind is constantly full of thoughts. Often pleasant ones, sometimes not so much. She rarely manages to unwind before bed, and even less frequently feels rested or peaceful upon waking in the morning.

Felicia sits in the candlelit room with her eyes closed, trying to focus solely on her breathing. *This is so annoying. How is a person supposed to not let their thoughts distract them? Therapists tried to get me to meditate in the past. They would tell me to picture my thoughts as leaves floating down a river. Just let the thoughts float down the river, they'd say. Definitely easier said than done. But it's okay, I can at least try. Practice makes perfect! I'm picturing this thought as a leaf floating down the river. And this one. And this one. Ut-oh! My river is clogging up with leaves, causing a dam.* Felicia inwardly chuckles. She finds herself hilarious. *A nearby town starts flooding. Children struggle to climb out of school bus windows as the water level in the streets start lifting the bus off its wheels, they start screaming for their mommies, 'I'm too young to die, I promise I'll eat all my veggies.' Pandemonium breaks loose. Pets are floating in the streets, doggy paddling for their lives—Jesus Felicia, stop this. Back to your breath.* She takes a few breaths. In and out, in and out. *Breathing is supposed to ground you, they say. Ground you? What does that even mean? Nicole and Sean use the term all the time. I've heard it from a therapist once or twice before as well. What was that one's name? Kristen? Katelyn? Kathy! I think it was Kathy. She was the one who put me on Valium. Now* that *is grounding. I sometimes couldn't move. I would literally be stuck* on the ground. *Good times. Haha. Shit, Felicia you're lost in your thoughts again. Just focus on your breath. Lets try counting to ten. Breathe in. One. Breathe out. Breathe in. Two. Breathe out. Ugh. This is going to take forever. Why am I even doing this? You know why Felicia. It's because not all the advice from Tweedledee and Tweedledum is useless. And even though you don't want to accept it, it's often quite helpful. Hey! It's not nice to call people names Felicia. They love you and you love them. Oh good. And now I'm arguing with myself. Great. Where was I? Right. Breathing. Focus on breathing.*

Felicia truly has benefitted from some of Nicole and Sean's advice in the past. They once suggested she try a relaxing hobby and even gave her a list of ideas, things to make her more mindful, as that was another way to relieve stress. She tried painting. That did not work out. She would start by spending hours scrolling through pictures on her phone for inspiration and then end up getting frustrated when she couldn't come up with anything. She tried jigsaw puzzles. They were good. Fun. But they ended up being counterproductive because her eyes kept drying out and she would develop soreness from her neck being bent looking at pieces. However, the last thing she tried was gardening. She started by planting some tomato seeds, which seemed boring at first, although she did enjoy the way the dirt felt and smelled. Once the first seed germinated, she was hooked. She felt a sense of accomplishment bringing something to life. And after several weeks of nurture, she had the best looking tomatoes she'd ever seen. And they tasted even better than they looked. She never knew so much flavor could exist in such a simple food.

She then moved on to planting spring bulbs, which was easier as there was no care involved once they were planted. They simply bloomed into these wonderfully smelling flowers nurtured only by nature itself. But she also loved getting her hands dirty. She started weeding the existing flower beds in the yard, a task Sean willingly gave up to her. She found that during these weeding sessions, she would be fully present in the moment and her mind did not wander from the specific task she was involved in. She spent as much time as she could planting and tending to the garden all season long. Then winter arrived again and Felicia became once again stressed without her outlet of gardening. She had a few houseplants under a grow light, but it just wasn't the same.

After twenty minutes of struggling through the meditation, Felicia says goodnight to Nicole and Sean and makes her way up the stairs for what will hopefully be a peaceful night of sleep.

CHAPTER TWO

FELICIA AWAKENS IN A small puddle of sweat and a large puddle of terror. She hears and feels her heart beating from inside her ears. Her legs start trembling. Her jaw seizes shut. The puddle of terror is rapidly growing and threatening to drown her. She still hasn't opened her eyes. Her skin starts buzzing with electricity; all of her nerve endings begin to fire at once. *It's just a panic attack Felicia. You've had a million before. You know what to do.* She opens her eyes.

Felicia has had many panic attacks before, though the exact number is unknown. If one were to ask her, she would say it falls somewhat shy of exactly six million. She started having the attacks as an adolescent, shortly after her grandmother passed away from cancer. After bearing six months of testing to rule out any physiological abnormalities or neurological disorders, she was handed a diagnosis: Panic Disorder with and without Agoraphobia. She was told it was a lifelong—albeit manageable—condition; a combination of therapy and medication should get her symptoms well under control.

There were two different targets for the medications. One was to be used in emergency situations. They were to be taken to calm an attack once one had already started. This was achieved by causing drowsiness, so unfortunately they could not be used in all situations; namely those which happened while driving, walking, working or other various activities when one wanted to properly function. The other medication was used to prevent the attacks *before* they started. This was achieved by the geniuses in the pharmaceutical industry, by creating walking zombies incapable of having any sort of emotion at all. Apparently, it's hard to zero in on just fear, so the solution was to just drown out all feelings. Aside from the side effects that were allegedly supposed to wear off once one's body got used to the medication, one too many *grounding* sessions convinced Felicia to give up on medications altogether.

Therapy, although it did not have the side effects of medication, was simply not very helpful. Just the thought of discussing her emotions with a stranger never appealed to Felicia. She did not want people knowing what was going on inside her head. She didn't see the point. She was, however, taught learning techniques focused mostly on relaxation. These included distraction techniques, breathing in and out on a count, and progressive muscle relaxation. Felicia found some of these marginally helpful in the past. She attempts to use one now.

You got this Felicia. Breathe in 1-2-3-4, hold 1-2-3-4-5-6-7, breathe out 1-2-3-4-5-6-7-8. The 4-7-8 breathing technique. The names are made simple on purpose so they can be easily remembered under stressful conditions. Felicia manages to do this a few times and the room finally stops feeling like it is closing in around her. Now that she's starting to relax, she suddenly feels the need to pee. Not just any need, but the 'I've been on the longest road trip of my life' type of need. This always happens when she calms down after panicking.

Felicia hops out of bed and runs to the bathroom. After relieving herself of what feels like a month's worth of fluids, she slowly makes her way back to bed. She checks the time on her phone. 3:46 am. *At least I don't have work tomorrow.* She settles back under the covers.

Ugh, my feet are freezing. It's okay. I'm sure it was just because I just walked on that cold tile floor. They'll warm up. Suddenly, a wave of terror hits her again. The cold from her feet spreads up her legs and she starts trembling. The cold she feels does not stop the sweat from starting to form around her hairline. Her nerve endings all start firing again as her body begins to shake. *It's just the residual adrenaline. You're going to be fine. It's just leftover panic.* She tries to settle down by forcing her muscles into relaxation.

But is it going to be fine? Maybe I'm coming down with something. It is flu season. And I come in contact with a lot of people at my job. Maybe these are chills and I have a fever. Felicia puts the back of her hand to her forehead, then her cheek, then forehead again. *How do mothers do this and just know if their child has a fever? I sure can't ever tell.* The trembling continues and now the sheets begin to darken once again with sweat. *No Felicia. You know better than this. It's just panic. Just panic? That's hilarious. Panic is the most extreme form of fear. I think that's the literal definition. Just Panic. Ha. Ugh. This is ridiculous. Why does this have to happen to me? It's fine. It'll go away if you just do your breathing exercises again. C'mon. Breathe in 1-2-3-4.* Felicia tries to focus on breathing but her chest is doing all the work while it feels as though an elephant is sitting upon it. Panic is flooding her system. Adrenaline is taking over and there is no way to stop it. The trembling escalates into full blown seizing, the bed continues to darken with sweat until a puddle forms around her. All sense of time ceases to exist. All sense of control ceases to exist. Nothing exists in this moment but terror.

Felicia's mind is flooding with thoughts, though she cannot grasp onto a single one. It's like being in a downpour while attempting to catch a single raindrop in your hand. She struggles with the push and pull of trying to control while simultaneously also trying to let go. *Fighting will only make it worse.* She knows this somewhere deep within her mind. Riding the wave is the only way to keep her head above water yet she just can't seem to stop the fighting.

Please, please, please, why won't this just end? I can't take it anymore. No one can handle this kind of stress and come out of it unmarked. Please just stop. Wait, no. This doesn't need to stop, that's fighting. I have to stop fighting it and just know that it will pass. My job in this moment is not *to end the panic, but to simply allow it to pass.* Felicia tries to go with it and just allow her body to do what it wants to do. Allow the tension, allow the sweat, allow the trembling, allow the pain, allow the fear.

She can't manage to stop fighting it. She will not give up control. She cannot give up control. She must get this panic under her control. *Be brave, be strong. It's just adrenaline. Idea! You can burn it up. I can burn it off.* Felicia gets out of bed and starts pacing back and forth. She is very conscious of the sound her footsteps are making. She doesn't want to wake Nicole and Sean. The only thing worse than being alone in panic is others witnessing her loss of control. *This is just your body pumping out adrenaline Felicia. Nothing terrible is going to happen. This will pass.* She continues pacing back and forth with the lightest steps she can muster. She takes another look at the time. 4:21am. The pacing is starting to tire her out, though not make her sleepy, just physically tired. Sleepy and tired are definitely not the same thing.

Felicia suddenly hears a loud noise come from outside. *That sounded like...like trash cans falling over. It's probably just some raccoons.*

She welcomes the distraction as she goes to the window, draws up the shade, and peers out into the early morning. It is not some raccoons. She sees a car halfway across the sidewalk, idling. The headlight beams are mostly blocked by the trash cans that seem to have stopped the vehicle's forward momentum. She continues to stare for a few moments, trying to fully grasp the scene in front of her. She thinks she is seeing movement inside the car, but the glare of the streetlight is making it difficult to understand exactly what is going on. Then the shape of a hand appears against the inside of the rear window. A child's hand.

Felicia grabs her phone and runs down the stairs two at a time, not paying any mind to the noise she's making with these steps. She runs into the street and approaches the vehicle, taking in everything at once. There is trash everywhere. There is the rumble of the motor running. There is a woman slumped over in the driver's seat. There is a child in the backseat whose cries

for mommy can be heard from the open driver's side
window.

Felicia tries to open the door closest to her. Locked.
She runs around to the other side of the vehicle, reaches
into the open window, and finds the button to unlock
all the doors. She presses it. She runs back around to
the other side of the vehicle, opens the front passenger
door, and is immediately assaulted by a pile of newspa-
pers. She kicks them out of the way. Her first concern
is putting the vehicle into park. Then she pulls the keys
from the ignition.

Meanwhile, the child is yelling, "Mommy! Wake up!,"
from her buckled position in the backseat.

"It's okay sweetheart," Felicia is softly saying to the
child as she is dialing 911 on her cellphone. She places
a comforting hand on the little girl. "It's okay. Just try to
tell me what happened." The phone is ringing.

Through glassy eyes, the little girl says, "Mommy fell
asleep."

"Nine-One-One. Where is your emergency?" Felicia's
attention is pulled to the voice coming from her cellphone.

"Outside of 242 South State Street, Newtown."

"Borough or Township?"

"Borough," Felicia says while being mildly confused.
*Don't they want to know why I am calling? I call bullshit
on television shows.*

"Name?"

"Felicia Gerhard"

"Phone number?"

"215-555-4870"

"What is your emergency?"

There it is. "There is an unconscious woman in a vehicle that lost control outside my home. We need an ambulance." Felicia hears some tapping of keys on a keyboard.

"Emergency units are en route. Is the victim breathing?"

Felicia looks over for signs of chest movement. "She appears to be. Is there something I should be doing?" The little girl has now managed to have unbuckled herself and gotten out of her car seat. She is leaning forward, shaking her mother. Felicia realizes she hasn't mentioned the child to the operator. "There is a little girl here in the car with her."

"Is the child injured?"

"She seems fine, just scared for her mom."

"Can you stay with her until EMS arrives?"

Sirens are sounding in the area and flashing lights can already be seen reflecting off the windows of the buildings down the street. "Absolutely. They're almost here already." Felicia hangs up the phone, not knowing whether or not she should have, but also not worrying about it. The calvary is arriving.

Officer Hibbs seems to be out of the cruiser even before it comes to a complete stop. He has the traditional blonde cop crew cut, is nicely built, and in his early twenties The look on his face is that of a toddler on Christmas morning. It is not often that the Newtown Borough police receive calls that could potentially require some of their academy training. His partner, Officer Dart, is more composed as he exits the cruiser. He has spent some time eating donuts and coffee, his body shows it. He is balding and looks like he should soon retire. This is clearly not his first rodeo.

The ambulance arrives soon after, and before anyone has the chance to speak, the two EMTs are already halfway into the vehicle checking on the little girl and her mother.

Both officers approach Felicia. Hibbs is shifting from foot to foot while Dart calmly starts in with the questions. "Good morning miss," he smiles, "Can you tell us what happened here?" Felicia does to the best of her ability.

After answering all the questions, with the ambulance is gone, Felicia finds herself back in bed. *Well, that was interesting.*

She is asleep before another thought can arise.

CHAPTER THREE

THE HOME IN WHICH Felicia lives with her sister was built in the early 1900s. Even after undergoing various updates and remodels by the previous owners, the historic charm can still be seen in certain untouched areas. It is 11:00am and Felicia is sitting at the kitchen table. She is drinking a hot cup of decaf green tea. The first time her sister had given a cup to her, she was on the fence about even trying it. Then, Nicole started to explain all the health benefits and how it is a sacred drink in many ancient religions. In an effort to stop the forthcoming lesson (ahem...lecture), Felicia took a sip and blurted out, "Who cares? It's delicious!" and smiled as big as she could. Tea then became the way she started each day. After all this time, she does actually like it.

Nicole comes in from the backyard. "Oh, hi! I didn't hear you come down. How did you sleep?"

"Great," Felicia smirks, "that was of course, after the police and ambulance left."

"Police and ambulance?" Nicole looks as if she might be physically ill. "What happened?"

Nicole and Sean both possess the uncanny ability to sleep like the dead. They claim it's from their meditation practices and Zen lifestyle, but Nicole at least, has always slept like that. Felicia never mentions this aspect when her sister brings up the positive side effects of meditation. She tries to be a good sister.

"I heard a noise last night, looked out the window, and saw a car crashed outside of the house." Felicia went on to explain everything that occurred.

"Oh my! What a night!" Nicole exclaims. After pausing for a moment to reflect, she adds, "My sister is a hero!"

"I wouldn't say that. All I did was make a phone call. I'm fairly certain the emergency response units were the heroes." It's too early in the morning for an eye roll.

"You always sell yourself short Felicia. Not everyone would have reacted as you did. You could have very well saved that woman's life, not to mention her child. You potentially saved that little girl from growing up without a mother."

"I think you're being a bit dramatic," Maybe it's not too early. Felicia rolls her eyes. Yet deep down, Felicia feels a twinge of something only vaguely familiar. *Could this feeling be a sense of pride and accomplishment? Stop. This is silly. All I did was make a phone call. Despite what my sister thinks, anyone would've done the same. On the other hand, Nicole could be right. Maybe I did save that woman and her child. I'll tell you what, this feeling feels good. Better than good actually. It feels amazing. 'Felicia the Superhero'. I like the sound of that. Feels a bit boring though. I should come up with an alter ego superhero name. The superman to the Clark Kent. The Spiderman to the Peter Parker. The Incredible Hulk to the—*

"Earth to Felicia!" Nicole is smiling at Felicia with her eyebrows raised.

"Sorry, I think I may still be half asleep." Felicia offers as a cover.

"Why don't you come outside with us? It's a beautiful day and Sean and I are working in the garden. Nature always helps us connect with the best the universe has to offer. Wakes you right up!"

It is a warm sunny morning—which do not come too often this early in spring—and Felicia would not mind taking advantage of it. "Let me finish my tea first. I'll be out in a few minutes."

"Perfect." Nicole walks towards the door and kisses Felicia on the head on her way by. "My sister, the hero," she says.

Felicia continues sipping her tea while musing about last night. She was mid panic attack when everything started. And she had simply forgotten about it by the time she was halfway down the stairs. It was as though a switch was flipped. Full blown panic attack. Flick. Completely calm. Alert and ready for action. Felicia has heard before that one surefire way to take care of your-self is to focus on taking care of others, but that never resonated with her. It always seemed like just another half assed distraction ploy that only works part of the way and some of the time. Who knows? Maybe this was something she could get into. If nothing else, she greatly enjoyed this fulfilling feeling afterwards. *Maybe I should find a new job. Something fulfilling. It's at least something to think about.* She finishes her tea—leaving the dregs as is customary—and puts her cup into the sink. She heads out into the yard.

The rear part of the yard is partially shaded by mature

oak trees. The rest is open sky and full sunshine. There is a vegetable garden with raised beds and trellises. There is a path of stones winding through two small ornamental beds. Nicole is kneeling on the ground, her hands covered in dirt. Sean, however, is simply standing there, facing one of the mature trees, arms out, not moving.

"Good morning Felicia. Beautiful day, isn't it?" Sean asks from his stationary pose with a child-like smile on his face.

"Good morning. Yes, it is a beautiful day. Are you giving the day a hug?" Felicia laughs.

"No silly. I'm doing Qi Gong—tree meditation," he pauses to take in and let out a breath, "although, that's not a bad idea. To hug this glorious day."

"I literally do not know how you deal with him," Felicia says to her sister, employing one of her all too common eye rolls.

"What do you mean? I think he's wonderful." Nicole genuinely means it.

"Never mind," Felicia smiles, "what can I help you guys with?"

"This bed here needs weeding so we can get the cool weather veggies in the ground. Do you want gloves?"

"No thanks." Felicia never wears gloves while gardening unless she's working around thorns. With all of Nicole and Sean's eccentricities this is one thing Felicia thinks they have right; gardening with bare hands. Feeling the earth and plants does something for your well-being.

After 45 minutes, the vegetable garden is ready. Felicia feels great and realizes she didn't get lost in her thoughts once the entire time. "I do love gardening.

Maybe I can get a job doing this," Felicia says, more to herself more than anyone else.

"That sounds like a great idea!" Sean chimes in, having heard. He pauses and then a smile spreads across his face. "Oh, I know! Let's manifest it! Spring is the best time for manifesting anyway!"

"Why must you make everything weird?" Felicia asks as she lets out a sigh.

"He's not wrong, Felicia," Nicole says with an air of seriousness. "For hundreds of years people have been manifesting their desires. I recently read an article online stating that the CIA actually proved its benefits. Manifestation really works."

Felicia is in a good mood today, so she might as well humor them. They just seem so incredibly enthusiastic about all this stuff. It would be like disappointing a child if she didn't let them run with their ideas every once in a while. "Okay," she says, "let's manifest it. What do I do?" Felicia is proud of herself for not rolling her eyes.

Sean is beaming. "You say, 'I have a career as a gard ener.'"

"Okay. I have a career as a gardener." Felicia nods and smiles. "Now what?"

"Now, believe it as it already has happened," Sean smiles back.

"Believe it?"

"Yup! Believe it."

"Okay. I believe it. Now what?"

"Now the universe will provide."

"Okay...?"

"Okay!" Sean's shoulders relax. "Time for lunch!" He scurries off inside.

Felicia turns to Nicole, "that's it? Is he for real?"

"Yes. And I wouldn't have him any other way." Nicole smiles, grabs her sister by the arm, and they both make their way into the house.

After lunch, Felicia finds herself upstairs in her bedroom. In the remaining daylight, we can see the room's plaster walls are painted a pale shade of blue. There isn't much blue to be seen however, as the walls consist mostly of windows. This bedroom is on the corner of the home and two bay windows with transoms are facing south and east. The window ledges are the perfect environment for growing flowers. Felicia lovingly waters her plants and pinches off a few browning leaves. Flowers always bloom sooner in her mini greenhouses and she can see some fresh buds starting to form, adding to the appeal of bright petals that have already opened. She smiles inwardly with anticipation of the next flowers.

Felicia looks over at the pile of boxes in the corner. She moved in with her sister and brother-in-law a little over a year ago, after her breakup. She moved to Colorado with her prince charming at the young age of 19. She was in love, so it was not even a difficult decision to leave her family and friends behind, pack up all of her belongings, and move across the country. Eight years later, she had just as easily packed up all of her belongings and moved back to the east coast to her hometown in eastern Pennsylvania. A stack of a few remaining boxes are still piled in the corner of her room. At first, she had been putting off fully unpacking because she always had it in her mind that this was a temporary living arrangement; a stopgap on the way to bigger and better things. Later, she simply hadn't had the motivation to unpack. In reality, she hasn't had the motivation to do much of anything. Survival has been the only thing on her mind. But today is a good day and she is going to take advantage of her uplifted mood and accomplish this unforgotten task.

Felicia prances over to the corner with a lightness in her step. She kneels down and pulls open the flaps of the top box. It is mostly full of small kitchen appliances and utensils . *No reason to unpack these.* She'll need everything in here when she moves into her own place, but right now it seems unnecessary. *Wait, should I be using these things? I use my sister and brother-in-law's toaster, is that weird? Should I be using my own? Stop it Felicia. No. It would be more weird to have a second toaster sitting on the counter. Whatever, next box.*

This next box is full of a potpourri of all sorts of things: a winter hat, small travel blanket, hairbrush, two tampons, picture frame without a picture, keys to unknown locks, a plastic figurine, one lonely glove without its mate, a slinky, and a pink Swiss army knife. And that's just what can be seen on the top layer without digging. *What am I going to do with all this junk? Why would anyone pack a box like this? I don't pack like this. What was I thinking? I'm normally so organized. Oh, that's right. David. David is why I did this. And it's also why I can't do this right now. My head hurts.* Felicia becomes aware of every heartbeat in her chest. The room is suddenly a tropical rainforest. It's hot and moist with a cold damp chill. The air is too dense to comfortably breathe. There is a droning sound that cannot be identified. Felicia is having a panic attack. Again.

She begins searching the recesses of her mind for all the tips and tricks she's gathered over the years. Nothing is coming to her. She's in for another hell of a night.

Chapter Four

THE SUN IS SHINING in through the open curtains of the bedroom windows. The boxes are still sitting in the corner. To say Felicia did not sleep well these past two nights is an understatement. Even the waking hours of the weekend are a blur filled with memories best forgotten. It is late Monday morning. The alarm on her phone is chiming for the 3rd time. Felicia cancels the alarm once again and glances at the time. She can't stay in bed any longer or she will be late for work. She gets up, brushes her teeth, and quickly gets dressed. She takes a peek at her plants. She notices a Gardenia bloom is all but spent, so she plucks it from its stem and places it behind her ear. She eats in a hurry and rushes off to the restaurant for work.

When Felicia arrives at the restaurant, she begins refilling the salt and pepper shakers—the closers must not have done it last night. The lunch rush doesn't start for almost an hour. A few customers are slowly starting to arrive for late breakfasts. An older couple is seated in Felicia's section. A woman with white hair in a modern cut, wearing clothing matching current trends, sits across from an older gentleman with gray hair who dons a business suit. She recognizes the woman—Betty. Betty comes in every week and always requests Felicia to be her waitress. She does not recognize the man. Felicia approaches the table with a smile on her face.

"Good morning. How are we doing today? Can I start you off with a beverage?"

Betty smiles and says, "We're doing just fine, thank you. We'll both have coffee. Black."

"Perfect. I'll be right back with those." As Felicia is filling their mugs with coffee, she notices Betty leaning in to talk to the man as they both keep glancing in her direction. Felicia starts to feel self-conscious. *They're obviously talking about me.* She glances down to make sure she has pants on and that both of her shoes match. She *was* in a rush this morning. She does, and they do. *Are my clothes stained? Ugh, I'm probably just being paranoid.*

She makes her way back to the table with the coffee for her guests while trying to push aside her paranoid anxiety. "Here you are. Are you ready to order?"

"Just the coffee is fine, thank you. We are having a business meeting."

Felicia now notices the papers and folders spread out on the table. "Okay. Flag me down if you need anything, I don't want to be a bother and interrupt your meeting." *Great, this'll be a large order; and if the order is small, so is the tip.* Once her back is turned, she rolls her eyes. *Just two cups of coffee and they'll probably be sitting at my table—taking up real estate—well into the upcoming lunch rush.*

Felicia enters the kitchen and starts to socialize with the other servers who are gathered around using this time to take a breather and get their bearings before the lunch rush begins.

"Ugh, I have a coffee only business meeting in my section," Felicia says to no one in particular. Complaining is and always will be a universal way to bring people together.

"Sucks to be you," says Kendall, a young server with blond curly hair and a permanent case of resting bitch face.

"Haha. I know, right?" Felicia replies. After all this time, she's learned many tricks to improve her tips and converse with customers, but she still does not know how to do friendly small talk with people her own age—ones who could potentially be her friends. She leans against the counter and tries to look as normal as possible. She has never been one to easily fit in.

"Nice flower," Kendall says, pointing to the gardenia behind Felicia's ear. Kendall starts to giggle and looks at Alyssa, another young server, who joins her in the giggling.

Damnit Felicia. You're not in Hawaii. People don't just walk around with flowers in their hair. Quick. Think of something. "Oh, I forgot it was there. I took my niece to school this morning. She asked me to wear it and I guess I forgot to take it out after I left." *Excellent cover Felicia. These people haven't ever tried to get to know you. They don't know you don't have a niece.* She takes the flower from behind her ear and carelessly tosses it in the trashcan. "I just can never say no to that adorable face." Felicia then walks away before she accidentally says something that ruins her lie.

She decides to check on her table. Before approaching, she glances at Betty and her business partner from the doorway of the kitchen. She sees they are looking in her direction again. Instead of getting paranoid again, she considers maybe they have decided to eat after all.

She approaches, "How are you two making out?"

"Fine, thank you." The expression on Betty's face changes to disappointment. "What happened to that beautiful gardenia that was behind your ear?"

Shit. I should've left it in. Betty likes flowers, I know this. It may have helped my sure to be meager tip. "Oh," Felicia reaches up and touches the place where the flower was, feigning surprise. "I was in the kitchen, leaning down to reorganize a bottom shelf, it must've fallen out." *Sounds plausible. Sometimes I wish lying didn't come so easily to me, it kind of makes me feel like I could easily become a horrible person.*

"What a shame. It was so pretty. Where did you even get a gardenia at this time of year?"

"It's one of my own. I grow them at home."

"You can keep gardenias alive indoors? And get them to bloom?" Betty steals a quick glance at the man she is sitting with. She returns her gaze to Felicia. "I knew you liked flowers, but I didn't know you also had a green thumb."

"I don't know about that. I like to think of it as my grandmother used to think of cooking. Love makes flowers grow better—just as it adds a little something special to food," Felicia says with a smile.

Betty is unmoved by the comment. "Exactly how much do you know about plants and flowers?"

"Quite a bit at this point. It's become a major hobby of mine, a passion really. I've only started learning recently, but I find so much peace in gardening and nature, that I just took to it quickly. Right now I'm living in my sister's house with a tiny yard and some windowsills to grow things. I'd love to have my own enormous garden one day. With a greenhouse too."

"Well, maybe it's your lucky day. This is my partner, Gerald," Betty raises a hand to indicate the man she is sitting with. She seems to be silently asking him if it is okay to go on. He gives a nod. She continues. "We happen to be reviewing applications for a new position at my nursery. We're looking for someone who loves flowers as much as I do. Who wants to make a lifestyle out of gardening. I don't think there is a single person in these stacks of applications who is as good of a fit as you. You always seem to be on top of things here whenever I come in. And you just told me how much you love gardening. Do you think you might be interested in working for me?"

A million thoughts start swirling through Felicia's head, yet she somehow manages to stay focused on the conversation at hand. "That does sound rather amazing. I would love to spend more time outside in nature. Just this past weekend I was wondering if I should try to get a job gardening. I wasn't even sure what that meant," Felicia pauses, running through some of the questions in her mind, "as great as it sounds, I don't have a car. I never saw the need while living in such a walkable area. So the commute might be an issue for me. Where is your nursery?"

"It's just up the road in the township. But the commute won't be an issue. I may have left some information out," Betty pauses. "There is a caveat that we believe attributes to why we haven't been able to find a good candidate."

Gerald is nodding in agreement. "But it seems like a bonus for someone in your situation. After what you just told me about your living arrangements, and lack of a vehicle, I do believe you'll consider it a plus." Betty shoots a quick smile at Gerard. "The position is more than just a gardener, we're looking for a groundskeeper. The nursery is on the same property as my home. There is a small guest house on the property. It isn't much, but I want whoever is going to work for me to live on site. It's what I'm used to." Betty shrugs her shoulders.

After a brief pause, Betty continues on in explanation. "I started off gardening over 40 years ago, just for pleasure. I still live in the same home I grew up in. Once you see it, you'll know why I couldn't leave." She says this as though Felicia has already accepted the position. "To be honest, the real reason I started gardening was because my family had a groundskeeper, he lived in the guest house—the one that I'm referring to which would be for the new groundskeeper—and I had a huge crush on him. Looking back, it's so silly. But I am so happy that I was once a hormonal teenage girl, because I couldn't imagine my life any other way.

"Anyway, his name was Bernard, and I had this crush on him. He was quite a few years older than me. I started to help gardening just so I could be around him. I couldn't exactly expect him to ask me on a date. Even without the age difference, he was one of my parent's employees." Betty paused to smile, looking as though she was reminiscing about some wonderful memories.

"As time went on, we became very close, and together decided I should start a gardening business. It had always been a dream of mine to run my own company, to follow in my father's footsteps. He had a successful factory in the 1920s and was blessed to be fortunate enough to sell before the Great Depression caused the economy to come crashing down. He made some proper investments and my family and I never went without. I wanted to build something for myself and my parents supported my decision—they even gave me start-up money. I was out looking at nurseries almost every day, trying to find something already established that I could purchase. While I was out trying to start a career, my mother had become very ill. I put my dreams temporarily on hold to care for her.

"She passed away within three months. My father followed her shortly thereafter, said to have died from a broken heart." Betty takes a moment to collect herself. "Now that I had inherited the 160 acres estate that was my childhood home, I decided I should start from the ground up so to speak. With all that property, it was an easy decision to turn most of it into a garden and nursery. With my groundskeeper's help, it has been thriving ever since." Another pause, this accompanied by a more somber look. "Bernard passed away two months ago and it's just too much work to keep it up and running by myself. This is why I am looking to fill this new position. Someone who will be more than just a gardener."

This was a lot for Felicia to take in. *Gardening as a career? Hells yes. Did I literally manifest it? Shush. I can't even begin to process that right now. But can I really live in this woman's guest house? Super creepy. I don't really know her and clearly she's looking to replace more than just an employee. Can I live up to that role? What does that even mean? I mean, she is a great woman. I always enjoy the chats we have together. I don't know. I did not think this manifestation through.* Felicia chuckles to herself at the ridiculousness of that thought. *What if I hate this position? Worse, what if I love it but suck at it and get fired? This is an amazing opportunity though. Come on Felicia. You know you'll love it and be great at it. But I just had panic attacks all weekend, my nerves are not ready for this. Or maybe it's a sign that I need this. Maybe I just—*

"Felicia," Betty interrupts Felicia's train of thought, "I can see this is not an easy decision for you to make, especially now that I put you on the spot like this, but I really need to make a decision soon. I spent a month grieving my dear Barney and I allowed things to slip at my business. I can't really wait too much longer for a replacement." She glances at Gerald, "I'm sure Gerald does not want me to say this and 'show you all my cards', but I am desperate at this point. I enjoy your company and would love for you to say yes. So, to help with your decision, I want to let you know that you would be given $60,000 a year, there is no rent to pay, and I also cover the utilities on the guest house."

Hold up. 60k? Living rent free? This woman barely knows me. Why does she want me so bad? Doesn't matter. Decision made. "I can't leave here without 2 weeks' notice. That's just not who I am, but," *I cannot believe I'm doing this. Jump Felicia. Jump. Take the leap.* "I'd love to come work for you."

"Wonderful! Gerald can take all your information."

"Thank you so much for this opportunity. I'm excited. And I won't let you down." Felicia reaches out and shakes Betty's hand. "Now, can I get you guys anything else? Any food?"

"Just the check please. Our work here is done," Betty winks at Felicia.

As Felicia gets their check and gives Gerald her information, the lunch rush is just starting. Felicia is excited and anxious about the decision she just made. The onslaught of hungry patrons is a welcome distraction.

CHAPTER FIVE

FELICIA ARRIVES HOME AND enters the kitchen. Sean is sitting at the table, for once doing something normal people do. He is having a cup of tea. Felicia is beaming a smile at him when she walks in.

"Hey Felicia! I assume that smile means you had a good day at work?" Sean asks.

"Work was okay." Felicia's ridiculously large smile is beginning to make her cheeks hurt.

"I don't even need to use my uncanny ability at reading people's energies to know you are very happy about something. Please share." Sean places his elbows on the table and rests his chin on his hands, awaiting the good news.

Felicia nonchalantly walks around the table, casually brushing her fingers along the backs of each chair as she passes. "Oh, it's nothing. I just got a new job is all," she tries to maintain her nonplussed demeanor, "as a gardener."

"That's incredible, Felicia!" Sean is now beaming as well. He gets up so fast that a bit of tea spills over the side of the cup. He doesn't take notice. "I told you the universe would provide! But wow, manifestation normally doesn't happen this fast! You must have a serious bond with the divine!" He embraces Felicia. It is the most demonstrative hug she has ever been a part of. They are both squeezing each other and jumping up and down like school children.

Nicole walks in and sees the two of them beaming with positivity. "Hey guys, what are we so excited about?"

"Felicia's a gardener now!" Sean blurts out.

"Oh, honey. That's great!" Nicole joins in the embrace. "Tell us all about it."

Felicia tells them the story. By the end, Nicole can't help but to feel a bit sad. She's enjoyed sharing a home with her sister again. She'll be sad to see her go. But she doesn't want to put a damper on Felicia's happy news. She doesn't want to disrupt all this happy energy by sharing these thoughts. So she doesn't.

A few days ago, Nicole was meditating on finding a way to help Felicia's low mood. She asked the universe to help her and give her a sign. The divine quickly provided insight, and she almost felt silly for not thinking of it sooner. Nicole is part of a local support group and thought that they could go together. Felicia may have trouble helping herself, but she's always been good at helping others and raising the vibrations of the room, even if she doesn't believe in that sort of thing. Nicole figured that if Felicia could see the positive impact she had on others, even if it was unintentional, it would lift her own spirits. Felicia was over the moon after helping that woman and her child in the accident. This was the confirmation Nicole needed that her idea was a good one. She hadn't gotten a chance yet to share her idea with Felicia. She can't help but feel a twinge of jealousy that this other woman, Betty is her name, beat her to the punch. This is what Nicole gets by holding back her thoughts. She never was one to rush into anything without first gaining insight. She wants to help her little sister. The support group thing might seem silly to Felicia, especially now that she doesn't exactly seem to need her help, but it's not until tomorrow night, so Nicole will sleep on it and decide whether or not she will bring it up tomorrow. "This is such great news Felicia. We're so happy for you," Nicole manages to say in a genuinely delighted tone.

"Thanks! I know it's not for two weeks, but I'm so excited that I think I'm going to start boxing up some things now!"

"Want some help?" Nicole asks, hoping Felicia will say yes.

"Sure."

The two women gallop up the stairs to Felicia's room. Nicole will spend every moment she can with her sister, now that she'll be leaving soon.

The following day, Nicole and Felicia are sitting at the kitchen table having lunch together. Nicole casually mentions the support group to her sister. After sleeping on it, she decided she will ask, but not be disappointed if she says no.

"Sure, why not?" is Felicia's reply.

Felicia isn't too keen on the idea of going to a support group—why does she need support?—but she knows she will be seeing less of her sister soon and doesn't want to turn her down for anything while she's still here. Nicole has been so incredibly generous to Felicia in her time of need; even if her and her husband's ideas of help are often quirky. "What's this support group for?"

"It's technically 'loss support'. It's run by one of the ladies from Feeling & Healing. She suggested it to me one day when I was shopping in the store, after my miscarriage. All the ladies over there were intimately involved in every aspect of my pregnancy. They're such wonderful women. The group's been really great. It's all about releasing trapped emotions. Even though I've already released most of my trauma, I continue to go in order to support others. It's become like an extended family."

Felicia was on the other side of the country when her sister became pregnant. She can still remember the phone call she received the day she had lost the baby. It was one of the only times she felt any regret for moving away from her family. She was so thankful that Nicole had found these ladies for support. The thought of meeting these women who helped her sister banishes her questionable thoughts. She is going to make the best of it. "They're not going to wave burning sage in my face and try to get me to cry...will they?" Felicia is smirking as she says this.

Nicole returns the smirk. "No. It's not like that. We're just there for one another. I figured you could—"

"Oooo! Are we smudging?" Sean trots in from the front room carrying grocery bags. Reusable cloth, of course. He's glistening with sweat.

"What?" Felicia asks Sean with a confused look on her face. "What are you talking about?...and why are you so sweaty?"

"When I was opening the door I could've sworn I

heard you say sage. I thought you guys were smudging. So I got excited and ran in here." Sean takes a few panting breaths. "So are we smudging? Did I miss it? Please don't tell me I missed it."

"No, sweetie." Nicole stands up and takes a bag from her husband. "We're not smudging. We were talking about support group tonight. Felicia is going to join me"

"Oh," Sean looks deflated. He is going on a weeklong seminar and will not be able to join them for support group. Or any impromptu smudging for that matter. He gets an idea. He quickly perks up, "Do you think the group would like some gluten free quinoa cookies?" He doesn't wait for a response. "I do! I'll make them before I leave! I better get started!" He resumes his trotting, now accompanied by humming, and begins putting away the groceries in the kitchen.

Felicia side-eyes her sister. "Are you sure you like him this way?"

"Absolutely."

Later that evening, with freshly baked cookies in hand, Nicole and Felicia head out to support group. Sean has already left for his trip. They take a few leisurely steps down the tree-lined sidewalk and quickly arrive at their destination. It is a neighboring house built in the 1900s. They walk up the stairs and onto a wraparound porch. They go inside and down the stairs to enter a basement filled with men and women making small talk. There is a circle of chairs in the center of the room and a table with edible treats and drinks off to the side. Nicole places the cookies on the table. The walls are painted in a soothing pale green and are adorned with all sorts of woven tapestries. There is soothing music and a faint aroma of incense. Large crystals and geodes are strategically placed around the room. A lone wind chime hangs in the corner. It doesn't matter that they are indoors where there is no wind. These are the type of people who believe moving energy will sound the chimes. *Did Nicole really see this as a normal environment? She told me it wouldn't be 'like that'.* Felicia is mustering up the self control necessary to not roll her eyes, she promised herself she was going to make the best of this evening and she will not break that promise.

A gong sounds softly, signifying the start of the meeting. The individual chatter stops and everyone takes a seat around the circle. A pleasantly plump young woman with waist length red hair begins to speak. "Welcome everyone. I see a few new faces tonight, so I will go over what our goals are and what to expect this evening." She pauses to softly smile. "My name is Roselia and I'm so pleased you could all join us. What we do here is release emotions.

Emotions, like all things in our abundant universe, are made up of energy. When we allow ourselves to feel and express our emotions—by doing things like crying while sad or screaming when angry—everything flows smoothly in and out of our bodies; like they were meant to. For those times when we feel ashamed or embarrassed by our emotions—or for whatever reason we may have to not allow ourselves to express these emotions—they become blockages, trapping the free flow of energy in and around our bodies." She pauses for effect. "This will not only lead to ease of repeating the same habits due to the blocks, but can also over time cause physical and psychological ailments due to the disruption of energy flow.

Here in this room, we release those trapped emotions. We also help raise each other's vibrations by sending loving, healing, positive thoughts and light to one another. This is a safe space to let your emotions go. We do not have any rules of who must speak when or what must be said; your subconscious will let you know when and how it is ready to release. Once anyone feels ready, simply raise your hand and I will call on you to speak. Feel free to say whatever arises in you. Try not to be nervous. Sometimes you will be compelled to speak of specific events that led to the entrapment of emotion, other times it will seem more symbolic or metaphoric. Allow yourself to acknowledge whatever arises.

We will first begin with a short meditation to clear the room and then we will open the floor. Are there any questions before we begin with the meditation?" Roselia glances around the room. No one is stirring. "Then let us begin."

Roselia's shoulders visibly soften. She adjusts herself slightly in her chair.

"Allow yourself to get into a comfortable position, adjusting yourself as necessary as you begin to relax. Softly closing your eyes, relaxing your body even more, allowing any thoughts, feeling any emotions. Without judgment. Allowing yourself to be."

Why did I agree to this? Felicia struggles to find a position that at least resembles relaxation. *You agreed because you love your sister. Just buckle down and deal with it.* Felicia decides to daydream about her new job instead of trying to meditate; it'll look the same to anyone watching. *This job is going to be amazing. The smell of fresh air and flowers. The exercise that doesn't feel like exercise because it is so enjoyable. The beauty of it all is almost too good to be true. Manifesting. Did I really manifest it? Is there any truth to it at all? That's just crazy. And I may have panic attacks, but that does not mean I'm crazy.*

Felicia's thoughts are interrupted by an audible sigh followed by Roselia's gentle voice. "Starting to become aware of the room again. When ready, slowly blink open your eyes at your own pace." Rose allows a few moments to pass. "Who feels ready to begin?"

One of the few men in the group raises his hand. He is in his early thirties with dark hair and dark circles under his eyes to match. "I'll go."

"Thank you Tim, we're glad to have you back."

"Well, um...as Roselia just said, I'm Tim. I've been really thankful for this group. I don't know where I'd be right now without it." He clears his throat. "It's been six months since our Johnny died of SIDS and uh...my wife, Crystal, still won't talk about it. She won't let us touch his nursery," he pauses to take a breath. "I just...it's just that, we should be grieving together, ya know...supporting one another. But I just can't find a way to get her to open up. She just...I dunno." Tim looks down and starts talking to his lap instead of the group. "I feel like it's wrong to think this way, but," he takes another breath, "I dunno, it's almost like it's easier to deal with the death of my son than to deal with her. I'm sorry. That doesn't sound right." He looks around the room, embarrassed by the words he just said.

"It's okay Tim. We're in a safe non-judgmental space.

Let it flow." Roselia kindly reminds him as the rest of the group nods in agreement.

"Thanks Roselia. Um, the truth is, I just...I just think she's lost it. It's like she doesn't understand and accept that he's gone. She'll sometimes...," Tim straightens up in his chair and resumes addressing the group instead of his lap. "So look. I'll give an example. Just last night, we were sitting at home talking over dinner. Out of nowhere, she cocks her head to the side and tells me to shush. Then she goes, 'did you hear that? I think Johnny might be waking up from his nap.'

"I'm dumbfounded. It's been six months. How am I supposed to respond to that?" He lifts his hands in frustration. "So I just say, 'um, sweetheart, remember Johnny passed away six months ago?' So then she just looks at me and I can literally see the clarity enter her face. She bursts into tears and leaves the room. I know I probably should have followed her, but I just don't feel like I can do it anymore.

"And that's not even the worst part. The worst part is, twenty minutes later, she comes back into the kitchen while I'm cleaning the dishes, and acts like nothing happened. Completely normal. She even asked me if I wanted to watch the new episode of Yellowstone." He pauses and exhales a long breath. "So that's it. I just, I dunno. I don't know how I'm supposed to deal with her. I mean, I've moved on from Johnny's death, gotten through it as well as can be expected. You guys really helped me with that, I couldn't have done it alone. And yet that's exactly how I feel. Alone."

Tim clears his throat. "And I know people grieve at different paces and in different ways, but c'mon, I want to move forward and continue to build a life with my wife. Now that she's gone crazy and refuses to talk to anyone, I just don't see how that's possible. I've tried to get her to come here, but no. She doesn't think she needs to. I'm just at my wits end. I don't know what to do. I definitely can't walk out on her while she's like this—that would make me feel like a horrible person—but it's also starting to feel like my only option."

Tim's body slumps into his chair. He looks down at his lap again. "Thanks for listening."

Well, that was depressing. Felicia looks around the room to see the looks on everyone's faces. To her surprise, no one else appears to be sharing her opinion.

Another person raises a hand to share a story. Then another. And another. Some stories are like Tim's. Others are more uplifting. Some stories aren't even stories at all, but more of a string of words put together like a poem. Some people just cry or laugh during their share without using any words. As more and more people begin to share, the more the atmosphere seems to lighten. Which is amazing and strange at the same time. One would assume hearing these stories would darken the room. But that is not happening at all. Neither of the sisters share, but both are grateful in their own ways for this evening. Nicole is happy to have been here to support the others and she knows her thoughts of love and kindness lifted them. Felicia is unsure of why she feels grateful. It was not anything like she expected—or even could have imagined—but she too is left feeling like her presence somehow had a positive influence on those around her. Both sister's sleep well this night.

Felicia awakens to a wonderfully delicious aroma wafting throughout the house. She cannot place what it is exactly, but it smells both familiar and fantastic. She inhales deeply to take more of it in and a lightbulb goes off in her head. "That's bacon!" She actually says this out loud as a smile forms across her face. Just as quickly as it appeared, the smile is then gone. *That can't be actual bacon. There is no meat allowed in this house. Sean would have a heart attack. He is so weird. I should probably tell him you actually need to consume the meat in order for it to cause a heart attack, it doesn't just clog your arteries through osmosis. What a silly silly man.*

She gets dressed, brushes her teeth, and heads downstairs. Sure enough, Nicole is standing in front of the stove cooking what appears to be bacon.

"It smells delicious in here." Felicia approaches Nicole at the stove. "Whatcha cooking?"

Nicole looks at Felicia and makes a confused face. "You don't recognize the sight, sound, and glorious smells of bacon?" Nicole inhales deeply and grins at her sister.

"Is that truly real live bacon?"

"Well, I'm certain it is no longer live bacon, but yes. It's real. Remember, Sean left for his weeklong seminar so I figured I'd make us a treat. Just like when we were young."

"We are still young." Felicia bumps hips with her sister and then plants a huge kiss on her cheek. "Nicole, you are amazing."

Felicia sits at the table. "Hey, remember that time when mom and dad went on vacation and you set off all the fire alarms while trying to cook us bacon?" She starts laughing.

"No, actually. As I remember it, you were the one who forgot to turn on the exhaust hood. So it was you who set off all the fire alarms." Nicole sticks out her tongue, but is laughing as well.

"Hey! You were supposed to be in charge of me that week. You were always so excited to go from big sister to babysitter and act all high and mighty. So I'm fairly certain that means *you* set the alarms off."

"That makes zero sense. It doesn't make me responsible."

"Oh my god! Yes it does! You were literally named the 'responsible party' when you agreed to the role of babysitter. So...you're definitely partly responsible. Plus, you were the cook, you should've checked the hood." Felicia playfully shoves Nicole.

"It was funny either way. We always had a lot of fun back then. Didn't we?"

"Yeah we did."

The two sisters continue to take a stroll down memory lane.

Chapter Six

The next two weeks go by uneventfully. Felicia is still getting trapped in her thoughts and having panic attacks, while Nicole is still trying to shower her sister with enough love to heal her.

Sean is the only one that changes. He returns home from his trip with about 50 pounds of extra weight. Actually, it is exactly 53.7 pounds of extra weight. Sean knows this because the extra weight was precisely weighed at the airport and cost him an additional luggage fee.

Sean's new and exciting hobby is sound healing. He bought every frequency of tuning fork they had to offer on the seminar. Ohm is his favorite. His new hobby has Felicia glad to be moving out. She has all of her belongings packed and is saying her goodbyes.

"We'll miss you so much!" Nicole embraces her sister for the sixth time today.

Sean hands her a gift box. "This is from both of us. For you to remember us by."

"Guys, I'm only moving a few miles away. I'll still see you all the time." Felicia rolls her eyes. She unwraps the gift box and peers inside. It is full of incense and crystals and a box of the green tea that she's become so accustomed to drinking every day. There is also a mug wrapped in bubble wrap. She takes it out and reads what's written on the side. "Namaste in bed?"

"Get it?" Sean asks expectantly. "Because you're always being cute with us. Making fun of our lifestyle while secretly enjoying it." He nudges her playfully with his shoulder. "I know you love the things we invite you to do. I saw this mug and couldn't resist. It's so incredibly you." He hugs her again.

"Thanks guys. I mean it. For everything." Felicia does mean it. She is grateful for everything they've done for her. She's just not so sure she'll miss all the weird activities that go on around this place—definitely not Sean's new sound healing hobby. "I'll see you next weekend and I can tell you how things are going."

"Sounds great. We'll see you then. Have fun!"

Felicia takes her last box outside and into the waiting Uber. Nicole and Sean stand on the front step, arms around each other, waving. It's as if they're sending their little girl off into the wild. They are still standing there waving when Felicia peers out of the back of the vehicle as it makes its way down the street.

The driveway is nearly unnoticeable from the road. The Uber driver Felicia hired to take her to her new residence has to make not one, but two U-turns after missing the entrance. Once the turn is successfully navigated they find themselves surrounded by mature elms and oaks, towering over the drive so densely that the automatic headlights of the vehicle turn on. The drive then opens up to rolling greens dotted with purple, yellow, and white crocuses that are just beginning to bloom.

They pass by a pond with a swan serenely floating in its center. After following the turns as previously explained by Betty, they arrive at a small cottage that looks as though it's been plucked right out of a fairytale.

The SUV comes to a stop and Felicia gets out to unload her belongings. Once unloaded, she says thanks to the Uber driver and wishes him luck. Hopefully he will be able to find his way back to the street without too much trouble.

"Good morning Felicia!" Betty is quite pleasant this morning. "Let me help you with your things."

"Good morning Betty. Thanks, I'd love some help. Nothing should be too heavy." Felicia hands her one of the lightest bags and then collects the heaviest box for herself. Betty opens the door with her free hand and leads Felicia in.

"This place is amazing. It's better than I could have ever imagined. This guest house is nicer than anything I've personally ever stayed in."

The inside of the cottage is just as whimsical as the outside. Ornate wood carvings surround all the windows and doors including the stained glass transoms above each. The furniture looks to be from the time period when the cottage was built. The furniture may have even been built before the cottage and shipped over from a place like London. Fine wood craftsmanship like this cannot be replicated. Two wing chairs frame a wall length fireplace made of stone and a fabric doily turned yellow from the sun covers the small coffee table between the two chairs. The Victorian feel of this cottage is not of this world—or at least not of this century. Felicia and Betty both put the bags and boxes down and head outside for another load.

Betty grabs a bag. "Welcome to my little slice of paradise." Betty notices the look of awe upon Felicia's face. "Wait until you explore the grounds. As a little girl, I used to find places that I felt like no one had stepped on before me in over 100 years. I always liked to think there was magic in these grounds. Truth be told, I still do." Betty winks at Felicia.

They make their way back inside, this time Felicia is carrying two boxes.

"It's simply incredible. Even though I'm lugging this stuff," Felicia deposits the boxes on the floor with a grunt, "I still feel more at peace than I have in a long time."

The ladies finish bringing Felicia's things inside.

"It's still early, so you can have a look around here and get settled for a bit. I'll be back to get you in," Betty looks at her watch, "let's say forty-five minutes?"

"That sounds perfect. Thanks for your help bringing in my things, and thank you again for the opportunity you've given me."

"I'm glad to have you." Betty smiles. "Bathroom's through there and the bedroom is the next door over. See you in a bit."

Betty goes outside, climbs into her golf cart, and takes off.

Felicia spends the next forty-five minutes acquainting herself with her new home and unpacking bags and boxes. The bedroom has a canopy bed with a handmade quilt lain over the foot. More doilies on the nightstands. The bathroom has a white clawfoot tub with wraparound curtain and gold faucets. Felicia is once again full of excitement and anxiety about her decision to take this job. The place is so incredible that the excitement is outweighing the anxiety for the moment.

She continues unpacking most of her boxes while finishing exploring all the nooks and crannies this place has to offer. It's not an incredibly large place, but anything this old is bound to hold some secrets. Felicia suddenly notices the time and is surprised. Betty should be arriving back shortly.

The temperature for the day has not quite risen yet, so Felicia changes into something a bit warmer. She's not sure what to expect on her first day, but she errs on the side of caution and chooses something she won't mind getting dirty. It is early spring, but Felicia likes to refer to it as mud season. *Why does spring seem to be the only season that plays tricks on us? When summer comes, the warm weather is here. When autumn arrives, the leaves don't change to their fiery colors and then switch back to green. When winter arrives, there may be a warm day or two, but once the cold comes in, it's here to stay. Why is spring the only season that seems to torture us with its pretending. Spring is supposed to signify rebirth, but come on, just get born already. One day it's nice and you think the cold spells are over, then bam! You're back in long underwear, turning the heat back—.*

Felicia's thoughts are interrupted by a knocking at the door. She opens it and sees Betty's eager smile. "Are you ready?" Betty asks.

"You betcha!"

Felicia gets into the golf cart with Betty. She's never

been in a golf cart before. She enjoys the feeling of the wind on her face, the openness of it all—although she would definitely enjoy it more once it's warmer. Betty is driving them around, pointing out to Felicia all the different growing areas on the property. They are following a wide gravel path that reaches out in various directions, like branches from a tree. Traveling in the open air, Felicia can now smell the early spring blooming bulbs that she saw on her drive to the cottage. She takes in a deep breath and savors the fresh new aromas. Betty cruises past some greenhouses, an old barn, and other buildings in various shapes and sizes.

"There are many buildings all over the property that have been standing since the late 1800s. Some are in need of a little TLC. Others should be knocked down," Betty explains as they pass an old building with only three walls and part of a roof. "If you do decide to venture off and explore the grounds in your downtime, please be careful." She pulls around another turn. "Now that I have a second set of hands, maybe we can get around to some repairs I've been putting off."

This is almost more than Felicia can handle. It's all just so wonderful. This property must have so much history hidden in its crumbling structures; if only walls could talk. She would hate to see any of this get demolished. It's all too surreal. Mystical might be the word.

Felicia doesn't recall saying anything during their ride. She has been awed into silence. She is surrounded by so much beauty.

Betty stops at a large plot beside one of the many greenhouses. "I assume you know how to divide tuberous perennials?" She asks Felicia, finally getting down to business.

"You mean like hostas and daylilies? Of course." Felicia responds with a smile.

"Great. This needs to be done before the plants start waking up for the season. They need to be dug up from the ground, divided and then put back. The removed plants will go into pots and be moved into this greenhouse here," she points, "to be sold throughout the season."

"Roger that!" Felicia is elated.

"I have to say Felicia, I am so thrilled you agreed to come work here. I think we'll get along great! I also have to say though, I was quite surprised you didn't have any reservations about uprooting yourself to take this new job and move out here."

Felicia feels a bit confused by these words. 'Out here' is less than 10 miles from where her sister's house is. That's nothing. Felicia had actually uprooted her life over a year ago and moved thousands of miles to get away from a bad situation. Moving a few miles down the road towards a good situation didn't even seem like anything special. She feels Betty must have lived quite a sheltered life to think this way. "It was nothing. I'll still see my sister and brother in law, they're only right down the road."

"The man in your life didn't have any issues with you not discussing this decision with him first?"

Betty's life was clearly not only sheltered, but old fashioned. "There actually isn't one." Felicia responds hoping Betty will not be shocked into cardiac arrest. She would really rather not have to call nine-one-one for the second time this month.

To Felicia's relief, Betty stays upright. "A pretty little thing like you is single?"

Felicia turns red at this comment. "Yup," she says, keeping it light. She hopes this conversation will end soon.

"Any reason why?" Betty is unsure if she should pry, but has never been one to mind her own business.

"Well," Felicia starts, and then hesitates. This old fashioned woman will never understand. And how much should she reveal to her anyway? How much *can* she reveal without spiraling down a hole?

Betty pats Felicia's thigh in a motherly manner. "I've been around long enough to notice unresolved heartbreak when I see it. You have to let that out girly. It doesn't have to be right here, right now, but if you don't let the pain out eventually, it'll eat you from the inside out."

Oh great. Another Nicole in my life. Why is everybody always so obsessed with letting your feelings out? "My sister says that all the time. But thank you. I'll keep it in mind. Right now I'd just like to get started if that's okay."

"Of course. Sometimes I can't help myself when I see someone in need. But yes, working is why you're here. I may need a reminder of that from time to time. I just enjoy your company so much! I hope you're as excited as I am." Betty pulls Felicia in for a hug.

"I truly am Betty. And I do thank you." Felicia gets out of the golf cart and begins to work.

Felicia spends the day dividing and potting perennials. Betty comes to check on her every now and then, but she mostly has the day to herself as Betty has other tasks to tend to. Felicia loves this work. She herself wouldn't even call it work. Yes, she was getting paid to do it, but she's finally discovering the old saying is actually true. 'If you love what you do, you'll never work a day in your life'.

As she is finishing up the last hosta, she sees the sun is starting to set. The sky is changing color, from blue to pink. There was not a cloud in the sky all day. Once the sun is gone, the night will become chilly, as a reminder that it is still early spring.

Betty pulls up in her golf cart. "Hey, look at this!" She scans the plot with a look of astonishment on her face. "I cannot believe you finished all of them. This is wonderful. I didn't expect you to get this all done in one day. Felicia, you're amazing!" She pauses to survey the plot as if she cannot believe her own eyes.

Felicia feels a sense of pride warm her through the dropping temperatures. She just assumed she was supposed to get them all done today. She didn't even think anything of it. "It wasn't that much work. And I was having fun!" Efficiency has always been one of Felicia's strong suits; that is, when she isn't getting distracted by her own thoughts. Now that she thinks about it, her thoughts were scarce today. She hadn't even realized it until now.

Felicia finishes up some loose ends and Betty drives her back to her cottage. They say their goodbyes, agree on a time to meet tomorrow morning, and Felicia enters her new home.

She immediately plops down on the couch. It is a wingback like the chairs, but with deep tufts and velvet cushions. She doesn't realize how tired her body is until she sits down. Now, she doesn't want to get back up. She stays sprawled out on the couch until her hunger forces her to move.

There was a welcome basket from Betty when Felicia arrived earlier today. It is sitting on the small kitchen island. She didn't get a chance to go through it before her workday started. Now she is sorting through the goodies and her ravenous hunger makes everything look delicious. *This is awesome. This woman is almost too nice. Too nice? Why do people say that? What does it mean to be 'too nice'? How is that possible? Like, if you become too nice something bad will happen to level things out? I don't get it. Perhaps it's because some people believe not everyone deserves kindness? That it has to be earned? Oh, I know. Maybe what people really mean is 'they are too nice so they make me feel like an ass for not being as nice as them'. Yeah, that's probably it. 'Stop making me look like a jerk' is what they mean to say. 'Lower the bar for me, asshole'. I dunno. Most people just say things and don't ever delve any deeper into the words that are coming out of their mouths. At least I assume that's what happens. Why else would people say things that don't make sense. Man, I wonder if everyone talks to themselves like I do. Probably not. A therapist once told me that I need to remember 'I am not everyone'. Zen masters would've had a problem with that guy. Don't they say we are one with the universe? Ipso Facto: we are in fact everyone.*

Anyway, what am I going to eat? It's getting harder to decide because I'm suddenly not as hungry as I was while lying on the couch. Felicia looks down and notices a half eaten loaf of bread in her hands and sees a chunk of cheese missing as well. *These damn distracting thoughts. Focus Felicia.* She sits down at the table and finishes her food while focusing on each bite she is taking. Once full, she puts everything away and into the cabinets.

After reading a few chapters of a hardcover fiction novel she finds in the living room, she takes a nice, long, warm shower and gets ready for bed. She settles under the sheets and drifts off to sleep while her mind is reliving all the special moments from the wonderful day she just had.

CHAPTER SEVEN

IT'S THURSDAY WHEN FELICIA awakens to the warmth of the sun peeking in through her sheer curtains. It is another mild spring day. The perfect weather for working outside.

Felicia gets out of bed, brushes her teeth, combs her hair, and makes sure to dress in layers. The sunshine may speak to the rising temperatures, but the mornings still start off quite cold. She heats up some oatmeal, still leftover from Betty's welcome basket, and makes herself a cup of green tea. She steps outside to take in the fresh air. As she closes her eyes and turns her head towards the sun, the rays warm her face. She smiles to herself, feeling gratitude for simply being here in this moment. She inhales deeply and slowly lets out the breath. Her smile broadens. The sound of leaves rustling on nearby trees and birds chirping in harmony takes her to a recent memory.

A little less than a year ago, Felicia and Nicole were sitting in the back garden together. Sean was there too, doing his Qi Gong practices close to the fence. It was early May, but it was a day just like today. The warmth of the sunshine was complemented by a light breeze drifting through the air.

"Can I tell you something?" Nicole says, as birds are chirping all around them.

"Of course," Felicia says, "we're sisters. You can tell me anything."

Nicole smiles. She seems nervous, but proceeds nonetheless. "Promise it won't make you think I'm weird?"

Felicia rolls her eyes. "No worries there. I already think you're weird." She sticks out her tongue and gives her sister an affectionate clap on the back.

"Be serious for a second. I know you don't agree with a lot of my spiritual beliefs and ways of life—and I'm fine with that because you seem to accept that it is just who I am. And I also never feel like you're actually judging me for my quirks. Because yes, I do understand they *are* quirks. But I just, I dunno. Just promise me you won't think your big sister is a looney toon and try to have her committed."

"You know me, this is how I always am. I am being serious. I seriously think you're weird." Her sister seems only minimally amused. Felicia stops with the jokes. Apparently, whatever her sister has to say is important. "But I'm being legit serious. You could never convince me that you're a looney toon. We grew up together. We shared a bedroom. I would have figured it out by now if you needed to be committed."

"I guess that's true."

Nicole stares off into the garden at the birds playfully splashing in the birdbath. She is contemplating how to put into words what she is about to reveal. She stops overthinking and just says it. "Sometimes I get feelings. More than feelings. Maybe visions is a better word." She looks up to make sure Felicia is taking this seriously. "And I'm certain that they are real. At first, I convinced myself I was going crazy, you know psychological disorders do run in our family, but then when the visions started becoming true, I couldn't help but accept that there is a bigger part of this world that most people cannot see. There has to be. It's the only explanation I could come up with that even halfway made sense."

"Well," Felicia starts, unsure how to continue on. Her sister is definitely not crazy; this she knows for certain. If these so-called visions were not predicting reality, yet she still believed they were, *then* she would be crazy. But that's not what she's claiming. How can someone be considered crazy if the visions they get are true? "I guess there are a lot of things in life that cannot always be fully explained. It doesn't mean they're not real. I get it. It just means we haven't figured out the why yet." She thinks of how often things are just chalked up as coincidence. Or how miracles have in fact been proven in the past. Felicia doesn't claim to have the answers, but she does accept that some things happen that do not fit the laws of science as we understand them. "How long has this been happening?" Felicia asks, genuinely curious.

"Actually," Nicole shrinks down to the smallest size possible, in order to be the smallest possible target for the attack she's expecting, "basically my whole life. As long as I can remember at least."

Felicia visibly startles. "What? You're whole life? And you're just telling me this now?" She claps her sister on the back again, this time not so affectionately. "Why in God's name did you wait so long to tell me? Better question...since you've been keeping this to yourself for like, ever, why decide to tell me now?" Felicia stares at her sister, arms folded, awaiting a reply.

"I guess it just never felt like the right time before. We've gotten so much closer these past couple months. I want you to be open with me, and in order for you to feel comfortable doing that, I decided I shouldn't be keeping anything from you."

"Okay." Felicia rolls her eyes. "I guess." she glances over towards Sean. *If anyone turns out to be crazy, it's gonna be him right there.* She lifts her chin in his direction, "does he know?"

"I did tell him, yes." Nicole looks ashamed. "I know you're my sister and all, but it's different with him. He gets feelings too."

"Whatever," Felicia says, with her nose in the air like a pouty six year old. She rolls her eyes. She is way too curious to waste time pouting over this infraction of sisterhood. "So, what are they like? These visions."

Nicole softly closes her eyes as she speaks. "There's actually a name for it. It's called claircognizance. I get this immediate knowing about someone or something. A word or scene will just pop into my head out of nowhere."

Nicole opens her eyes to take in Felicia's response. She looks slightly put off.

"It's not like I can predict the future or anything, it's just...I'll give you an example. The moment I met Sean, I saw a bottle of alcohol, then a heart came down and shattered it into a billion pieces. This told me that he was an alcoholic and love would break his habit. The visions are almost always symbolic, but I am almost always certain that I do—for lack of a better word—*decode* them correctly."

This conversation is starting to make Felicia extreme-ly uncomfortable for a reason she cannot quite put her finger on. Perhaps it's because Felicia herself sometimes knows about a person or thing—although it definitely never comes with these symbolic images; it's just a gut feeling. And if it did come to her in visual images in her mind, she would be convinced she must've been bopped on the head and now had brain damage. Nonetheless, she does not want her sister to share in her current feeling of discomfort. "That's cool I guess. I mean, it's definitely weird. But no weirder than a lot of the other stuff you've said to me." Felicia nudges her sister play-fully on the shoulder which causes the conversation to return to the light playfulness it had prior to this new disclosure by Nicole.

Felicia is snapped back to the present moment by the sound of tires crunching on gravel. Betty has arrived in the golf cart to pick her up. She is wearing a daring floral ensemble that would feel at home as a costume choice for any of the Golden Girls—at least she skipped the shoulder pads. She must be in an interesting mood to be dressed so flamboyantly.

"Good morning, Betty!" Felicia croons. What do you know? Betty's outfit sparks some flamboyance in Felicia herself.

"Good morning, Felicia! It's another beautiful day in paradise!"

Betty's chipper mood is due to the fact that her monthly Bridge Club meeting is tonight and it's her turn to host. Joanne, one of the Bridge gals, had the flu last month. Since you can't play bridge with four, the meeting was canceled. The month before that they also skipped. Sue, another one of the fabulous four, was hosting her out-of-town family for the holidays. The host couldn't leave to play a silly little card game—at least that's what Sue's sister-in-law would have said and she'd never hear the end of it. It's been three months since the Northeast Golden Girls have sat around the table and 'talked shop' over a deck of cards. Bridge Club always makes Betty—as well as the others—feel young again.

"You're right. It sure is a beautiful day in paradise. What does my Virgil have in store for us today?" Felicia says as she gets into the golf cart.

Betty raises her eyebrows and smiles. "I love the Dante reference! And speaking of—since you've been doing wonderfully this week, and I seem to keep underestimating your efficiency—I figured I'd mostly let you make the decisions about what you can and can't achieve. If you ask me, Dante no longer needs his Virgil." Betty smiles at their witty banter. It's nice to know Felicia is not only a lover of nature, but a lover of classic books as well. "I know it's only your first week, but I already feel comfortable stepping back a bit."

They take a turn onto the paved drive. "I'm going to show you the things that need to be done. If you end up getting everything I've pointed out completed, then you're on your own to explore the grounds. Roam around and make a list of things that seem like they need doing. I trust your assessment. You can bring the list to me tomorrow."

Betty points out a few tasks along the road that need completing. They soon arrive at the main garden. The vehicle stops and they both get out. Betty is grinning and signaling towards a paint faded, missing hubcapped, in need of love golf cart. "For you!" She says as if she's presenting a Bentley.

"I get to cruise around in this bad boy all day?" Felicia appreciates the dramatic irony.

"Why not? You've proven yourself already. Today will be a test to confirm I haven't jumped the gun with my decision to let you go off on your own. The keys are in it."

"Thank you Betty. You will not be disappointed."

Betty hands Felicia a notebook and pen. "Call me if you need anything." With that being said, Betty gets back in her own golf cart and takes off down the path.

"This is so effing awesome!" Felicia has not driven any kind of motorized vehicle in over a year. She rented a van to drive across the country after her breakup, but never bought a car back here on the east coast. Even though she greatly enjoys driving, she never had a need to buy a car as she lived in a walking town where parking was not ideal. She'll have to get one now that she's not in walking distance from—basically anything, but all in due time. She is just happy to be behind any kind of wheel again.

She turns on the golf cart and sees the batteries are fully charged. She releases the parking brake and sets off towards her tasks for the day. She will be cleaning the fall and winter detritus from all the ornamental beds around the property.

She drives to the furthest point away, choosing to start at the furthest point and work in a spiral inward. One hundred and sixty acres is a lot of ground to cover, and one can easily lose their bearings. Felicia has a pretty good handle on the layout after spending almost a week here. Plus, she's always had a great sense of direction.

She pulls out her notebook and pen along her journey to clean up all the beds and jots down things she notices need some attention as she passes them. Felicia sees so much potential to carve additional beauty from this little slice of paradise. The ideas she has makes her feel alive inside. Creating beauty—not just for her, but others as well—fills her with a sense of gratitude and awe. She will have to go over everything with a fine tooth comb once her assigned task of cleaning the beds is completed, but this simple act of writing and imagining is a great start. She wants more than anything to continue to make a good impression on Betty.

CHAPTER EIGHT

"BREAKFAST IS READY!" CHARLES calls down the hall to his father, Ron. Ron seems a bit more like his old self this week, which is good. Charles will exploit this opportunity and try to convince his father to go to the doctors for a check-up. "I made your favorite!"

"Bacon and eggs?" Charles jumps as Ron is suddenly standing right behind him. He almost drops the frying pan. How a 64 year old man in this state of health can manage to repeatedly sneak up on him will never cease to amaze. Although, perhaps it speaks more to Charles' observation skills than it does his father's agility.

"Of course, dad. Bacon and eggs, sunny side up, with whole wheat toast."

"Look at all this food. And toast too? Who's going to eat all this?" Ron Pulls out a chair and grunts as he collapses into it. "Are we expecting visitors this morning that you neglected to tell me about? I would've put on a nice shirt, had I known."

"No, dad." Charles shakes his head. He puts two plates down on the table and takes a seat across from his father. "No visitors. It's all just for us. You haven't been eating enough lately. You're losing too much weight, I figure it might be because the food isn't to your liking; that's why

I cooked your favorite. If you keep losing weight, you won't be able to beat me in arm wrestling anymore. And then where would we be?"

"Don't be a smart ass. I'm just not as hungry as I used to be. I like the food enough 'round here."

"But you're wasting away. I'm only trying to help."

"You really wanna help me?"

"Of course dad."

"Then lets you and me take a walk out back and you can put a bullet right between my eyes."

"Please dad, don't start."

Charles starts eating his food and attempts to change the direction of the conversation. "Mmm, this is good. I have to say, I am one hell of a cook." He winks at his father.

"You want to know who was a hell of a cook?"

Here we go. Charles exhales and slow blinks his eyes.

"Your mother! Boy, she knew how to cook, let me tell you." Ron continues, "not this thing you kids call cooking nowadays. No siree. She would make everything fresh. Everything. She would go down to the butcher every single day and get her own choice of cuts. Then she'd spend all day marinating the meat in her own mixes, none of this premade packet junk you kids pick up at the big chain groceries. Oh, and her bread! She'd make it fresh from scratch. She'd mix up the dough and leave it sitting in the pan to rise. I'll never forget the one time I peeked under that dish towel to see what she was making. Well, you bet your ass that was the one and only time I'd ever did that! Your mom walked into the kitchen and saw me with that towel in my fingers. You woulda thought I was peeking under a ladies skirt—not a dish towel—with the look she gave me. I could just about hear the vein popping out on her forehead. So guess what she says, she says—"

"Ronald, if you ruin our bread, I'll ruin your head," Charles finishes before his father has the chance. "You've told me that one before." *About a million times.*

"Well, I'm so sorry for boring you, son." Ron stabs a piece of bacon with a fork and shoves it into his mouth.

Charles immediately feels guilty. "No, dad, I'm the one who should be sorry. I should've let you finish. You're not boring." Charles takes a deep breath. This morning is not going at all as planned—such is his life lately—but he still feels he should try and make his move. "I've just been worried about you. I really would like you to have Doctor Morgan take a look at you. Just a routine check-up."

"And why do I need this routine check-up?" Ron stares at his son directly in the eyes. He knows what Charles is trying to do.

"I already said, whether you'll admit it or not, you're losing weight. You can barely get up and down from a chair. I can hear you grunting. You've stopped working almost entirely."

There was a long silence.

"There ain't nothing no doctor can do for me. Even more importantly, there ain't nothing I *want* a doctor to do for me. I want to be with your mother."

Charles lets out a long sigh. "Dad, don't say such things. You no longer even try to hide what you're implying. Please don't talk like this."

"Don't 'please' me. My kids're grown. Your sister married that nice fella and they're all set down in Georgia.

You're taking to the family business end of things quite nicely. I've done my part and now there's nothing left for me. I don't know how to live without your mother and frankly, I don't want to. I just want to be with her." Ron takes another bite of bacon as if to say 'end of story'.

"Well dad, a wise man once told me, 'we can't always get what we want'," Charles smirks at his father, they both know this 'wise man' was Ron. "It's been two years since mom passed. It's time to start living again." He reaches across the table to place his hand on his father's. "I know it's hard, and I knew it would be a major adjustment for you, which is why I've given it all this time, but two years should be enough time for you to at least *try* to start living again. Just let me make an appointment for you."

"You don't *know* anything. How could you? Did you lose your wife? You ain't never even been married, you wouldn't understand." Ron pauses to eat a mouthful of eggs. "But you don't need to understand. The only thing you need to know, is it's not gonna happen. I'm not going to no doctor." Ron Pushes his chair back from the table with a screech. "And I think it's time for you to get off to work." He stands up and starts down the hall. He pauses for a moment and begrudgingly—without turning around—says, "I love you, son."

"I love you too, dad," Charles murmurs to no one, as his father had already continued to make his way down the hall.

Charles finishes eating, cleans up breakfast, and heads out the door. He walks down the wooden stairs, heads over to the adjacent building, unlocks the lower level door, and steps in. He flicks on all the lights, walks down the hall, and settles into his desk.

The building is like most of the others in Newtown borough—old. The floors all have a gentle slope to them, the plaster is crumbling in places, even though it is mostly held in place through several layers of paint. There is conduit running down the walls; the electricity was installed several years after being initially built during a time when oil lamps were the only thing to provide light after the sun went down. However—also like many of the other buildings in town—it retains a beauty that can only be found in historic places.

Charles was unintentionally forced into taking over the family business, in this beautifully historic building, after his mother had begun her chemotherapy treatments. The transition hadn't been too difficult, as he had been being groomed for this his entire life. It was only the timing that was unintended.

A little over two years ago, Dorothy Yaniero, known to her friends and loved ones as Dot, was diagnosed with cancer. She was a devoted wife to Ron and doting mother to her children, Charles and Shannon. The diagnosis came as a shock to all parties involved. Dot was 58 years old at the time and had been healthy her entire life. A rare form of cancer had been unknowingly growing inside of her. She was given 6 months upon her initial diagnosis; the chemotherapy was never supposed to rid her of cancer, it was just supposed to prolong her life. Once it was decided that a chemotherapy life was not one to be called a life at all, she had made the difficult decision to end treatment. Shortly thereafter, she passed away. The services honoring her death were that of the royal family—which is simply what happens when your family business is running a funeral parlor.

Charles reviews the messages from the answering machine. He finds himself distracted by thoughts of his father. *Does he really want to die and join mom? I mean, it's actually sorta sweet when you think about it. One day I can only hope to love someone as much as mom and dad loved each other. But life is not a fairytale or a Hollywood movie. The dead have passed on, they have completed their time here on earth. The living must go on living until some higher power decides their time is up. It's not up to the individual to decide. I will figure out a way to help dad to start living again.*

The front door of the parlor opens. A young woman walks in.

Charles hears Patricia enter and gets up from his desk.

"It's just me Mr. Y. I hope you don't mind—I'm a little bit early. I've got a lot to catch up on."

Patricia is a petite young woman that would feel at home on the set of The Addams Family. She has long straight black and skin that is so pale it is nearly translucent. She always wears dark colors. Her look may scream death, but her personality screams life. A good combination for her career choice.

Charles peeks his head out into the lobby. "Good morning Patricia. Of course it's fine. I just was making sure you weren't a client. Mrs. Willis is going to stop in this morning to finalize the flower selections for her husband's viewing tonight. I thought you might've been her." He starts back to his desk, then stops, and sticks his head back into the lobby. "And how many times have I told you to call me Charles?"

Patricia started working at the funeral parlor a month ago. She is not yet trained as a mortician, but she answers the phones and handles the overflow of paperwork while training at school. She has been a Godsend. Her personality suits the grieving, which is ideal, as she is the first contact clients have with the business. She has a healthy respect for both the deceased and their loved ones. Her bright bubbly personality isn't too in your face to the point that it is offensive; the dark ensembles help to calm that down. She's just the right mix of everything.

"Sorry. I've just always been used to referring to my elders by mister. I was taught it as like, a sign of respect." Patricia smiles.

Charles chuckles and shakes his head. "I'm barely your elder. The stress of running this business may be aging me, but we're only 5 years apart. Just try to stick with Charles."

"Okay...Charles," Patricia replies. The word feels weird on her tongue. "And I'll take care of Mrs. Willis when she comes in. I may be backed up, but I know you also have a lot on your plate as well," she smiles. "Did you have the talk with your dad?"

"I did." Charles is thankful to have Patricia. Not only for the sake of business, but to have someone to talk to about what's going on in his life.

"How'd it go?" Patricia genuinely wants to know. Her youth allows her to still retain the curiosity that comes with being young.

"It went as I expected, I guess. I can't seem to say the right thing to get him to care about living," Charles shakes his head, "he started again about being with my mother."

"I'm sorry to hear that." Patricia bows her head. "I like, totally regret never having met your mother. From everything I've heard, she seems like she was an amazing woman."

"That she was."

The conversation is interrupted by the door once again opening. Mrs. Willis walks in.

"Good morning Mrs. Willis," Patricia says. "Let me help you with your coat." She takes the elderly woman's jacket and hangs it on the coat rack by the front door. "Please, have a seat. I'll be helping you today."

Back in his office, Charles once again begins thinking about what to do about his father. His health has been deteriorating ever since their family's loss. One does not need to be a doctor to see it. Charles doesn't want to lose the only parent he has left.

CHAPTER NINE

CLEANING THE BEDS TAKES less time than Felicia had originally anticipated. She has a few hours left before the sun takes its nap for the evening. She had begun making a rough sketch of the property as she was driving around. She is looking at it now. She decides to explore the north side of the property in greater depth.

Felicia heads that way and finds a building at the far northwest corner of the property with a root cellar still intact. The building appears to have once been a work area used to sort through crops before storage in the off-season. If Nicole or Sean saw this place, they'd say it had a good vibe.

She makes notes of all the things that need to be done in order to get the place back up and running. The structure itself seems quite solid, but the path back here is overgrown and should be trimmed down for ease of travel. She envisions a large stone lined ornamental bed out front, which should only be a matter of some tilling and planting, and bringing in and placing the border. The soil all over this property is incredibly loamy and fertile which makes planting effortless. The existing vegetable beds need some railroad tie edging replaced, as they have rotted out over the years. The shrubs are overgrown, misshaped, and in need of some pruning, but their placement is fantastic. She makes notes of all these things and continues down the path to her next destination.

Feeling like she has notated everything that needs work on the north side of the property—as well as feeling like her map is complete—she glances at the time. She estimates she has twenty minutes before losing the remaining light completely. She decides to head over to the main garden center; maybe she can catch Betty there and show her the list early. She feels that wonderful sense of accomplishment warming her body. She hopes Betty will be as proud of her as she is of herself.

Betty is in fact there when Felicia arrives. She seems flustered. She is sprinting back and forth between the garden center and a delivery van, her floral shirt bouncing with each step.

"Oh thank God, Felicia. Help me with this please." Betty is still bouncing back and forth from the garden center to the van while she talks. "I have an order for flowers that needs to go out before seven tonight. With everything going on, it completely slipped my mind. Thank God Charles just called me to make a minor change or I may not have remembered at all!"

"Don't worry, Betty. I got you. Just tell me what I need to do."

"All those flowers there need to go into this van," she points. "Then they need to get driven over to Yaniero's Funeral Home in the borough."

Betty stops to catch her breath and rubs her temples in frustration, her dirty fingers leaving gray-brown streaks on her face when she removes them. "Also, I was in the middle of transplanting some things that can't be left out of the ground overnight," she takes a rattled breath, "and to top it all off, I'm hosting Bridge Club tonight so I need to get ready for that! I know it's late, but do you think you could take care of this flower run for me?"

"Of course." Felicia has already started moving the plants to the van even before she finishes her words of agreement. "I just need the address and I'll get them there."

"Thank you." Betty shakes her head in frustration. She is flustered and having difficulty thinking straight. "I don't remember the exact address. It's on the corner of Lincoln and Washington, are you familiar?"

"Yup! The big yellow building. It's right down the street from where my sister lives." Felicia is familiar with the place because every time she passes a funeral in progress she can't help but make the sign of the cross out—a compulsion still leftover from her Catholic up-bringing.

"Anyone in particular I should see?"

"Ask for Charles. And make sure you get the delivery slip signed, I already put it on the passenger seat of the van so I wouldn't forget."

"Sounds good. I'll take care of this. You go back to doing what you were doing."

"Thank you Felicia!"

"I'm glad to help. It's what I'm here for."

Felicia finishes loading the van. Poor Betty is so over-whelmed. Hopefully Felicia can help get this business back to running smoothly for her.

Felicia backs into the funeral home parking lot. She is around the back of the van, fumbling with the door. Like a lot of the things from Betty's business, this van is older and in need of some maintenance. With sweat forming on her brow, the handle finally releases and the doors swing open. As she is making sure nothing got damaged during the drive over, she hears the door to the funeral home open behind her.

She turns around, ready with her best customer service smile plastered on her face. Her heart stops. Time stops. The most gorgeous man that has ever graced this earth with his presence is standing before her. Everything brightens. Sounds fade away.

His gray eyes seem to be peering into her soul. The smooth muscles of his arms glisten in the sunlight. His smile has just the slightest hint of a smirk to it.

"Next time, come in first, that way I can help you." Adonis in the flesh, with not only the body, but also the grace of a God, steps towards her. "You must be Felicia. Betty just called and said her new head gardener would be headed over soon." He extends a hand towards her for a handshake, "I'm Charles." He winks.

Felicia suddenly realizes she's been holding her breath and lets out an audible sigh as she reaches for his hand. She manages to get control of the swarm of butterflies that have taken up residence in her stomach.

"Yes, I'm Felicia. I just started this week."

His hand is the perfect combination of softness and ruggedness. A man who clearly doesn't mind work, but who also takes care of himself. She can't seem to let go. *Stop it Felicia. You're being creepy. Let go. Close your mouth and stop staring*. She wants to look away, but can't.

She manages to let go of his hand. She cannot seem to find any words, but she finally manages to close her mouth as her lips instinctively form a smile.

"Let me get those for you." Charles leans past her and into the van. She gets a whiff of his scent. *This must be what heaven smells like.*

Felicia watches his forearms and biceps dancing under the weight of the boxes of flowers. She lets out another sigh. *Stop it Felicia. You're acting like a lovestruck teeanger.* But she doesn't even care. Victorian novels speak of women swooning. This must be how it happens.

She's snapped back to reality by the sound of Charles' voice. "Follow me," he says as he winks at her a second time and walks towards the door.

Did he just wink at me...again? I literally cannot even right now. Felicia walks—no—floats through the door behind him.

Charles is walking down the hallway with his back to Felicia, shaking his head to himself. *Did I just wink at this woman? Twice? Yes. I did. What has gotten into me? Play it cool man.*

A few moments before, Charles had looked out his window as he heard the van pull up. When the door opened and Felicia emerged from the van, he was immediately taken aback. She seemed to glow. An aura of sparkling purplish-white light surrounded her and he felt that light enter himself. He previously believed 'love at first sight' was a myth made up by romance novels and rom-coms in an effort to make money off susceptible women who think life mirrors fairytales. But this is real life, and the glow that he just experienced could not be called anything else.

CHAPTER TEN

NEWTOWN'S CRIME LOG NORMALLY contains some telephone scams that lose people money. The ones that are hard to believe anyone actually falls for. The ones that are reported only after several gift cards were purchased at the local Rite Aid. And were only reported because the 17 year old behind the counter making minimum wage thought it was strange that a 72 year old woman was buying two thousand dollars worth of gift cards on a Friday night at 9pm, so she asked her why she was doing it and convinced the elderly woman that it was a scam. These types of scams.

Sometimes the crime log includes a noise disturbance or two. Other times a driver operating a motor vehicle presumed to be under the influence of alcohol—charges pending results of a blood test. So when a missing person is included in the report, it immediately gets noticed.

Betty is checking her Facebook feed and sees the missing person report as she's scrolling through. One of her seasonal helpers, Kaylee, downloaded the app for her last year. She told Betty she should have more of a social life.

Scrolling through a phone app was apparently this teenage helper's idea of socializing. 'It's called *social* media,' Kaylee informed her when Betty questioned the idea.

It may not be the type of socializing Betty is used to, but she quickly becomes addicted to learning the intimate details of others' lives.

When she finally manages to click on the crime log link to read it—she still has trouble with links—she sees the news of the disappearance. At first, she is a bit concerned for the woman's well-being, yet this emotion is quickly overtaken by excitement. This news was just released. The Bridge Club gals will be here any minute and maybe for once Betty will be able to share some gossip that Gladys doesn't already know.

If one were to ask Gladys, she would gladly share with you the fact that she hates gossiping. The reason she hates it? It is because of Shelley, the gossip queen who lives on her street. The one whose son went back to rehab—again—after he had been seen flirting with the mayor's daughter, Katie. Katie—who anyone who's anyone knows is sleeping with Johnny, the produce man, who is old enough to be her father. Shelley is the biggest gossip Gladys knows and she hates that she always shares everyone else's business. Finds it despicable. Maybe Shelley will at least stop spreading rumors now that her daughter is having her fourth child, which means Shelley will have to spend time taking care of her grandbabies since her son-in-law has been known to favor the bottle. Anyone who's anyone knows this.

"Heyloo!" A chorus of voices chime in from the front porch. "We brought wine and brownies!"

Betty greets her guests and escorts them to the bridge

table in the sunroom—which already has four empty wine glasses ready and waiting.

The ceramic tiled room is full of white wicker furniture with flowered cushions and a flowered area rug to match. There is no sun during this hour at this time of year, but during the late spring and summer months, the sun shines in creating an exquisite atmosphere. The crystal chandelier and string lights create a different—albeit still magnificent— type of atmosphere in early spring. And the cooler temperature is convenient for when the frequent hot flashes of this group start arising. The ladies always blame their flashes on the wine, not their hormones.

Gladys, Sue, Joanne, and Betty all sit down around the table in their usual seats. Joanne, a short jolly woman with dyed black hair and bright red lipstick, uncorks the wine bottle and starts filling glasses. Sue, another jolly woman but with voluminous blond hair, starts shuffling the cards. Gladys the self proclaimed gossip-hater, a tall and thin woman with natural gray curls, cuts up the brownies.

There is a bubbling energy in the room that always seems to join these ladies during their monthly Bridge gathering.

Not wanting to seem too eager about her new gossip, Betty begins by asking the group, "So, what's new ladies? How have you all been?"

After not seeing these ladies for several months, she is genuinely interested.

Joanne speaks first, "I've been wonderful. My Julie is expecting again! That will make grandbaby number six!" She's positively beaming with pride.

"Oh how wonderful, Joanne. Tell her we said congratulations," says Sue. "My husband and I are planning a cruise now that all of our grandbabies are finally in school and Tabitha doesn't need the extra help."

"I don't know how you managed it, Sue," Gladys puts in. "I need a nap just thinking of chasing around our Danielle's little one. And your Tabby has three!"

The group chatters on about the difference between raising children versus grandchildren. They all decide it's better to be a grandmother than a mother at any stage of the child's life.

Betty feels excluded from the conversation, as she never had any children of her own. She tries not to let this bother her as she deals out the first hand. To Betty's delight, the topic of conversation shifts without her needing to do so.

Gladys says, "My Dan is finally retiring. That man sure loves to work. I almost cannot believe he is finally doing it."

Her husband, known to most as Officer Dart, had worked at the Philadelphia Police Department for the first portion of his career. He then semi-retired to Newtown Borough, where there is much less action. "It will be so nice to have him home and around the house. Maybe he'll finally start on the honey-do list that has been growing for the past 40 years."

The ladies all join in a laugh.

"Gladys, you may think you want him home, but ever since Joe retired, he's been bored out of his mind. Which obviously means he's driving me crazy," Joanne says. This makes the group laugh some more.

"Well, it's not official yet. But so long as nothing pressing crops up, he'll be making his announcement at the end of the week."

Bingo. Here is Betty's chance. "Then I am going to assume that you did not hear about the missing person?" Betty says, thanking her lucky stars for this perfect lead-in to her gossip.

"Missing person? No." Gladys glances around the room to see if anyone else is showing signs of recognition at this news. Even though no one does, she is not pleased with her own ignorance. "When did this happen?"

"The article I read says the missing person's husband reported her missing late last night. The couple lives in the borough. I'm surprised you didn't know." Betty rubs salt on Gladys' wound.

"How scary!" Joanne says. "I hope she isn't hurt or anything. Perhaps she just ran away." She pauses and laughs to herself. "Maybe her husband had recently retired and she couldn't stand him anymore!" Joanne is chuckling, but seems to be the only one who finds her joke amusing. She never has been good at reading a room.

"I'm surprised Dan didn't share this with me," Gladys does not seem to care that she's not hiding the fact that she is more concerned that she wasn't the first in on the news than she is about someone missing. "I'm sure I'll get all the details later on. I really hope she is found quickly." *So it doesn't ruin Dan's retirement plans*.

Gladys then changes the subject. "Anyway, Betty, have you hired a new groundskeeper yet? We all know you've been looking for quite awhile. And honestly, I hate to say it, but it shows in your landscaping that I saw on the way in."

Gladys clearly makes this comment in retaliation to Betty's embarrassment of her. She notices the other women are staring daggers at her. Maybe she should lessen the blow. "I was sorry to hear of Bernard's passing. My condolences." She solemnly bows her head.

"Thank you," replies Betty. *You could have offered them sooner if you had actually shown up to the funeral.*

Betty tries to stop being petty. "I did, actually," referring to the groundskeeper question.

Thoughts of Felicia help Betty to forget Gladys' slight, as well as her desire to be crowned 'all knowing'. Every time she thinks about Felicia she is warmed from the inside with gratitude, especially after her coming to her rescue tonight.

"Her name is Felicia and she is absolutely amazing. I sent her out just a short time ago to deliver flowers to Yaniero's. I feel like I can trust her entirely to work on her own. Things should be getting back to normal around here very, very soon."

The night continues on. The mood is once again full of bubbling energy. Maybe it is because they are back to sharing happy achievements and future goals instead of attempting to one-up each other—or perhaps it is simply because the first bottle of wine is empty.

CHAPTER ELEVEN

THE RADIO TURNS ON. *I Think We're Alone Now* by Tiffany starts playing.

God, I love this intro! Such a good beat! I can't help myself but to dance. I sway my hips as I start to sing along.

I sashay over to the storage room, open the door, and flick on the light. The room is cold, and there is no furnishings except the single chair that Crystal is sitting on. I continue to set the mood with my singing, but since it's always nice to share an experience I shout, "take it away Crystal!"

"Mmmph mmmph."

"Oh, sorry. Brain fart!" I rip off the duct tape and remove the rag from Crystal's mouth. "*Now* take it away!"

"HELP!"

I slap her across the face. I tilt back my head and let out a burst of laughter. "Oh Crystal, Crystal, Crystal. Do you really think I'd be asking you to sing if there was even a small risk of anyone hearing you?" I pout at her. "Now sing! This line's for you!"

I sway my hips and snap my fingers, trying to get her in the mood." Why is she being so difficult? Classic Crystal. I shake my head. "I can see your lips moving but I can't heeeaaar you!"

Crystal manages to mumble the lyrics through her sobs.

"Great job Crystal!" I would've liked a bit more oomph, but I appreciate your effort. I knew you could do it! Things are looking up! Didn't I tell you I'd make it all better?"

I've seen Crystal a few times over the past couple weeks and she always just seemed so damn sad. Obviously, I couldn't help but befriend a woman in need. Helping others is my purpose in life and it brings me so much joy.

I continue to sing and dance. Hip shimmy. Hip shimmy. I pull the blade from out from my back pocket. "Fast or slow Crystal? Fast or slow? Your wish is my command!"

"Please, please. Don't. I'll be happy. I promise."

"Oh Crystal. You say that now—and I want to believe you—I really do. But how do you expect me to believe you when you're not even smiling?" I push up on the corners of her lips in an attempt to get her to smile.

On the ride over here, Crystal and I had a nice little chat. I told her how wasteful it was to not enjoy one's life fully and just really live it. She completely agreed. She told me that she wanted to, but she couldn't figure out how to get rid of the overwhelming sadness she feels everyday of her life. She tries to shove the pain away, but that ends up causing all sorts of other problems. She asked me to help her. Asked me.

So, I then asked her if she was willing to trust me. She said—and I quote, 'At this point, I am willing to do anything to take away the pain. Of course I trust you'.

Now, here we are and she won't even sing! So much for her claim she'd do anything.

I sometimes just can't understand people. They ask for your help, but they obviously don't *really* want it. It's okay though, if I need to be the 'bad guy' in order for others to be happy, well that's a burden I'm willing to carry. I know I'm not *exactly* a saint, but I'd be willing to bet that I am as close as you can get to sainthood while still walking around God's green earth.

Suddenly, I notice something shift in Crystal, I can feel it in the room.

"Fast," she mutters to my surprise and delight.

I look directly into her eyes and see that all the pain and suffering is gone. I see acceptance. Such a wonderful emotion. Acceptance. All the weight that has been resting on one's shoulders just floats away. No tension. No stress. Just pure relief. This is the part that I enjoy the most, watching those who have been suffering for so long finally catching a break. Is that a smile I see on her lips? I believe it is.

"Fast it shall be." I swing the blade across the left side of her neck and gracefully flip it over and bring it down across the right. "Say hello to Saint Peter for me."

And now what do I see in her eyes? Not only acceptance, but peace. As I gently lower her eyelids, I feel the peace consume me as well.

CHAPTER TWELVE

FELICIA HAS MADE IT through her first week living on her own using only the food from the gift basket left by Betty to fuel her nutrition. But now she needs to get some groceries. She still doesn't have a car. She could always Uber, but Betty has said she can use the delivery van for short trips until she gets a vehicle of her own.

Felicia travels the four short miles necessary to get to the closest grocery. She made a list before she left, so this trip shouldn't take too long. She is carrying a basket up and down the aisles, expertly navigating her way around all the other patrons. It is crowded on this Saturday morning.

Felicia is scanning the labels of two different protein bar boxes, comparing ingredients. She has no idea what she is actually looking for. She is used to shopping with Nicole and Sean. They would check the ingredients of everything she was prepared to buy and then either tell her yes—or make a face that said 'are you sure you want to poison yourself?'. She had no idea there were so many alleged 'poisons' in massed produced food. Isn't that what the FDA was for? She mentioned this to Sean once, and after the 45 minute lecture about the energy that each individual food group released which the FDA was not concerned about—not to mention the toxins released in the environment depending on the methods used to produce and ship foods—she decided it was easier to just keep her mouth shut. She just followed their suggestions and replacement ideas during their weekend grocery adventures together. Later, she would take secret solo trips to the grocery, to stock up on real food that she would hide in her bedroom—like Oreos and Cheez-its.

She gives up on label reading and instead chooses whichever is cheapest. She heads around to the produce section to pick up the last of the items on her list.

As she's rounding the last aisle, her heart skips a beat. Charles is at the tomatoes. He is squeezing each one before placing it in his cart.

Oh, he looks good. Felicia almost swoons once again as the feeling of butterflies comes into her stomach. She doesn't want him to see her here. Not like this. She just threw on some clothes this morning and pulled her hair back in a messy bun. Granted, it's not like the last time he's seen her she was done up, but she had an excuse the day because she was working outside before delivering those flowers. She doesn't want him to think she dresses like a hobo all the time.

And let's also not forget the fact that she's holding a handbasket full of junk food that would be more at home on the arm of a pot-vaping college kid than her own.

She steps back out of the produce section and bee-lines for the register. She never really knew how to select produce anyway. And it would have more than likely just sat on her counter until it went bad, while she finished off the more appealing foods, like the cheesy poofs that are already in her basket.

She finishes scanning her items, swipes her card, then grabs her bags and practically runs to the van.

Now in the safety of her borrowed vehicle, her heart rate returns to normal. Why does he make her feel this way? She obviously likes him—a lot—but she has never had a hard time talking to guys she likes. She's never gotten all medieval swoony before.

Now's not the time to ponder these questions as she realizes that she is still not one hundred percent safe from being spotted. She is sitting in a moving billboard advertising the nursery. She doesn't know what he drives, she could very well be parked right next to him.

She pulls out of the lot—now feeling safe—and decides to make another stop before heading home.

Last night she finished the novel she found in the cottage and realized how much she missed reading. It's something to take up her time when her body is too tired after all the physical labor of each day. Conveniently, there is a small bookstore in the shopping center adjacent to the grocery.

This bookstore is independently owned and not very large, but Felicia likes the ides of shopping local. The bookstore smells like—you guessed it—books.

Felicia loves the smell of books almost as much as she does the smell of flowers—or bacon. She takes a deep demonstrative inhalation and a woman approaches out of nowhere to ask if she needs help finding anything.

Startled and embarrassed, Felicia tells her no. Which is not accurate. It's been awhile since she's read anything and would have actually liked to have asked this woman for some recommendations. Too late now. She guesses she'll just have to start browsing instead.

She heads to the back corner of the store hoping the embarrassment of this woman catching her huffing book aroma will fade a bit.

Felicia wanders once again towards the front of the store and over to a shelf labeled 'staff picks' that she noticed upon entering. The bookstore employees get to select a few of their favorite titles and display them in the front of the store.

She scans a few back cover blurbs and decides on one about a man trapped at sea. This pick comes from an employee named Paul. According to Paul's bio, he is an avid reader—aren't all readers avid? Why else would they be reading?—he loves summer, and volunteers at the local fire department on his days off.

The firefighter factoid triggers Felicia's memory of her favorite book during her teenage years: *Fahrenheit 451* by Ray Bradbury. She hasn't read it since then and is curious if she'd still enjoy it. She decides to buy herself a copy. She asks the worker—Ann says her name tag—where she can find it.

Ann is a petite woman in her 50s. She is dressed in modest attire, something you would expect a librarian to be wearing. She tells Felicia the book is located in the classic section in the back and she was actually headed back there for something else, so she'll grab a copy for her.

As Felicia is scanning some more book blurbs off the 'staff picks' shelf, the bell hanging over the entrance door jingles. She casually glances in that direction and cannot believe who she sees. Charles has just entered the book store.

Felicia stares hard at the book in her hands. This time the butterflies are in her chest instead of her stomach.

I don't think I can hide from him in here, it's too small. Get your shit together Felicia. Yes, he's hot. He's supernova hot. He takes your breath away and makes you feel all weird on the inside. But it's no big deal, you've spoken to plenty of hot men in the past. You barely spoke six words to him the other evening at the funeral parlor. You need to pull it together or else he's going to think you're on the spectrum.

"Felicia?" His voice sends chills down her spine in a good way. She manages to look over at him and smile. She can't quite manage any words yet.

He steps near her. "I thought that was you." He smiles. "It's Charles, remember...from the funeral home?"

Felicia stares at him. *He doesn't even think you remember him. Say something you buffoon!*

"Hi, Charles. Yes, sorry, I was distracted by this fascinating book." She looks down to read the title she holds in her hand. *It Starts With Us* by Colleen Hoover. *Eek!* She puts down the book as if it's burned her fingers.

"Anyway, how's business?" she asks. *How's business? Great question for a man who runs a funeral parlor. Idiot!* Her internal self is rolling her eyes at her own blunder.

"Business is good. I just wish I had more flower orders." *Real subtle.* "I mean, I've been hoping to see you again." *Less subtle.*

Charles cannot seem to hide how much he loves this woman. He hasn't stopped thinking about her since her delivery the other night. That enchanting aura is pulsing around her. He would have thought it impossible, but it seems even brighter today than it did the first time he saw her.

Felicia hasn't responded, so he adds, "I know it's very forward of me, but I'd very much like to take you to dinner." *Screw subtle*.

Felicia feels like she could burst. First this new job, and now this stunning man wants to take her out to dinner? It's surreal.

Her smile turns into a grin and she is shocked to hear that she can actually manage to speak. "I'd like that very much."

"Great!" He somehow manages to step even closer to her and his smile grows, "How's Monday night?"

"Monday works for me." Felicia's heart is pulsing in her ears.

"I'll pick you up at Betty's around 7?" He expands, "She told me you moved into the guest house."

He's been talking to Betty about me? "I did. And 7 sounds great to me." *I can't believe this is happening.*

"Great! I'll see you then." Charles walks out of the bookstore and once out of view, pumps his fist in victory. Felicia doesn't seem like much of a talker so it was hard to figure out whether she likes him or not. She agreed to the date and that's all that matters. Hopefully she will talk more on Monday night.

He's halfway to his car before he realizes he just entered and exited the bookstore without making a purchase.

Chapter Thirteen

"OH HOW WE'VE MISSED you!" Nicole and Sean both simultaneously envelop Felicia in a hug. She accepts the embrace.

"I've missed you guys too," They step out of their hug, "but it's only been a week, so I don't see why we're group hugging in public."

Nicole, Sean, and Felicia meet for brunch at their local coffee bar. It's Sunday, midmorning, so the place is packed.

The modern décor seems out of place in this historic town. The outside of the building may be the original stone—repointed after decades of weathering—but inside is all new. Stark white walls are accented with vibrant pinks and purples in art deco patterns. The sleek chairs are finished in various bold neon colors—all metal, not a single piece of wood in the entire room. All the tables are topped with translucent glass.

The trio manages to find an open table and sit down.

"So, how's the new job going?" Nicole asks with a sympathetic smile. She wants Felicia to feel comfortable enough to be honest even if it has not been going well.

"I am loving it! Spending all that time in nature has been making me feel so calm. I haven't had any trouble sleeping." Felicia brightens as she continues on, "and I haven't had even a hint of panic all week!"

"Calm? You're positively glowing!" Sean practically shouts while wearing a smile from ear to ear. "There has to be more to it than just the job. I know it's a dream come true, but you're throbbing with positive energy," he turns to Nicole, "Can you feel her?"

Nicole has a look of concern on her face. "I guess." She hesitates. Nicole is having one of her visions. She is skeptical to share, not wanting to start this gathering off on the wrong foot. She sees two figures, bound together. The binding breaks and then dark smoke consumes them. She doesn't know exactly what it means, which is not normal for her. It makes her nervous. "Honestly, something seems off to me."

"Off?!" This time Sean is more than just practically shouting; he is actually shouting. Some of the other customers shoot him awkward leers. He doesn't notice—or maybe he just doesn't care. "She's radiant!" he turns back to Felicia, "Tell us. What else is going on?"

"Well, you're right, there is actually something else," Felicia remarks, "I met someone."

"Yay!" Sean claps, "Our Felicia is in love!"

"Whoa. Whoa. Whoa. I didn't say that. All I said is I met someone."

"Sure, sure. Whatever you say. But I can feel it. It's love." Sean puts his elbows on the table, resting his chin on clenched fists while he looks dreamily towards the ceiling.

"Hun, why don't you grab us some drinks?" Nicole says to her husband as she lovingly pats him on the shoulder. She wants to attempt to have a private conversation with her sister—at least as private as can be in a packed public coffee house.

"Green Tea I presume miladies?" Sean asks, with arms spread and knee bent.

The girls nod their heads in agreement and Sean gallops away. They both adoringly watch his prancing.

Nicole looks at Felicia. "I don't want to start anything off weird, but are you sure you're ready for a relationship?" Nicole places her hand over her sister's. "You've got a lot going on with the move to a new place and new job. When our emotions are strong, it can sometimes override and influence all other aspects of your life. You may think you're ready and are in love, when it's just these existing strong emotions spilling over. I'm concerned."

"It's nice that you're concerned," Felicia manages to hold in an eye roll, "but I never said anything about the L word," she pulls her hand out from under her sister's and tosses a thumb over her shoulder, "that was your weirdo husband. I simply said I've met someone. I am loving this job and this place that I find myself living. It's like it's been ripped right from a fairytale. I am really, really happy. But it's not causing me to make any rash decisions."

"And I am happy *for* you. Just be careful with this guy you met." Nicole does not yet want to reveal her vision. Not until she understands exactly what it means. "I don't want to see you heartbroken again. And it's my job as your big sister to worry."

"Again, I appreciate it. But I just think you may be being a little dramatic."

"You can call it dramatic if you want, but can you

honestly say that your break up didn't almost destroy you? Your panic attacks were as bad as I've ever seen them. It's like when we were teenagers and you couldn't even go to public school."

Felicia puts a hand up to interrupt, but Nicole keeps talking.

"I don't want to hear that you're good now. It's been a week. It's not enough time to say you're better. And I also don't want to hear that you just *met* a guy, Sean's not wrong about the love thing, I can feel you glowing as well. There is definitely something more to this."

"We're going on a date this week. That's all. I know you're my big sister, and I love you to death. But I'm a big girl too, ya know. You don't need to watch over me. The breakup may have been bad, but clearly it didn't destroy me." Felicia spreads her arms, palms up, to show that she is still here—clearly not destroyed. "And I know its only been a week but I feel different. On the inside. You know how you just *know* things sometimes? Well I do too. And I know I'm great and that this is not a passing thing."

"The tea fairy is here!" Sean interrupts as he prances to the table with their drinks.

"Speaking of dramatic," Felicia rolls her eyes.

"What? Does my fullness of life bother you?" Sean blows Felicia an air kiss and winks as he hands Felicia her tea. She returns the air kiss. He places Nicole's tea down in front of her as well. He can feel the vibe coming off her and doesn't think his air kiss would be accepted.

"We don't need to get into it anymore right now. I said my piece. I'm content with that." Nicole blows on her tea and takes a sip. "I'm glad you love your new job and new place."

"Oh yes, me too! Tell us all about it." Sean says, lightening the mood.

Felicia tells them all about the magical aspects of her cottage and the landscaping. She tells them about how she's been getting along great with Betty and how she trusts her to be on her own. She tells them about her ideas for fixing up the property. Then, because Sean clearly cannot contain his excitement, she tells them both about Charles.

"I was making a delivery of flowers when I met him. He's a customer of the nursery. Then a few days later, I ran into him and he asked me on a date."

Felicia expands to explain about her hiding from him just to see him again moments later.

"How serendipitous! Sounds to me that the universe was using fate. Right?" Sean raises his eyebrows first to his wife, then to his sister-in-law, waiting for one of them to agree with his discovery.

"Of course, hun." Nicole says more to placate him than anything else, she can't shake this sense of unease. "Be a doll and grab us some scones and muffins?"

"Sure thing!" Sean leaves on his next mission for baked goods.

Nicole finds herself a bit distracted by trying to decipher her vision. She shakes off her unease and directs her attention back towards Felicia. "So what's Charles do for a living? Do you know much about him?"

"Need I remind you that we only just met?" Felicia sees that this answer is not satisfying her sister. She goes on, "I do, however, know a little bit. He runs his family's business, which he just took over a year or so ago. He's lived in Newtown his whole life. He has one sister, older, who is married and lives in Georgia. His mother is deceased, cancer, also a year or so ago. He currently lives with his father who has not been handling his wife's death well." Felicia is thankful Betty can be a bit of a gossip. All of this information she gathered from her, not Charles. Nicole doesn't need to know that.

"What's the family business?" Nicole asks, as if Felicia's response still does not satisfy her.

Felicia intentionally left this part out. She worries that Nicole and Sean will find it creepy that he's around dead people so much.

It's not creepy to Felicia. She has a different way of viewing death than most. She doesn't associate dead bodies with dead people. A body is just a body once the soul moves on. As inanimate and mundane as a lamp. The soul lives on eternally. When someone dies, they're not gone, they're just somewhere else. We are not bodies with souls, we are souls with bodies.

Felicia decides she has to tell them. It's not like she would be able to hide it for very long. All she needs to do is mention his last name; everyone in town knows of the funeral home that's been in the borough as long as any living person here. "It's a funeral parlor, Yaniero's." Felicia prepares herself for Nicole's response.

Before she can respond, Sean arrives back at the table with their delicious treats. "Did I miss anything?"

"Felicia was just telling me a little bit about Charles." Nicole looks from her husband to her sister. "Felicia, why don't you tell Sean what he does for a living?" She smirks at Felicia. Nicole may or may not have a problem with this job, but Sean sure will.

Felicia squints her eyes at her sister displaying a look

that says 'thanks a lot'. Felicia regains her composure and turns to Sean. "He runs his family business. They've been helping people for three generations now. It's Yaniero's, over on the corner." Felicia shoots a thumb over her shoulder, indicating its location right down the street.

"Oh, how nice. I think it's wonderful that he's involved with the family business. You need someone who knows family is important. And he's successful as well, so that's a plus." Sean pauses, clarity dawning on his face. "Yaniero's? That's the funeral home, isn't it?"

"That's the place." Felicia waits for an outburst. She is both surprised and relieved when Sean continues on as normal.

"That's actually quite interesting. You think maybe he'll be willing to show me around the place?"

"Ew, honey. Why?" Nicole interjects.

"I just said, I think it's interesting. I wonder what the energy would be like." Sean looks whistfully towards the ceiling and starts rubbing the bottom of his chin.

"Anyway," Felicia's eyes go wide, she would like the conversation to change; she can see Sean's wheels turning and knows what happens if this is allowed to continue, "how have you guys been?"

They continue to chat about their week. Sean has added drums and sound bowls to his ever growing sound healing collection. Nicole is still loving him exactly the way he is. Life is continuing on as normal—their version of normal.

CHAPTER FOURTEEN

"DAD!" CHARLES YELLS DOWN the hall to his father, "have you seen my shirt?"

There are piles of unfolded clothes all over Charles' normally military neat bedroom. "The charcoal one that I wore to—Jesus!" Charles jumps. Ron is standing directly behind him.

"No need to yell. And watch your language, son." Ron's smirking.

"You scared the sh—, you scared me half to death. Stop sneaking up on me like that."

"I'm not doing any sneaking. You called for me." Ron looks around at the piles of clothes. "What happened in here? It looks like your sister's room used to look after one of her fashion show slumber parties."

"I can't find my charcoal shirt."

"What do you need it for?"

"Well." Charles has not told his father about his date yet. He worries that he'll feel abandoned.

For the past two years, Charles has spent most of his free time with his father. He worried about him being alone after his mother's death. He still worries about it.

"I'm just going to meet someone for dinner and I want to look nice."

"Look nice? Listen Nancy, are you trying to tell me that you're going on a date? You want a manicure too? Maybe some nice lace panties to go with it?" Ron lets out a roaring laugh. He enjoys teasing his son. Men aren't supposed to care what they look like. That's a woman's job. He's always teased his boy about his tendency to be fashionable.

"Knock it off, dad. Yes, I have a date. And No, I don't need a manicure or any lace panties." Charles shakes his head. "I just need to find my shirt."

"It's probably in the laundry room. I saw a bunch of shirts hanging in there."

The laundry room, of course. Charles feels like an idiot. This date has him so flustered that he had forgotten to check one of the most obvious places.

"Thanks dad."

He starts to head to the laundry room and then turns back. "And I made Chili for you for dinner. It's in the crock pot. Make sure you eat some. I won't be home late."

"Come home as late as you want. You're a big boy. And I hope this date goes well. Maybe if you found yourself a woman you'd leave me the hell alone a bit."

Charles doesn't respond. He just smiles at his father and heads off for the laundry room to see about his shirt.

He'd miss me if I wasn't constantly badgering him, I know it. Ron used to complain about his wife all the time while she was still living. Referring to her as 'the pain in his ass'. It's just Ron's way. He'd never admit to it now. You don't speak ill of the dead. It's also just Ron's way.

Charles arrives at Felicia's cottage at exactly 7:00pm.

The clocks sprung forward last Saturday, so there is plenty of light to take in the awe-inspiring surroundings. He knocks on the door, and as it opens, the surroundings are no longer the only thing that is awe-inspiring.

Felicia is wearing a simple low-cut black dress with equally simple heels. A chain of teardrop diamonds hangs around her neck. Her long dark hair is cascading around her shoulders with a soft wave.

"Hi." She smiles at Charles. This time, he is the one who is without words.

"Let me get my coat," Felicia says when she realizes he isn't speaking, and heads back inside.

Felicia spent the days leading up to her date fretting over it. She had asked Betty if it was okay, him being a customer and all. Betty has always been fond of Charles and there are no laws against dating customers; she told Felicia as such. Betty loaned Felicia a necklace to wear that would 'draw a man's eye to her goodies'. Felicia rolled her eyes at this comment. Betty could sometimes be inappropriate. She accepted the necklace anyway.

Betty had said they should call it quits early today and helped her get ready for her date.

Felicia is much less nervous now, after having spent the last few hours with Betty and hearing her words of wisdom. It's a shame Betty never had children, she has such an easy calming maternal presence.

Felicia is back in the doorway with her jacket. They walk towards the car.

Charles opens the passenger door of his black 540i BMW.

"Milady." He takes a bow—just as Sean did yesterday—and motions to the seat. Felicia welcomes this charming albeit nerdy gesture.

Charles manages to stop himself from implementing a *Dukes of Hazzard* slide over the hood of his car. He doesn't want to be away from Felicia even a second longer than necessary, and a hood slide would help, but he's already ashamed of his 'milady' comment; a hood slide would definitely be too much.

The couple arrives at *La Trattoria*, an upscale Italian restaurant in the center of town. Felicia has never been here before, it's too expensive, but Nicole and Sean always choose it for themselves when celebrating special occasions.

There are two large statues framing the entrance upon the cobblestone path to the door. The atmosphere inside is much like that of Felicia's previous employer, with the added tranquility of opera music softly playing. It has more of a Coppola vibe than Scorcese.

They are escorted to a table by a hostess named Bianca wearing entirely too much make-up and showing entirely too much leg; what is it with hostesses in Newtown restaurants?

Charles pulls out Felicia's chair for her. Bianca hands them a wine list and tells them their waiter will be with them shortly.

Although Felicia has managed to overcome the swooning sensations she previously experienced around Charles, she is still met with—although not *assaulted* like before—the sensation of butterflies in her stomach. Her heart rate increases as she peers over the wine list and into his penetrating gray eyes that are laser-focused on nothing but her. He smiles and his eyes sparkle with the gesture.

"I have a confession to make." Charles says, putting down his wine list and leaning in towards her. Felicia matches his movement. She holds her breath. The swooning sensation has made a reappearance.

With a low volume that screams pleasure he says, "I have exactly zero idea how to select a wine." His smile turns into a smirk and he can't hold back a the ensuing laugh.

Felicia lets out the breath she's been holding and chuckles herself. "That makes two of us."

They laugh together. It's a comfortable laugh. One that is usually reserved for lifelong BFFs and is rarely experienced on a first date.

The waiter arrives to take their order; a Roman God chiseled from stone whose biceps are struggling to breathe in his tight black shirtsleeves. "My name is Andrew and I will be guiding you on your culinary tour this evening." He smiles and twists the ends of his handlebar mustache.

"Have you chosen a wine, or shall I offer the beautiful couple a suggestion?"

With Andrew's help, Charles and Felicia place their orders.

After the waiter has left, Charles opens the conversation.

"So, how did you end up filling the role at Betty's? I know she's been searching for a replacement for Barney for quite some time."

"Right place, right time, I guess? I was waitressing over at Tony's and she offered me the job. I had known her for a couple months—just from her coming into the restaurant—and we always got along. We chatted about flowers quite a bit, but I never even realized she had a nursery. She's a wonderful woman."

"You're liking it then? The job?"

"Of course! It's not like waitressing was a calling for me, it was just something I did to make money. But gardening? I think it may in fact be my calling, as silly as that sounds. The peace I receive from having my hands in the dirt has changed me. All the beauty I'm surrounded by. For the first time in my life, I feel truly happy."

"I get it. And I think it's wonderful. You radiate happiness."

"You sound like my brother-in-law," Felicia smiles, "he told me I'm glowing." She laughs.

"He's not wrong." Charles grins in a way that only he can. "So, are you from the area? I'd have to imagine no, or else I would have been sure to have seen you before. You are not exactly the type of woman who can walk around going unnoticed." Charles winks at Felicia. She adores his flirty personality.

"I grew up around here, in the borough, right down the street from this restaurant, actually. I moved away when I was nineteen, to Colorado. That turned out to be a mistake." Felicia rolls her eyes. "I just moved back last year."

"I see," he nods his head, "and why do you believe it was a mistake to move to Colorado?"

Felicia feels like pouring her heart out to this man. Something deep inside of her says she can and should trust him. She has never felt comfortable revealing what happened to anyone else. She cannot explain why, but he just feels right. Like this is where she is meant to be. Like he somehow already knows her intimately and loves every dark recess of her mind. Normally when she talks, she feels as though her words do not make any impact. With him, it feels like he is not only absorbing every word, but the spaces and pauses in between them as well. He is interested in what she has to say, not in order to judge her for her words, but to use them to get closer to her, to understand her and become a part of her.

"Charles?" A disheveled man in his late twenties approaches the table. He is wearing a button down shirt, heavily wrinkled with the sleeves pushed up, and only half tucked in. "Holy shit! It is you!" The man sticks out his hand for a shake.

As Charles grabs his hand, he is yanked out of his chair for a standing embrace. The man is still clutching Charles in the bearhug while he continues on. "How are you man? It feels like forever since I've seen you!"

Charles is finally released. He steps back. He can still smell the alcohol on this man's breath from here. He remains standing.

"It's probably been," Charles pauses to think, "eight years?"

The man is Mike. He and Charles went to school together. He was a bit of a loose cannon back then. Charles hasn't seen him since he left for the military. USMC.

"Yea man, a lifetime! I'm so glad to see you. How've you been?" Mike wobbles a bit.

Charles prepares himself in case Mike falls over.

"I've been great. How about you?"

"To be honest man, not too good. Not too good." He looks down and shakes his head. "I got kicked outta the military. Apparently, they weren't too fond of my drinking. The bastards took away my VA benefits as well. It's completely fucked."

Charles can't say he's surprised. "I'm sorry to hear it. You'll make out alright, you always did."

Which is true. Somehow, no matter how many situations Mike got involved in back in the day—which was a lot—he always managed to land back on his feet.

"I dunno man. Maybe not this time. Turns out I not only earned myself a dishonorable discharge, but also a raging case of PTSD. I can't even function without some kind of dulling to the good ol' memory keeper." He taps on the side of his head. "I went to a doc for drugs. Turns out alcohol not only works better, but is cheaper considerin' I ain't got no bennies anymore." He shrugs his shoulders. He glances to Felicia, noticing Charles' companion for the first time. "And who's this hot piece you're having dinner with?" He moves towards Felicia, stumbling.

Felicia blanches. This man is making her a bit uncomfortable, but she's used to dealing with men like him. She had to do it all the time at her old job, they were mostly harmless. It always seemed more sad than anything else. She begins to speak as Charles steps towards the man and speaks for her.

"Her name is Felicia. And although she is extremely attractive, I would never use the term 'hot piece' to describe her. It's degrading."

"Alright man, no sweat. No sweat. I was just saying she's hot. You did always have a way with the ladies."

Charles gives Mike an 'it's time for you to go' look. Mike takes the hint. "I'll leave you to it. You guys have a good night."

"You too, Mike. And good luck with everything." Charles reaches out to shake Mike's hand. He's simultaneously bracing himself for the incoming bearhug, but this time it is only a handshake.

"Sorry about that." Charles takes his seat. "Mike's a good guy. He just likes drinking way too much and sometimes gets himself into trouble with his lack of filter. He's harmless though. If you ask me, he seems more depressed than anything else."

"No need to apologize. It's fine."

Andrew the waiter comes to the table with their meals. The conversation turns light. Felicia's opportunity to share her history is long passed. She's unsure whether she is grateful or not.

CHAPTER FIFTEEN

CHARLES PULLS INTO HIS driveway—technically the parking lot of the funeral home—and sees through the windows that all the lights are on in the house. It's after 10 pm. His father should have turned everything off and gone to bed by now. He rushes up the stairs in a hurry, worried that something has happened.

He gets up the stairs, fumbles with his keys, finally manages to open the door, and finds his father sitting on his Lay-Z boy watching the news.

"Hey there Charlie, my boy. You're home early." Ron mutes the TV. "No hot cockles? You didn't slip her the old salami?"

Charles' heart is thudding in his chest. "Dad, don't be crass."

Charles shuts the front door behind him and manages to settle down a bit. His father is fine. Not fine in the sense that he doesn't have a seriously disturbing sense of humor, fine in the sense that he is safe.

"It was only a first date. I really like this one." He glances at the television. "And it's not that early. The news is already on."

"It's early enough to know you didn't have a horizontal refreshment." Ron smirks.

"That's enough, dad." The color has returned to Charles' face now that he sees his father is fine—or it could be that his comments are making him blush? Charles sits down on the couch.

"I'm just breakin' your stones. I guess I'll be done now. All kidding aside, how was it? You said you really like this one."

Charles doesn't feel like going into it with his father. He is honestly a bit embarrassed by the strength of his feelings towards Felicia. His father is a man's man and romantic feelings aren't the sort of thing they talk about.

He instead tells him about his night focusing only on something real men discuss—food. "I had veal parm. It has about a pound of cheese on it and the meat was incredibly tender. It was fantastic. Best I've ever had. La Trattoria. Me and you should go over there sometime. It's expensive, but worth it. You'd love it."

"That don't sound like too bad of an idea."

Charles thought the mention of good food would spark a conversation with his father. He was wrong. Maybe his appetite really has gone away. Charles tries to keep the conversation alive. "I ran into Mike. Remember my buddy from back in the day? The one you always said had 'shifty eyes'?"

"Of course I remember him. The two of yous always would steal my liquor. After I started questioning how much was left and I started markin' the bottles, you boys'd fill it with tap water. You thought you were so clever, but I was onto your tricks."

"That's the one." Charles chuckles at the memory. His voice turns somber. "He got discharged from the military and is taking it pretty rough. He was never a bad guy. Says he's got PTSD. It's a real shame."

"Yeah, I heard. The military does that to some people. Not me. Not real men, but—" He leaves the sentence unfinished.

"Wait...how did you hear?"

"Wayne, the UPS guy. He clucks more than any hen I've ever met. He gives me more solid news than these jamokes ever do." Ron gestures towards the muted television. "He stopped in last week while you were out at the distributor. He told me all about Mike being back in town."

"Huh. How is Wayne these days? I haven't seen much of him in awhile."

"Retiring. He's using up all his leftover PTO days before he does. That's why he ain't been around much."

"Huh. Good for him."

"Yessir."

Charles has drug this conversation on as long as he can, his father has never really been a talker, unless its about the good old days.

"Well, it's getting late, I think I'm going to call it a night." Charles gets up to head towards his room. He looks at the television as he rises and sees MISSING PERSON FOUND DEAD IN QUIET SUBURB upon the screen. Newtown Borough is written smaller below it. He recognizes the wine and spirits store the reporter is standing in front of. "Dad, gimme the remote, quick." Charles unmutes the television.

"...missing just last week. Her body was found early this morning by local sanitation workers on their usual morning route. There are not many details as of yet. Police suspect foul play. The investigation is still ongoing.

Bucks County detectives have been brought in to assist. We will have more information as the story develops." The news then shifts to other stories.

Charles turns the television off. He and his father exchange a look at one another. The only sound is the grandfather clock ticking in the corner.

A moment goes by. Ron breaks the silence. "What's the world coming to? No place is safe anymore."

"Nah, don't think like that. Terrible things can happen anywhere, but the world is full of much more beauty and peace than violence. The police will do their job and figure out what happened. We don't even know what foul play means. Maybe the woman committed suicide or something."

"Maybe. But I don't like it. Not one bit."

"Try not to worry about it too much. I'm going to bed. Goodnight, dad."

"Goodnight, son."

Charles is lying in bed, but unable to sleep. He's distracted by thoughts of Felicia.

He had a fantastic time this evening. He believes they both did. But he's nagged by the idea that there is something hidden behind that glow of beauty that surrounds Felicia. He could sense her uncomfortableness in talking about herself. She talked of a mistake. He tried to bring it back up after the interruption from Mike, but Felicia shut down.

Charles wants nothing more than to break down any walls Felicia is hiding behind by showing her that his love can heal whatever pain she is suffering from. Because he's certain that's what it is. Pain. He's witnessed it before. If he could discover who or what caused this pain in such an astonishing woman, he would find them and make them wish they were never born. Charles is not a violent man by nature, but if anyone messes with someone he loves, he becomes a different person altogether.

Chapter Sixteen

The seasonal employees arrived last week, which leaves Felicia with a lot of extra time on her hands. She does not have to do as much physical labor since they've arrived and to be honest, she misses it.

Felicia is working on her side project, the old building and surrounding land on the northeast corner of the property. She wants to not only restore it to its original function and put the cold storage to good use, but something deep inside of her is also urging her on to add to the beauty of its already astounding presence.

Storage Wars—as she calls it—has been sort of an uphill battle. It has been a push and pull the whole way through. Every time she fixes one thing on the building, she turns around to notice something else wrong. But she has set her mind to it. She will win this battle. Felicia is re-securing some of the vertical wooden posts on the cellar steps when she hears Betty's voice.

"Yoo-hoo! Felicia?" Betty hollers from above.

"I'm down here." Felicia emerges from the cellar. "Hi Betty!"

"Good morning, Felicia."

Betty looks around the place. "I cannot believe how much work you are getting done around here. Everything is really coming along."

"Thanks!" says Felicia, as her and Betty both head outside to take in the sunshine. Spring seems to have officially sprung, the chilly days seem to have passed.

"I was going to come up with some excuse and pretend I needed to find you for another reason, but I think we know each other better than that by now. I'll just cut to the chase." Betty sits in the back of her golf cart and pats the seat next to her for Felicia to join. "How was your date? Dish girly, dish!"

"Oh Betty, he's just amazing! I can't even put it into words." Felicia lets out an exhale that forms a smile on her lips.

"Well, try! I wanna hear about it." Betty is as eager and excited as a tween at a Justin Beiber concert.

Felicia smiles at Betty. "I dunno. It's just...I feel so...normal with him. It's effortless. I feel like he already knows me. The butterflies and stuff that I felt when the first time we met have settled down. They've been replaced by something so much deeper, more profound." She hugs herself and raises a shoulder to her cheek. "It's like being wrapped in a blanket fresh out of the dryer. It's like nothing I've ever felt before. I dunno."

"Oh sweetie. I'm fairly certain that's called love." Betty rubs a soothing hand up and down Felicia's arm.

"Love?" Felicia feels a chill run up her spine. "I don't know why just hearing that word makes me cringe. You sound like my brother-in-law."

"Your brother-in-law sounds like a smart man." Betty places a comforting hand on Felicia's thigh. "Do you think maybe the word makes you cringe because your heart isn't ready for it? You seem completely fine with the way you feel, I see the joy pour out of you when you talk about Charles. It seems to only be the label of love—which is obvious that that's what it is, mind you—that you're not okay with."

I know this woman is just trying to be kind, but she really needs to learn to back off and stop with the love stuff. Everybody needs to start minding their own business a bit. "Now you sound like my sister."

Felicia rolls her eyes, but also nonchalantly places her hand on top of Betty's. A part of her doesn't want Betty to remove the comfort. She just doesn't want her to make assumptions or pry.

"I am fine with how I feel, better than fine. Maybe you're right and it is just the label thing. I've never liked labels. Mostly because I never seemed to fit any." She shrugs. "But I dunno about this whole 'heart not being ready' thing. Hearing that makes me more than just cringe. It makes me want to throw up."

"I don't know sweetie. The day I asked you about why you're single, you remember that day? I told you I saw heartbreak. And I meant it. I saw something in your body language. You have pain inside of you that wants to come out. I believe that's what makes you cringe."

Felicia doesn't respond.

Betty continues on. "I read a book once called *The Body Keeps Score.* One of my Bridge Club ladies had to read it for her Book Club. She liked it, so she gave me a copy. It says that even if we don't acknowledge traumas in our minds, the body does. These things need to be acknowledged and let go of."

Ugh, this is too much. "Great, now you sound like that kook at the grief counseling meeting. Honestly, I'm not sure I agree with you *or* that book. Actually, I'm kind of sure I *don't* agree. My breakup was just a breakup. No big deal. It was bad, but there was no *trauma*."

Felicia now shifts her leg to remove Betty's hand. "I don't know why people have to keep telling me there's something wrong inside me. I'm fine. I'm happy. It was just the job I had and the fact that I moved across the country. A lot of stuff was going on. That's all. If, and this is a big if, if there was anything wrong with me, it's better now." *Simmer down Felicia, this woman is clearly just trying to help.*

"You could be right. Maybe you *are* right. I'm sorry."

Betty realizes this is not the time or place to have this conversation. She sees the pain inside Felicia, but she also sees that this girl is a fighter. Betty is not prepared to be her opponent right now. Felicia may seem happy, but she's always seemed happy to Betty. It's only when talk of her last relationship is brought up that the obvious heartbreak comes to the surface. She doesn't want to keep pushing.

She changes the subject. "How are the seasonal guys making out?"

Felicia is grateful for the change in topic. She doesn't want to argue with Betty. She likes Betty. She just *really* wishes sometimes she'd mind her own business. "It's going really well. I have most of them pulling bulbs to make the flower pots for Easter. Which reminds me, we're good on pots, but we need more wrapping foil."

"I'll add it to the order; I'm putting one in today. Anything else you can think of that we need?"

"No. I think that's it."

"Okay, dear. Just let me know."

Betty glances around. Felicia has done a lot, more than she could have ever dreamed, but there is still much more to be done.

"Back to work!" Felicia gets out of the golf cart.

Betty starts to pull away, then stops. "And Felicia. I'm sorry about prying. I know you're supposed to just be an employee here. But Barney was like family. And I know I shouldn't expect you to feel the same way, but I really think of you as the daughter I never had. I'll try to be more boss and less mom if that makes you more comfortable. You're just going to have to cut me some slack if I slip up, like I said, Barney was like family so this is an adjustment for me."

"No, Betty. I'm sorry I snapped a bit. I love how you treat me." Felicia doesn't know why she snapped because she is telling the truth right now. "It's quite wonderful. And so are you. I think we're on the same page. Enjoy the rest of your day."

"You as well! Toodles!" Betty appreciates Felicia's response. She wasn't sure she'd be capable of looking at Felicia as just an employee. Thankfully she won't have to find out. She resumes her driving.

Felicia doesn't know what has gotten into her lately. She's been flooded with emotions of such strength. It's not that any of the emotions are necessarily new, unidentifiable, or uncomfortable, they're just so incredibly strong and ever changing. One minute she is overcome with joy and peace which feels like it will never end. The next she is boiling with rage brought on by the minutest of incidents. These upsets pass quickly; she doesn't go down the doomsday spirals that she used to. That's a definite improvement. Felicia is better than she's ever been in her life.

Like she told her sister the other day, she is better—she knows this with certainty. She hasn't had any panic over the past two weeks, which is a record for her. If people would stop focusing on the bad and instead focus on the good—and stop having to label everything—the world would be a much better place.

Felicia goes back to the task she was working on before Betty came to chat. She gets the screwgun out now that everything is dry-fitted into place. She secures each piece of wood using rust-proof screws with Torx heads. Once she's completed inserting the last screw, she steps back to observe her achievement. A warming sense of accomplishment fills her. Even though her work here is never-ending, and somehow the scope keeps growing everyday, she still takes a moment to appreciate that once a single task is completed, it's completed. And that makes her feel great. There is nothing more frustrating than that of incomplete tasks.

She gathers her tools and heads up the newly reinforced steps. She stops midway up and takes a few pounding jumps to make sure she did a satisfactory job. Just because it looks good, doesn't mean anything. The steps don't even rattle. She has done not only a good job, but an excellent job. She continues up the steps. Onto the next task. She thinks she'll head back outside. The day is beautiful, she might as well take in every ounce of it that she can.

Felicia kneels down in the front beds and begins removing the rotted railroad ties. The anger from Betty's prying is ancient history at this point. Felicia actually thinks the prying is quite sweet. It shows Betty cares about her. Maybe she'll try and remind herself of that next time something like this happens. She pulls up a piece of wood that crumbles in her hands. Ants scatter in all directions. She shuffles back a bit to let them relocate. Their world was just torn apart by a force much greater than their tiny size. Doesn't that happen to all of us at one time or another? The hand of God reaches down and throws your world into chaos. But all we can do is pick up the pieces and find something new—perhaps better.

Felicia takes this moment to ponder how this has happened to her. Greater forces beyond her control set in motion the circumstances that led her to this precise moment. She is working her dream job, making great money, surrounded daily by the astounding beauty that is nature. She has a wonderful boss who looks at her as more of a daughter than employee and truly seems to care for her. She has a mystical cottage all to herself that she gets to call home. She is spending time with a man more incredible than she ever thought possible. Her panic is almost entirely non-existent. Life is perfect.

CHAPTER SEVENTEEN

CHARLES ARRIVES AT THE office a bit late today. He spent the morning at Staples looking for a new desktop for the office. He arrives while Patricia is on the phone. He nods a greeting, she nods back. He walks down the hall into his office, takes off his jacket, and settles into his desk. He's thinking about Felicia this morning and is pondering on whether or not it's too soon to text her when Patricia walks in.

"Knock knock, Mr. Y."

"Charles." He smiles.

"Right. Knock knock, Charles." She has an excited look on her face. "Guess who's coming in today."

"Who?"

"That poor man whose wife was murdered. He wants us to do her funeral!"

"You look awfully happy."

"I mean, I like, obviously feel terrible that she passed on the way she did. And I also feel terrible for her loved ones. But like, I think it's cool that I'm going to see a murder victim."

Patricia is a huge fan of podcasts like *Serial* and shows like *Snapped*. Now she gets to feel like she's a part of it.

Charles finds this hobby a bit on the disturbing end

of the spectrum, but true crime is hot these days, and Patricia is a good kid with no other odd obsessions.

"I shouldn't need to tell you, I know you know better, but don't let Mr. Strathie see you this elated."

"You know I wouldn't. I'm just trying to like, burn all this excitement off now, before he gets in."

"What time is he coming?"

"Mr. Strathie should be arriving around 11. Mrs. Strathie won't be coming in for a few days. She's over at the county coroner's office getting autopsied."

"Thanks Patricia. Let me know when the husband gets here." *There she goes again, calling the body by her living name.* She does this all the time. At first it was confusing. Charles thought she was speaking of a relative, always formal with her misters and misseses.

Charles once asked her about why she did it. She said she was taught it at school. They seem to think that referring to the bodies by their names will ensure people treat them with respect. It is to help remember that they were once a living person and people still love them; they are not just an inanimate object and should not be treated as such. Charles was not taught this, he honestly finds it weird. The same way Felicia believes the bodies are not what defines us; it is instead the soul, which leaves the body at the time of passing. He still treats the bodies with dignity and respect, but not for any other reason than it is the right thing to do. If he thought these bodies held any remainder of what their souls once shared, he'd probably be too freaked out to work in this industry.

Charles heads down to the morgue to make sure they'll be ready when the body arrives. It's a few days away, but sometimes getting supplies takes time.

Charles arrives in the morgue below the funeral parlor and turns on the lights. The fluorescent bulbs hum as they begin to warm up. The familiar aroma of formaldehyde can still be detected beneath the more prominent odor of cleaning agents. Charles rolls a metal table off to the side and opens the doors of the cabinet beside the work table to make sure they are well stocked on all necessary chemicals and equipment.

Charles knows who Tim Strathie is. He's been on the news quite a bit over the past week. Charles has been following the developments closely. Not for any reason other than the unusualness of the situation.

Newtown is one of the safest places in the country. People do not go missing around here. Mostly all of Bucks County is safe. Sure, there was that one kid five years ago in the town over who murdered a bunch of other kids and then either burned their bodies or buried them with a backhoe. That was absolutely crazy. But there are crazy people everywhere. And it wasn't even in Newtown. People don't go missing here. And they surely don't get murdered.

Or apparently, now they do—at least this one did. Charles is sure the killer will turn out to be someone she knew—probably the husband, to be honest; it's almost always the husband. Thinking about it, that's almost certainly the reason Patricia is so excited, she is enough of a true crime fan to know it's always the husband, she probably thinks a killer is coming by. Her detective hat will definitely be on when he arrives. Charles just hopes she doesn't embarrass the business.

Charles has always found the morgue peaceful. He even used it as a quiet place to do his studies and homework as a schoolchild. In light of recent events, he can't help himself but to begin pondering what makes people do bad things. What could make someone take another's life? Is there such a thing as bad people? Are some born inherently evil? Or is it possible that everyone is born with both a seed of good and one of evil? Are they lurking deep inside us waiting to see which one will be fed?

Charles believes all humans to be inherently good—not evil. There are no bad people, only good people who do bad things. He's found that those who do bad things most often justify their own actions, believing what they did was not, in fact, bad at all. Even Hitler believed he was making the world a better place. He never considered himself a monster. He was doing what needed to be done on behalf of the greater good. The greater good. How often people hide their misdeeds behind the pretense of the greater good. Charles could ruminate this topic all day. But he knows he has work to do and has spent enough time on the subject for now. Maybe one day we'll have all the answers. But he doesn't believe he'll see it in his lifetime.

Charles turns off the buzzing lights and heads back upstairs.

"Mr.—I mean—Charles. I have some messages for you." Patricia hands him a stack of call-in slips. "Sorry, the excitement of a potential murderer had me distracted."

"Murderer?" Charles cocks an eyebrow. He was right in his earlier assumption.

"I didn't mean that. I meant—okay fine. I did. It's almost always the husband you know. And like, did you see him on the news back while she was still just missing? He seemed relieved that his wife was gone. Not worried that she wouldn't come back."

"I think it's too soon to make any assumptions. Remember, be professional when he arrives. For all we know, he's a grieving husband who lost his wife in a horrific way."

Both Charles and Patricia spend a moment staring at nothing.

Charles breaks the silence. "Anyway, I better get to these messages."

"You got it Mr. Y!" Patricia slaps herself in the forehead, harder than she intended. "Ugh, sorry. I totally meant Charles."

Charles chuckles as he shakes his head and walks down the hall to his office. His phone vibrates in his pocket as he sits down at his desk. Its a text from Felicia.

Thanks for last night. I had fun :) Meet again soon?

Charles feels a warmth envelop him. He hurries to respond. He was only worried about texting too soon in case she didn't reply. Now that she has made the first move, he has no fear of coming off too eager. He responds.

Me too :)

How about this weekend?

The weather is supposed to be beautiful. We could make a day out of it?

Charles doesn't even have a chance to put his phone to sleep before Felicia replies.

Saturday?

Yes. Pick you up at noon.

Dress is layers. And comfortable shoes

I have something special in mind

And don't even ask, it's a surprise

Ok :(

See you then! :)

Charles puts his phone back in his pocket and gets

busy returning the phone calls Patricia gave him. He's happily humming to himself while cheerfully punching numbers in on the phone. He leans back in his chair and puts his feet up. He couldn't be happier.

CHAPTER EIGHTEEN

THERE IS A BIT of a light breeze this Saturday morning. Falling cherry tree petals are skittering around the sidewalks. The sun is shining and temperatures are unseasonably warm in the high 60s. It turns out to be a splendid day for a hike.

Charles decided he wanted to take Felicia to his favorite overlook while he was in the shower the morning after their first date. He was reliving the evening in his mind and remembered the word she used to describe her new home; magical. She is someone that appreciates the beauty in the world, and the place he is taking her to is the most awe-inspiring thing he has ever seen; until he saw Felicia, that is.

He arrives at Betty's—he wonders if he'll ever stop thinking of it as Betty's—a little before noon. Felicia is already outside. She is sitting on an ornate garden bench below the front bow window, dressed in layers and comfortable shoes as requested.

"Hi," Felicia says with eagerness. "Can you tell me where we're going now?"

"Nope." Charles smiles as leans in to give her a peck on the cheek; as natural as could be. Felicia feels her breath catch in her chest. He picks up her hand and leads her to the passenger door of his car.

They take a short ride north through the winding roads of Bucks County. Felicia dreamily gazes out the window towards all the beauty that surrounds them. The images from the window start to slow as Felicia realizes they must have arrived at their destination.

She exits the vehicle and sees sprawling meadows and hills beyond the nearby towering trees.

"A Park?" Felicia asks.

"Yup." Charles pops open his trunk. He reaches in. "And lunch prepared by yours truly." He pulls out a basket—a real honest to God wicker picnic basket—and a blanket. "I'm a man of many talents." He winks at her. "Ready?"

Felicia gives him a grin from ear to ear. "Absolutely."

She takes the elbow that is not bearing the basket, and they start towards the path.

After a short leisurely walk down a well worn path, Charles steers Felicia onto lesser traversed terrain that Charles appears to know by heart. The going is a bit on the difficult side. Various degrees of grade, ranging from gentle to steep. Overgrowth along the path that Charles holds out of the way for Felicia to pass. A few rambling brooks that require the pair to methodically leap from rock to rock to make their way across. But Charles guides Felicia's steps, not once second guessing his strategic decisions.

"We're almost there," Charles says to Felicia, wondering if she will ever agree to a third date after this. Yet in his heart, he knows she will after they reach the top.

After a short steep slope, wherein Charles has to place

the basket down and help pull Felicia up it, they step out into a clearing.

Felicia is covered in sweat and panting from exertion as she stands in the clearing, but she is awe-struck at the view. She almost cannot believe her eyes. Charles steps in close behind, placing his arms around her. She snuggles into his arms, pulling his body against hers.

"Do you like it?" He whispers in her ear.

"Like it? I love it."

Felicia lets out a deep exhalation.

"Thank you, Charles." She settles into his embrace, taking in the view in front of her and the softness and comfort behind her.

The view is astounding. The sky is clear with just a few white puffy clouds scattered about, their animal shapes aching to be named by viewers. There is a sea of green grass dotted with the pink of cherry trees bursting with blooms. The eye can hardly discern the winding snake of a river far below that flows in and out of the shadows. As high as this apex is, there is still a backdrop of an even higher mountain in the distance, topped with an old stone tower, barely visible through the throng of bare trees. No other living creature can be seen or heard.

"This is proof of God," Felicia purrs. Her panting has been transformed into a low smooth rhythm. She has never seen such a stunning view in her life.

"So are you," Charles whispers into Felicia's ear. His hot breath on her skin sends chills down her spine.

Felicia sinks deeper into his embrace. There is nothing sexual in this movement. She is consumed by another feeling altogether. The profoundness of this moment envelops everything that ever was and everything that ever will be. Nothing else matters.

An eagle soars past their vision and lets out a peal. Felicia is shaken from her state of reverence.

"Food," she suddenly blurts out as she untangles her arms from Charles. She steps forward and turns to face him. "How about that picnic? I'm getting hungry."

"Um, yeah, sure. Of course."

Charles picks the blanket up from where he dropped it and spreads in on the ground before him. He is confused by what just occurred. One minute he was holding his dream woman, getting lost in the rhythm of her body against his, fantasizing about what he assumed would soon occur, the next minute she's looking up at him asking about food.

He tries to shake it off. He starts unpacking the food as Felicia gracefully folds herself onto the blanket.

This is not the meal he believed she was hungry for. Did he do something wrong? Or was he simply a fool to believe he was truly worthy of her intense essence?

Felicia notices the change in Charles' demeanor. She didn't mean to ruin the moment like she did, but she had suddenly felt an overwhelming sense of terror. It's gone now; it was just a flash for a moment.

She once again has been brought back to that sense of rightness and comfort in his presence. She doesn't know why that bolt of terror shot through her body. Perhaps it was simply the piercing sound of the eagle. She wants to apologize for her sudden shift, but feels it's probably better to not make a thing out of it.

"Everything looks delicious," says Felicia.

"I've made two different types of stromboli, one with spinach and sun dried tomatoes, the other with pepperoni and *ricot'*. Pasta salad with provolone and *capicol'*. Both my mother's recipe. And some homemade cannolis for dessert. But that's not my mother's recipe, it's grandma's." Charles smiles. "*Salute!*"

Felicia loves the adorable way Charles leaves off the ends of certain Italian words. It makes him the quintessential Italian American.

She takes a bite of stromboli. "This tastes even better than it looks!" *This man; he is stunningly gorgeous, says the most ridiculously flattering things, and now I learn he also knows his way around a kitchen. What was with that terror I felt? Who cares?*

"I'm glad you're enjoying it." Charles is happy that Felicia is happy. Maybe he misread her sudden shift. Her aura is still shining brightly. He has never wanted anything so badly in his life, and maybe it is clouding his perspective.

They finish their picnic; the dessert left almost uneaten after the deliciously filling lunch. Felicia is satiated in a way she doesn't ever recall feeling before.

Charles packs up the leftovers while the blanket remains spread. He and Felicia both lay back, allowing their full stomachs to take a rest.

"This place is wonderful. How did you ever come across it?" Felicia is speaking to Charles but gazing at the blue ocean of sky above her.

"After my mom passed, my father and I would argue all the time. One day, we got into a particularly heated argument and I stormed out, feeling a rage that I had never felt before. I got into my car and just started driving. Something inside me suddenly realized driving was probably not the safest thing to be doing in the state I was in, so I just pulled into the first place I could to take a break. It happened to be this park.

"I parked and then got out, thinking the fresh air would do me some good. But it seemed like every group of people I came across were happy families; sharing their time together, making memories," Charles pauses.

"I wanted to get away from it so I headed off the path, with no goal in mind other than being alone."

Charles pauses a again and shuts his eyes. He takes a few deep breaths, "I was just so angry. Angry at every-thing and everyone. I found myself cursing God for what he did to our family—what he took from us. As I'm barreling through the woods, my foot slipped off a rock and I fell face down into a silty stream. That was the point where I switched from being angry at God, to not believing he existed at all. I just turned over and sat down in the mud and sobbed.

"I didn't shed a single tear when my mom passed. I guess I was just too concerned about being strong in front of my father. I never felt like I had any time alone for myself. I was busy running the business without much help—my father was in a bad way. So I just sat there completely soaked and sobbing like a child.

"Once I felt as though I could cry no more, I became angry again. I got up and ran through the nearby stream. I just wanted to keep running forever. I didn't know where to, but I felt I just had to *keep going*. I came to a turn in the stream and instead of following it, I climbed. Climbed up through the trees and brush, get-ting pummeled in the face and arms—not even feeling it. I emerged into a small clearing. Here. I fell to my knees, soaked and panting, my heart banging in my chest, blood dripping from the scrapes on my face and arms."

Charles, for the first time since starting his story, turns to look at Felicia.

She's been lying on her side, looking at him the whole time. He smiles and continues on.

"I slowly peered out at the view. Suddenly everything just made sense. My anger was gone. My grief was gone. This was where I was running to. I had found it."

He looks back up towards the sky. "I can't really put it into words, but everything just felt right. Peaceful. There is a God and he made this. All of it. He not only made it, but He made me find it. He is part of me and everything and everyone. Who was I to judge his methods? He isn't the vengeful God I learned of in Catholic school; he is in everything. In all the beauty and all the pain and with a profound sense of wonder and awe, I just knew everything was going to be okay."

Felicia cannot speak. She doesn't know what she's feeling, but notices a tear has fallen down her cheek. She quickly wipes it away.

Charles rolls onto his side so he can face Felicia without turning his head.

"Sorry about all that. I used to be quite a private person, but ever since that moment, I've been searching for situations where I could be my true self. I don't like hiding anymore. I feel the same sense of wonder and awe when I'm with you, so I wanted to bring you here and share it."

"I appreciate you Charles. For bringing me here, for sharing your story with me—and for the delicious food." She smirks. "I like you. A lot. And I like how I feel when we're together. But I'm not special. I'm just like everybody else."

Felicia rolls onto her back looking up towards the sky—but scoots over close to Charles. He puts his arm around her. Felicia continues to stare towards the heavens while Charles continues to stare at an angel here on earth.

CHAPTER NINETEEN

THE RADIO TURNS ON. *Take Me On* by A-Ha starts playing.

Just another glorious day in the life of a savior. I skip over to the other side of the room, driven to movement by the music filling the air. The fast beat of this song always gets me hopping up and down.

"Good morning sunshine!" I remove the sack from his head. It's not morning, but removing the burlap sack that was on his head all night should make this meager light seem like morning to him.

"Time to make the bagels!" Wait, is that the saying? That doesn't sound right. Doesn't matter!

"Let's get moving!"

He slowly blinks his eyes, but otherwise doesn't stir. He looks exhausted.

I frown. I really had high hopes for this one.

But who can stay sad with this music? I start to sing along, snapping my fingers, really nailing the high notes.

Mike's been here for days. I swore he would've changed his attitude after the DT's wore off. I thought I was gonna lose him there for a hot minute—it was actually quite scary. I've never seen someone withdraw like this, but I knew he'd thank me for forcing this sobriety on him.

I continue singing and bopping up and down, adding in the occasional head tilt. Now that the tremors and hallucinations are gone, he just looks angry and tired. No thanks to be had! Can you believe it?

But alas, I do not do this for the thanks.

Mike mumbles something. I move closer. "I'm sorry, what was that?"

"I said I need a shot of something you fucking psycho." He starts laughing. And I mean *really* laughing. This makes me feel good, I enjoy making people happy. And laughter is—after all—the best medicine. I could have done without the 'fucking psycho' comment, but what are ya gonna do?

"No more alcohol for you sir, but I'm at least glad to see you're smiling!"

I bebop over to the table and pick up a tool to use as a microphone. Another refrain is coming up and I really intend to give this high note my all. I take a knee in front of Mike and really let it go. Yes. Nailed it once again. After a fist bump with the makeshift microphone in my hand, I stand up to take a bow. Mike may not be applauding—probably only because of his restraints—but he *is* smiling. Finally.

I step forward and plunge my microphone into his chest. The forward momentum has lined my ear up with his lips. Was that a 'thank you' I just heard? I believe it was.

CHAPTER TWENTY

"HAPPY EASTER!" FELICIA, NICOLE, and Sean all find themselves in a group hug—again. They reluctantly let go of the embrace.

Several weeks have passed since the last time they all saw each other. Felicia has been busy with her job at the nursery and other things—mostly with her relationship with Charles. She has been meaning to meet up with these two— especially now that she has a car— but she hasn't felt like she's had any time. Felicia hadn't worried about it because she'd talked to her sister on the phone and knew they'd be spending the holiday together. But now that she's here seeing them in person, she realizes she's missed them.

The three of them are standing on the front porch of the home they used to share. Felicia hadn't even made it in the door before the embrace began.

"I've missed you guys. Really." Felicia says, as the trio heads inside.

Felicia peers around the house, taking in everything she sees that has changed. The house is fully decorated for Easter. There are flowering bulbs on every flat surface, bowls and baskets filled with grasses and candies, small ornamental bunnies popping out from behind the various flower pots, baskets, and bowls. There are even freshly dyed eggs strategically scattered about. Felicia does not recall this from last year.

"The place looks festive," she says.

"Thanks!" Sean replies, as he takes in the room himself. "Some of what looks like Easter decor are actually offerings to Mother Earth in celebration of Ostara. If we expect to take from the earth, we must also give back."

"Yay! You're making it weird!" Felicia gives Sean a friendly pat on the back. "Can you believe I've missed that as well?"

"We're just so incredibly grateful for all She provides." Nicole says, fighting back tears. "We are so blessed."

Nicole now cannot stop the tears from falling. She lets out a wail. Sean pulls Nicole into his chest and starts rubbing her back. He's whispering something in her ear.

Felicia is a bit taken back by her sister's emotions. It's been a few weeks since she's seen them, but this is a bit dramatic— even for Nicole. Felicia is starting to feel guilty for not making time for these two. Family has a way of doing that—causing self inflicted guilt.

Felicia starts towards Nicole, but Sean puts up a hand in silent protest. She switches directions and heads for the kitchen. If Nicole needs space, she'll honor that. Yet, Felicia can't help but to feel a twinge of anger by the snub. She heads through the kitchen and out into the backyard to get her building anger under control.

The yard is spruced up for spring. The vegetable bed is fully prepped and planted; she sees the wooden stakes labeling each variety of food. She closes her eyes and takes in the warmth of the sunshine on her face. Her anger has quickly abated. She realizes she hasn't felt any anger recently—not since she moved out. Sure, she was frustrated at Betty for prying that one time, but that wasn't true anger. She lets this welcoming realization encompass her body. Life has been wonderful over the past few weeks.

The door to the kitchen opens and softly closes as Sean comes outside to join Felicia.

"What was all that about?" Felicia asks.

"My queen has been a bit emotional as of late." Sean is his usual perky self. "But have no fear, we just confirmed with the universe, it is time to talk to you about it. C'mon inside!"

He takes Felicia by the hand. But Felicia does not want to talk about it. She enjoys her life and does not want guilt mixed in with her happy emotions tainting everything. It's been years since she's felt this way. It's actually quite possible that she's never felt so good before. It may be selfish, but it also may be time for Felicia to be a bit selfish. She'll listen to what they have to say but she will not allow their negativity to invade her space. *Oh God, 'Negativity invading my space'? Did I just think that? I'm becoming like Sean. Is this just what happens when people become joyful? I'm not sure I like it. It's creepy.* Felicia gives her head a shake and comes back to the present moment. She reluctantly allows Sean to drag her inside.

Once inside, she removes her hand from his grip and is shocked when she registers what she sees before her. Her mouth first drops open, but then quickly closes and curves upwards into a smile. "Oh my God! You're pregnant!"

Nicole is holding a sonogram. Sean steps over to join

his wife.

"Yes we are!" Sean screams—dragging out the 'are' like Oprah Winfrey; he even has his arms spread wide and is shaking her hands like she does.

Nicole cuts in to Sean's viral display, lowering his still raised arms.

"We didn't want to tell you until I was out of my first trimester. I'm only at 14 weeks, but we got an early ultrasound yesterday—everything seems safe this time around—and the universe agrees that it's time to share the good news!" Nicole and Felicia meet each other for a hug. "Plus, my emotions are a wreck and I didn't want you to think it's because of something you did."

"Ha! I would never." Felicia laughs at herself for worrying. "This is awesome news! I'm so happy for you guys!"

"And I'm having sympathy mood swings myself!" Sean boasts. "That's what happens when you're spiritually connected to your partner. It's like I'm pregnant too!" Sean has a proud smile on his face.

"Of course you are, you little weirdo." Felicia says while grabbing Sean's cheeks and shaking them. She's smiling as she does it.

"So let's eat! I'm starving. Eating for two and all," Sean says as he skips towards the kitchen.

Felicia rolls her eyes and glances at her sister. Before Felicia can even open her mouth, Nicole says, "Yes. I do like him this way."

In the kitchen, the sheer quantity of food alone would have tipped Felicia off to something being up. Sean loves to cook, so their meals are always abundant, but there is enough here to feed an army. There is a heaping basket of dinner rolls, crescent rolls, and breadsticks neatly piled with their own seasonings. A colorful bowl of salad with lettuce, onions, carrots, cucumbers, and croutons, drizzled with a homemade dressing. A hot and bubbling casserole of baked ziti, its cheese melted to golden perfection. A steaming dish of green bean casserole, also baked to just the right crispness. There is broccoli, cauliflower, snap peas, and corn, all steamed just enough to be cooked, but not enough to diminish their nutrients. Mashed potatoes of both the sweet and the red variety. And finally, stuffing— which apparently you do not need a bird to stuff it in to make it taste wonderful. Nothing will go to waste no matter how much or little they consume. Sean and Nicole always take all the leftovers from holiday dinners to the local shelter.

The trio begins to chow down while discussing the upcoming birth. The due date isn't until December 21st—on the cusp of two astrological signs. Sean is hoping for a later birth, a Capricorn, so he can have another ambitious perfectionist in the house. Nicole is hoping for an early birth, not just because she doesn't want to be pregnant longer than necessary, but also because an adventurous Sagittarius would be better than living with yet another stubborn earth sign. Sean is a Taurus and he never lets anyone forget it.

They all laugh with one another, enjoying the conversation. After the pair has given their list of top baby names—which included true Sean inspired gems such as Dusk, Peace, and Moon—the discussion shifts to Felicia and her new boyfriend.

"Are we ready to admit we're in love yet?" Sean asks,

seemingly unaware of his bluntness.

"You know what Sean?" He braces for the impact.

Felicia does feel something deep, but she is not ready to admit anything aloud yet. She feels her body has known it was love since that second date in the park, but her mind has not fully decided to accept it yet.

Felicia smirks, "Let's just say I'm deeply in like—is that good enough?"

"Of course. Oh goodie! I'm so happy for you!" Sean claps his hands before digging back into the last of the ziti on his plate.

"By the way, we're going to a sound bath later this month," Nicole says. "We wanted you to come. Perhaps we could make a double date out of it? We still haven't even met this guy."

Felicia can sense Nicole's unease. "I don't know about bringing him to one of your guys' rituals just yet. But I still might like to go solo—if you wouldn't mind telling me what a sound bath is first. I hope Sean doesn't wear his infamous speedo." Felicia hopes her joke will ease Nicole's tension, but she simply gives her a look.

Thankfully, Sean cuts in, "It's not that type of bath, silly! We are fully clothed and simply bathed in sound. The vibrations are healing." Sean cocks his head. "But also, what's wrong with my speedo? I thought you loved my speedo. I feel like I always notice you smile when you see me in it."

"Honey, how about some dessert." Nicole interrupts, before Felicia has a chance to reply to Sean's question. "The pies are in the oven keeping warm. And grab the ice cream from the freezer. And whipped cream and cannolis from the fridge, please."

"Your wish is my command! Let me clear off the table of this food first. Felicia, are you done with the dinner portion? Ready for dessert?"

"I'm done with the dinner, thanks. Hopefully I can fit in some dessert. I'm the only one at this table eating for one, you know."

Felicia smiles at Sean. He enjoys her willingness to acknowledge his part in this pregnancy—even if she is only humoring him. He starts to clear away some of the plates and bowls.

After he's out of the room, Nicole quietly says to Felicia, "I've been having some visions." She awaits Felicia's response.

"Oh?" Is all Felicia manages to say.

Nicole meditated long and hard about whether or not she should share these visions with her sister. Sean thought maybe Felicia could help shine some light on them, as Nicole is still having difficulty with the full deciphering of the messages. Nicole never wants to share her un-decoded visions. But, after going back and forth about it, she decided it couldn't hurt. She believes it has something to do with her sister.

"I keep getting the same one over and over again—with slight modifications. This is what happens when I can't decode the symbolism." A pause. As much as Nicole swears by these visions, she is still uncomfortable sharing them with anyone but Sean. "Its two entities bound together. The binding breaks and they are consumed."

"That's...interesting." Felicia gives her sister an awkward smile. *Why is she sharing this with me? How am I to respond to this? No judgment, but seriously—okay, a little judgment. Creepy.*

Nicole still has not said anything. The silence is more awkward than this conversation.

"So, what's it mean?" Felicia side-eyes the kitchen, willing Sean to come back with the dessert.

"Well that's just it. I'm not sure. All I know for certain is that it's bad. Even if it didn't always come with the emotion of dread—which it does—I'd still know it's not good."

"And why are you telling me this?"

"Well, I didn't know if maybe you could help me decipher it."

"As titillating as that sounds, I don't think I can be of any help. To me, it only means what you said. People are broken apart and then things seem not good. Doesn't seem like anything special to me." Felicia shrugs. "Why's it matter anyway?"

"I dunno. I guess an ounce of prevention is worth a pound of cure? I figure if I can decode it, then I can stop it from happening."

"Has that ever happened in the past?"

"Actually" Nicole ponders for a moment. "No. It hasn't."

"So there you go."

Perhaps Felicia is right. Nicole has never been able to avert anything in the past. She doesn't even normally get this hung up on her visions—decoded or not. She decides to let it go for now.

Sean comes back into the dining room balancing entirely too much food in his arms. Felicia gets up to help him before he makes a mess.

"Thanks. I totally had it though."

"You totally did." *Stubborn. Nicole is right about not needing another one in the house.*

Felicia manages to have a small slice of pumpkin pie with whipped cream on top. She—as well as Nicole and Sean—are completely satiated. They all lean back in their chairs and the topic returns to the upcoming baby.

CHAPTER TWENTY-ONE

"WE GOT ANOTHER ONE." Dart drops a folder onto Hibbs' desk.

"Another what?"

Hibbs opens the file.

"You shitting me? Another missing person? That's twice in a month." He continues to read.

When Daniel Hibbs graduated from the academy at the top of his class, he had his sights set on action. Newtown Borough was not usually the place to find it. The only reason he took the position here was to get his foot in the door. No other departments were hiring at the time, and as much as he wanted to wait for something better, he needed the money.

Hibbs looks up from the file. "Says the missing person wasn't seen since the end of last month. Why is this just being reported now?"

"Keep reading. Apparently, he's a loaner, doesn't have anybody. The only reason it was reported at all is because his family says he never misses a holiday. He never showed up to Easter. They started asking around and turns out, nobody's seen him. So they filed."

Dart has a personal issue with everything that's been happening in town. He was set to retire, but there is no way he can leave with all that's gone on in the past month. They have that unsolved homicide still hanging. He knows the county guys are taking the lead, but he's been putting in his hours as well. Now he has to take the lead on this Missing Persons.

"I seen this guy around. Big boozer. Hell of a guy though. But he's always closing down the bars in town. I didn't even realize I had stopped seeing him around," says Dart.

"Yeah. I know he had some issues. Should we start by checking the local rehabs? Maybe he's just trying to get clean?" Hibbs is hoping to impress Dart with this suggestion.

"Nice idea. He is a practicing Catholic, I seen him over at Saint Andrews once or twice. Maybe it was a Lent thing, giving up the booze. I gave up sweets this year, just doing my part."

Hibbs laughs. "Yeah, doing your part to keep the wife happy. I know you don't buy into the religion mumbo jumbo."

"What do you know rook? Nice observation. You might just make it as a cop after all." Dart winks. "Go ahead and get started on making a list of the rehabs. I'm gonna go check on the County Boys."

"You got it."

Dart goes down the hall towards the room the County Boys have taken over. He gives a light rap on the door out of courtesy before entering; they may be higher up on the payroll, but this is still his town, he doesn't need permission to enter his own domain. He opens the door and finds Lewis and Bell scrambling to make it look like they've been busy.

"Workin' hard or hardly workin'?" Dart chuckles at his own sense of humor and closes the door behind him.

"We were just taking a five," says Bell.

"Don't bullshit him," says Lewis. "He's been around long enough to see through it." He shakes his head in defeat. "We've got nothing. We're at a dead end. There's nothing more to go on."

"He's right. The husband's been cleared. His alibi is rock solid. We don't even have any other suspects. Evidence is a joke. We didn't get shit off the body that couldn't be attributed to the dump site." Bell leans back in his chair with a matching look of defeat. "No DNA or latent fibers. No tire tracks. No cameras in the back of the store. No witnesses. No nothing."

Dart pauses to think. When there is no physical evidence, you have to talk to people. Learn the life of the victim. These guys don't seem like they know how to do that. The younger generations grew up watching CSI and think there will just be evidentiary paths to chase. More often than not, you have to follow hunches. These younger guys don't understand how to use their little gray cells. "How many times have you talked to the husband *after* you cleared him?"

Lewis and Bell exchange glances at one another.

"Uh, maybe once?" Bell offers up hesitantly.

"What does maybe once mean? Does it mean once—maybe twice? Because I'm hoping it doesn't mean once—maybe not at all." Dart says with a look of frustration on his face.

"Look. We had a conversation with him after clearing him. It just happened to be in the same sitting as telling him we checked out his alibi."

Bell looks to Lewis for help.

"We asked him if he knew of anyone that would want to hurt her. If she had any enemies. He said nobody he could think of," Lewis adds.

"And that's it?" *These guys.* If Dart's granddaughter was here, she'd be rolling her eyes—hard.

"Well, yeah. What else was we supposed to ask him? You think he's hiding something?" Asks Bell.

"No. It's not that I think he's hiding something—not intentionally at least. Look, this is Newtown. People don't just get murdered here. It's not a violent area. There has to be a specific motive for what was done. We just need to find it. And since our victim can't tell us anything, the husband is the next best thing. Set up a time to meet him at his home, or wherever else he wants to meet, just not here. The more comfortable he is, the better off."

"And what are we going to ask him?"

"Just talk to the guy. Have a conversation. Find out what she did, where she went."

Dart can see the look of confusion on both of their faces. In the modern world of texting and social media, having a conversation with someone in person is not common. And it's a shame because there is no substitute. "How about I go with you? Show you how we used to do it in the city."

"I guess that works. We're out of options otherwise." Lewis shrugs his shoulders.

"Set it up. And make sure he knows this is voluntary. Let me know when it's happening."

Dart walks out and returns to his desk. Instead of

feeling a sense of accomplishment on being involved, he feels a sense of disappointment in what the new generation has become. He doesn't think he'll ever be able to retire. His wife is not going to be happy.

Dart and Bell—Lewis doesn't go; he received a last minute call to babysit his stepchildren, his wife had an appointment she neglected to tell him about—head over to a pizza place in town to hold an interview with Tim.

The Clubber is more of a dive bar than a pizza joint. One wall has a bar running along it, there are slot machines on the walls, a jukebox, and a pool table. They grab one of the tables on the elevated platform in the back corner. This is the best they can do for a bit of privacy. Yet the place is fairly empty, so it should suffice. Only one elderly man at the bar—Skip, he's always here—and a pair of younger men playing pool. Privacy is not too necessary in this situation anyway. If it was, this meeting would've been held at the station. Comfort is the priority right now. They order a pie and some wings for the table and await Tim's arrival.

"So what's the game plan? I assume I just let you do the talking?" Bell says.

"I think that's best. I haven't met with him yet and so between the two of us sitting at this table, I'm the only one here who never accused him of being a bad guy. That should help him be more comfortable with me. I don't want him nervous. The guy's been through enough. I just want to ask him about his wife's habits and who she hung around with. Get a clear picture in my head. Then I'll see what crops up."

"Okay. That works." Bell suddenly looks like he's gotten an amazing idea. "Oh I know! I'll take notes."

Dart lets out a deep sigh. "That would be good, Bell. That would be good." He cannot believe this guy made County detective.

Tim walks through the door, sees them in the corner, and heads towards their table.

Dart stands up and motions for Bell to do the same. As Tim approaches, he sticks out his hand for a shake. "Good to meet you. Wish it was under better circumstances. Sorry for your loss."

Dart lets go of the handshake. "My name is officer Dart. And you already know this fine gentleman to my left." \

Tim shakes Bell's hand.

"Have a seat and I'll be sure to make this as painless as possible. I've already ordered a pie and some wings for the table. Feel free to order anything else. It's all on us."

The three men take their seats.

"Again, I'd like to extend my condolences for your loss. I can't imagine what you're going through. Our focus is on catching the bastard who did this. I know it won't bring her back, but hopefully it will offer a bit of closure."

"Thank you. I appreciate the effort you guys have been putting in. I don't know how I can help, but I'm obviously willing to try."

The pizza arrives and Tim immediately takes a slice. Bell starts in on the hot wings, adding red pepper flakes. That man has a stomach made of lead.

Dart isn't eating yet. He is confused by Tim. He understands now why he was the prime suspect, besides the obvious reason of being the husband. He says the right words, but something is off in his behavior. Dart has talked to his share of grieving people who lost their loved ones to violence—it happened all too often in the city. Tim's behavior does not fit. Appetite is often the first thing affected when a loss occurs. This guy is reaching for his second slice. And he looks down-right...happy? Dart takes in all this information. He files it away for later.

"No thanks needed, we're only doing our job. Now Tim—do you mind if I call you Tim?"

"Not at all."

"Tim, run me through, if you wouldn't mind, a day in the life of Crystal. What she would do on a daily basis, let's say, over the past month? Where could I find her on any given day? Did she keep to a routine? Who were her friends?"

"Well, definitely no routine. No real friends either. But you could pretty much always find her at home. She didn't really do much of anything to be honest. Not since our baby passed away."

"I'm sorry to hear that. It must've been tough losing a child. I can't even imagine."

"Thanks. I mean, it was absolutely the worst thing that has ever happened to me. Ever. And I can't imagine any-thing ever happening again that even compares to it. But enough time has passed, that I grieved and moved on. Crystal was still having a hard time with it. She left her job—to distressed to work—that's why she was home most of the time."

"Okay, you say most of the time. What did she do when she went out? Did she have any counseling appointments or anything like that?

"Nothing. I'm telling you. I don't know what else I can say. She was home all day. Occasionally she would go to the grocery to get food, or the drug store for medication, but otherwise, she stayed home. Then one day I came home from work and she's not there. Her car's still in the driveway. Her phone and purse are still there. She was just gone. I don't know what more I can tell you."

Tim is starting to get angry. Dart can see it in his face. This is not going as he planned. He'll have to try a different tactic.

"Okay. I can see that you're telling us all you can, I'm sorry. Let's look at this from a different angle. I don't want to upset you any further, but hear me out. What if you were the intended victim? I mean—you are the one suffering here. Can you think of anyone who would want to hurt you?"

Tim lets out a smirk. "You think someone killed Crystal to hurt me?" He shakes his head. "I'm 100% certain that's not what happened."

"How are you so certain?"

"Because. I was filing for divorce. It's not that I didn't love her, I did—and still do. I always will. She just became too much for me to handle recently."

"Huh." Dart shoots a look of ice at Bell. How did no one tell him this? Or did they not even know? His look goes unnoticed as Bell is not paying any attention. He's too focused on the plate of hot wings in front of him.

Dart needs to rethink this entire thing. Of course Tim looks happy. He no doubt was just saved thousands of dollars by her death coming prior to their divorce. His alibi may be rock solid, but maybe someone was doing him a favor. Dart needs to get his head right. He is boiling with anger on account of not having this information prior to now. He needs to calm down and regroup. He looks down at his smart watch, feigning an alert.

"Well, thank you for your time, Tim. I apologize, but we need to get out of here." He rises, backhanding Bell on the shoulder to get his attention. "Like I said—the tabs been paid—you can take your time and enjoy the rest of your lunch. We'll be in touch."

CHAPTER TWENTY-TWO

"I DON'T KNOW WHY you had to drag me out this morning."

Ron is grumpy as usual. His son came to him earlier today and invited him to join him on a trip to the park. At first, it didn't sound like too bad of a plan, he figured they'd go fishing. But when Ron got in the car and noticed the lack of fishing poles, his mood soured. He'd rather be watching the game.

"It's a beautiful day, dad. You rarely get outside anymore. Sunshine is good for your health."

Today's trip is not just about his father's health—although the sunshine is a fortunate bonus.

Charles pulls into one of the upper parking lots, backs into a spot, and turns off the car.

"Ready?" He is out of the car before his father can respond.

The passenger side door opens and Ron steps out.

"This way." Charles heads off towards a picnic area.

"Slow down boy. Your old man isn't what he used to be." Ron is breathing heavily. Charles stops to allow him to catch up.

"Let me tell you, if you don't use it, you lose it. And there's no way to get it back—not at my age. You know, I used to do fifty push-ups and fifty sit-ups every single morning. It's a habit I started way back in the military. The day your mother died, I stopped. And look at me now." Ron raises his arm to show the lack of muscle and definition. "I tried doing push-ups the other morning. I couldn't even do one. Not even from the nancy position."

Charles assumes his father means from his knees. His political correctness is something that needs work, but one thing at a time.

Charles resumes walking, this time at a slower pace. "Ah c'mon dad, I'm sure it's not that bad. You can get your strength back. I'll help if you want me to."

"You wouldn't understand. You're young. It's not the same for me."

"You're not that old at all. You still have plenty of years ahead of you."

"Well, I don't want them."

"You say that now, but if you start getting your health back in order, I believe you'll think differently."

"It's not about my health, you know that. It's about—

"SURPRISE!!" A chorus of voices yell from the picnic area upon their arrival. There is a group of people surrounding the tables and benches. The area is adorned with balloons held down by weighted bundles, streamers draped from tree branches, and a large sign strung from the pagoda stating 'Happy 65th Birthday'.

Two small children run up to Ron and wrap their arms around his legs.

"Happy birfday grandpa!" The little boy, with a headful of blond curls, says.

"Yeah, happy birfday!" Echoes the little girl with matching curls.

Both children step back and run over to their mother, who is approaching. Sharon leans in and gives her father a kiss on the cheek. "Happy birthday." She scoops up her littlest and balances her on her hip. The older boy clings to her leg.

"My God. Don't you know you're never supposed to throw a surprise party for anyone over the age of sixty? Look at all this." Ron dramatically clutches his chest. "You're bound to give an old man a heart attack."

"It's good to see you too, dad." Sharon smiles.

She and her family flew up from Georgia to celebrate this day with her father. When Charles called her to invite her up, she had excitedly secured her tickets while still on the phone with him. It's been awhile since she's seen everyone. She knows her father is happy to see her and his grandchildren; this is just his way.

Sharon leans over and gives her brother a peck on the cheek. She looks down at her children,

"Guys, are you going to say hello to your Uncle Charlie?" Sharon says as she swings the toddler on her hip in his direction.

"Hi, Uncle Charwie" Both children say in unison.

"Hey kids," Charles gives a small wave to his niece and nephew, smiles, and turns to his sister.

"How was the flight? Did Greg come?"

"The flight was good. Greg's here. He's over on the grill."

"That's good, I'm glad." Charles turns to his father, "Let's say hello to everyone else, dad."

Charles and his father make their way through the throng of excited faces. Many hugs and well wishes are exchanged. They both take a seat on one of the benches attached to a wooden picnic table.

Charles is scanning the area. Felicia is supposed to be here. He was nervous about her meeting his entire family all in one go, but this seemed like the right time. When he realizes Felicia isn't here, he pulls out his phone to send a text. Just as he is about to press that little paper airplane, he feels a warmth spread over the back of his neck. He looks up to find Felicia arriving. She has a shy look on her face as she waves to him. *That glow.* He puts away his phone and gets up from the bench to greet her. They swap a short kiss; its length does not diminish its intensity.

"Sorry I'm late. I was actually hanging back in the parking lot. I was a little anxious showing up here alone. By the time I worked out my silly nerves, I saw you and your father headed up the path and figured it couldn't hurt to wait a moment longer—as to not ruin the surprise."

"You're here now and that's all that matters. Let me introduce you to everyone." Charles places his hand in the small of her back and guides her to the cacophony before them.

Aside from Charles' sister and her family, many other friends and relatives are present as well. Charles introduces Felicia to his Uncle Joe and Aunt Judy. Their adult children. Joe Jr, who has a wedding planned to his fiancé Ashley next year, and Jessica, who is expecting her first child—rather children—as she has been artificially inseminated and is pregnant with twins. He then introduces her to his dad's war buddies, Matt and Jake, who share some colorful stories about Ron as a Gunner's Mate in the Navy.

The duo makes their way through the crowd. Felicia attempts to remember names but finds herself forgetting the previous name as soon as she's introduced to someone new. They finally settle down next to the birthday boy himself. Ron is seated alone at the table.

"Having fun dad?" Charles asks as he seats himself across from his father. The question only elicits a shrug.

"This is Felicia, the woman I've been telling you about."

"Nice to meet you!" Felicia says, reobtaining her long dormant waitress smile. She is seated across the table at Charles' side.

"It's nice to meet you too. I was starting to think my boy had made you up in his mind." Felicia giggles at the comment. Charles is smiling as well. "You two sure have been spending a lot of time with each other."

"You have a wonderful son. He's easy to spend time with."

"Says you. Try living with him," Ron harrumphs.

"Easy now, dad."

Charles is getting nervous. He wants to change the subject before his father decides to go off on one of his rants. "Why are you sitting here alone? These are family and friends you haven't seen in quite a bit."

"This. Do you see? This is exactly what I mean." Ron ignores his son and is speaking only to Felicia. "He's always telling me what to do. Let me tell you a little story."

"That's quite alright," Charles interrupts, "I don't think Felicia wants to hear any stories about me." He looks to Felicia with an apologetic shake of the head and shrug of the shoulders.

"Oh no Charles, this is where you're wrong. I would love nothing more than to hear stories about you from the person who knows you best—your father." She bats her eyelashes playfully at Charles. He smiles. She looks towards Ron eagerly. "Go on, Mr. Yaniero."

"Surely darling, but please, call me Ron." He clears his throat. "So this charming boy of mine, who you seem to be so fond of, is not so charming all the time. He has another side." Ron spreads his open hands, palms facing forward in the shape of a rainbow. He is really getting into the theatrics of his story. It's been a long time since someone has actually seemed interested in what he has to say.

Charles says, "You guys carry on without me. I'm not sure I want to be around to hear this. Also, I'm hungry. I'm going to grab some food. Do you guys want anything?"

Ron shakes his head.

"Not yet, thank you. I'm too excited about this story to eat." Felicia grins broadly at Ron with her eyebrows raised.

Charles kisses her on the top of her head and heads off in search of food and less awkwardness.

"Please Ron, go on."

"As I was saying. Wait...what was I saying?" Ron pauses and rubs his head.

"You were going to tell me a story about Charles. About how he's always telling you what to do." Felicia flashes another smile of encouragement.

"That's right. That's right." Ron pauses again. "Charles is my son. And you're the woman lovely who lights his eyes." The words come out jumbled.

"Are you feeling okay, Ron?" Felicia asks as her heart rate suddenly increases.

"I'm alright, bit of a headache is all." Ron rubs his temples again. Felicia notices not only the slur of his speech, but a droop in his face. She doesn't hesitate. This man is having a stroke. She pulls out her phone and dials 911 while simultaneously beckoning for Charles.

"Nine-One-One. Where is your emergency?"

Felicia knows the drill now. "I'm at Tyler State Park in Newtown Township. My name is Felicia Gerhart. My phone number is 215-555-4870. My boyfriend's father is having a stroke. We need an ambulance."

Charles' ears hear the words come from Felicia's mouth but his mind does not immediately register what is happening. He doesn't move.

"Emergency technicians are en route. What's the victim's name?"

"Ronald Yaniero. Is there something we should do while we wait?" Felicia asks the operator.

"If he is not already on his back, see if you can get him into that position to help the flow of blood to his brain. Otherwise, just sit tight until the techs get there. They will be to you in less than 6 minutes."

"Okay." Felicia turns to Charles. "Help him lie down."

Charles snaps out of his shock and steps towards his father. "We're gonna lie down now, dad. Okay?"

Ron looks at his son with confusion. Charles helps him off the bench.

"You're having a stroke. Felicia is on the phone with 911. You're going to be okay."

"I like her, son." Ron turns to Felicia. "I like you Felicia. And I also think you're really pretty." He turns back towards his son. "Isn't she pretty?"

"Yes, dad. She's pretty."

Charles is in agony. He is trying to stay calm and strong for his father. His insides feel like they are tearing apart. He looks up at Felicia, who still has her phone held to her face. She sees him looking and offers that familiar smile highlighted by the glow around her. She doesn't look nervous at all. Her smile settles Charles a bit.

The dispersed crowd of family and friends has closed into a tight knot. They stay close, but still allow Charles and his father space. Sharon has knelt down to be with her father and brother.

"It's okay dad. The ambulance is on the way." Sharon says through glassy eyes.

The ambulance arrives and takes Ron to the hospital. Charles and Sharon ride together in Charles' car. Felicia follows behind in her own vehicle. She wasn't sure that Charles would want her with there, so she asked if she should come. He gratefully accepted her offer.

The ride to the hospital was short, but the pacing in the waiting area is long. After an indeterminable amount of time, a doctor arrives through the doors to the waiting room.

"Mr. Yaniero?"

Charles stands up. "Yes? How is he?"

"Your father is fine. We confirmed that he had a stroke, but he is already responding to treatment. His vitals are stable. He will be here for a few days, but he's a young man. He'll overcome this. We'll have to run some more tests to see the extent of the damage, but our initial findings are hopeful. We'll be moving him to a room as soon as one becomes available."

"Can we see him?" Sharon asks.

"As soon as we have a room ready. A nurse will let you know."

"Thanks, doc."

Charles is not thrilled with the idea of not being able to immediately see his father, but he is where he needs to be.

Charles pulls Felicia towards him and takes a moment to drown himself in the comfort of her presence. He would not have been able to react the way she did; so calm and determined. He snuggles closer and breathes in the deep awe of her, thanking the heavens above that they sent her into his life.

CHAPTER TWENTY-THREE

FELICIA—SURPRISINGLY—FINDS HERSELF LOOKING FORWARD to this sound bath with Nicole and Sean. Charles' father came home from the hospital yesterday and he could use some time to get his father settled in.

She drives to the address Nicole had texted her earlier in the day. It's not far, but she has never been to this particular area before. She turns off the street, down a long paved drive, and over a small wooden bridge. There is a large pond to her left flanked by seven different color Adirondack chairs positioned in a rainbow. She pulls into a parking lot in front of a large Victorian style house with a separate building off to the side.

She steps out of her car and is greeted—assaulted may be a better word—by Sean.

"I'm so glad you came!" He says 'I' and not 'we' like he usually does. His embrace lifts Felicia off of her feet. "Are you ready to take this magical journey of sound?"

"I am. Where's Nicole?"

"Oh, she's already inside, getting us a good spot. And don't worry, we brought you one of our extra yoga mats for you!" Sean smiles and claps his hands. "Let's go! It's almost time."

They enter the building next to the home and remove their shoes. They step into the sound therapy room. There is a large gong on the rear wall, surrounded by various sized chimes. The ceiling is painted black and littered with tiny moving colored dots projected by lasers from below. There are a plethora of candles of various heights sitting on all the window sills and ledges. Upon closer inspection, the candles are battery powered—yet amazingly lifelike with a flame that flickers in every direction. A man is sitting on a yoga mat at the head of the room. He is surrounded by translucent bowls in various sizes and colors. Nicole is lying down on her back in the front row with a bolster under her knees, her eyes closed. On either side of her are two vacant yoga mats. Sean takes the one on the left and sits down in lotus position. Felicia settles onto the one on the right, kneeling down and sitting back upon her calves.

"Hey, sis," Felicia says, "how are you doing?"

"Fine, I guess." Nicole responds without opening her eyes.

Felicia looks over at Sean who waves a hand across his throat signaling that she should let it go. Felicia ignores his warning.

"Only fine? That's not like you."

Nicole opens her eyes and abruptly sits up. "Not like me? Well I'm so very sorry to disappoint you. Maybe you should try being exhausted all the time and peeing all the time and feeling your body swell up. Maybe you wouldn't be 'like you' if you were met with a river of blood from brushing your teeth every morning and even more blood every time you blow your nose. Try having a craving for foods that don't even seem to exist without traveling to a foreign country to get them. Then, you let me know if you still feel like you!" She crosses her arms and slams her body back down on the yoga mat.

Felicia looks to Sean for some assistance. He gives her an 'I told you so' shrug.

"Pregnancy is not going well I take it?" Felicia courageously asks.

"I'm fine."

"Welcome." The man in the center of the bowls begins to speak. "My name is Pierce and I will be your guide for our sound bath experience this evening. I like to refer to myself as your guide, because tonight we will truly be going on a journey.

"I will start off with some drumming, followed by gongs, closing with the crowd favorite, the sound healing bowls. If this is your first journey, please be aware that your body may go through different phases throughout the night. You may be met with dissonance as the vibrations make contact with your energy. Do not fight it or struggle, just focus on your breath until the dissonance turns into harmony. I assure you it will." He smiles as he makes eye contact with all the participants around the room.

"I'd like you all now to join me in a relaxed seated position, to do some breathwork before we begin the sound part of the evening. Once we begin with sound, you will want to lay back and get as comfortable as possible. Shifting around is okay. Falling asleep is also completely acceptable. You will still receive the healing benefits of the sounds even if you are not awake and aware. Allow your body to do what it needs to do."

Once everyone is in a seated position, Pierce begins again. "Softly close your eyes, take in a breath, and let out an audible sigh. Releasing anything that no longer serves you."

The group inhales and lets out their sighs, barely audible.

"Let's do that again, but I would really like to hear you this time."

This time the group's sighs are loud enough to be heard but Pierce still wants more.

"One more time. And really release with an audible sigh."

This final time the group has it. The sound of sighing in the room is so loud that a few people start to giggle. Felicia is one of those people.

Pierce goes on to instruct everyone to let out a specific sound with their exhales. Each different note coordinates with a different chakra and is supposed to open them in their body. Felicia does not know what a chakra is, but she does know she is having a wonderful time. After the round of breathwork is completed, everyone lies back, closes their eyes, and gets comfortable in preparation for the sound bath.

Over an hour later, Felicia is shaken back to the present moment. She is overcome by an immense—yet fleeting—sense of terror. She blinks a few times to take in the room around her. Her nerves have settled.

"Take your time coming back into your body." Pierce's soft words fill the room. "Wiggle your fingers and toes, stretch if you need to stretch, and once again join me in a seated position when ready."

Everyone slowly starts to sit and Felicia finally gets a chance to survey the people around her. It's mostly women, ranging in ages from young to middle aged. Sean is not the only male present aside from the instructor. Felicia recognizes Tim, the man from the grief group. He catches her gaze and nods a smile in recognition.

"Hey," Felicia taps Nicole on the shoulder and gestures with her eyes towards Tim. "that guy from grief counseling is here."

"Yeah, he comes all the time." Nicole responds in a hushed tone. "I can't believe somebody murdered his wife."

"Murdered his wife?" Felicia does not watch television or listen to any kind of news. She is not aware of what's been happening in her town. She's taken aback. "When did this—"

Felicia's question is interrupted by Pierce's closing words.

"Ah," he lets out an exhale. "I hope everyone enjoyed their journey this evening. Thank you for coming. Please make sure you all drink plenty of water over the next few days. Let's close by taking one final breath together."

The group synchronistically breathes in and out.

"Namaste."

"That was super amazing! Did you guys go on a journey? I sure did! I was soaring above the ocean looking down at a school of dolphins who seemed to be leading me to serenity." Sean is beaming with a sense of self-satisfaction.

"That's great Sean," Felicia says quickly. "Nicole, what do you mean his wife was murdered?"

"Keep you're voice down, he's coming this way. I'll tell you about it later." Nicole says in a strong but quiet voice.

Tim is approaching. "Tim, how good to see you."

Nicole reaches out to embrace him.

"It's good to see you as well. Sean, you're looking elated as usual."

Tim shakes Sean's hand. He turns to Felicia. "And...Felicia, right? How are you?" He shakes her hand as well.

"I'm good. This was a weird night huh?" Felicia is having trouble focusing on the conversation with thoughts of murder floating through her head.

"Oh, I love it. You'll be feeling the benefits over the next couple days."

"Well that's good I guess."

There is a long awkward silence. Felicia can't come up with anything else to say.

"Well, I should get going. It was nice seeing you all. And I'll see you two at grief counseling on Thursday?"

"We'll be there." Nicole answers for her and Sean.

"Alright, well, have a great rest of your evening." Tim saunters away.

"Dude's weird. Right?" Whispers Felicia to Nicole and Sean with a confused look on her face. "Seems a bit too jolly considering the stuff he's been through, no?"

Felicia eyes go wide and her eyebrows raise, insinuating that this should be an obvious fact.

"I dunno. People react differently to different things. It's not our place to judge." Nicole replies. "Let's get out of here. I suddenly have a craving for ice cream. Stop at the parlor with us on your way home?"

Felicia nods her head. "Okay."

"Sound bath and ice cream? All in one night? Yule has come early this year!" Sean smiles showing all of his teeth.

Felicia, Nicole, and Sean get their ice cream and have a seat outside in front of a propane fire pit. The days are warm but the nights are still chilly.

Nicole rode over in the car with her sister and explained all that she knew about Tim and his murdered wife. Nicole also told Felicia about the other missing person. Felicia found this information hard to swallow. She is out here living her best life, all the while tragic things are happening around her. She licks her soft serve cotton candy ice cream while trying to digest all this tragedy.

"How's Charles' father?" Nicole asks.

Another tragedy. "He came home today. The tests all came back pretty good, no long term damage. But it turns out that he's a diabetic. He just has to make some changes in his diet and get some exercise. They put him on medication, for now."

"What a shame. How's Charles handling it?"

"Honestly, I think he's fine. He seems a bit stressed, but no more than usual. He's spent most of his time worrying about his father's health for the past two years anyway, so this is nothing new for him. I almost think it's a relief to have his father forced to take action. The burden is off of Charles to convince his father that he needs to start taking care of his health."

"At least that's something." Nicole takes a moment to eat another spoonful of ice cream. She ordered pistachio with gummy bears and caramel on top. She is not ashamed of her weird cravings. "So when do we get to meet this Charles?"

"I guess whenever. We'll set something up."

"Oh! How about The Awaken festival next weekend?" Sean excitedly suggests. He seems to be enjoying his vegan vanilla ice cream.

"No, Sean. Nothing weird." Felicia rolls her eyes.

"Is The Awaken festival weird?" Sean is working out his apparent confusion in his head. The girls ignore it.

"How about we just meet for dinner?" Nicole suggests.

"Works for me. I'll check our schedules and let you know."

They finish their ice cream, say their goodbyes, and head home for the evening.

During Felicia's short drive home, she turns the radio off. She wants to spend these moments alone with her thoughts. Something happened to her tonight during the sound bath, but she doesn't quite know what. She can't remember what was going on during that hour or so. There are some memories—piecey and fuzzy just like a dream—but she knows with absolute clarity that she was not asleep. She doesn't know *how* she knows this, but she knows it all the same. Another thing she knows for certain is whatever happened is important. She must remember what happened.

Felicia pulls up to the cottage and parks her car. She turns off the engine but isn't ready to get out. *I remember hearing drums. Then I felt like I was watching myself from above. But not myself as I appear now. I was someone else entirely. And in a different era of time. I am dressed in Victorian clothing. I'm walking towards the edge of a cliff. Then everything goes hazy. I don't know if it is a lapse in my memory of tonight, or if I did not experience a continuous stream of events. The next thing I remember is being on a wooden platform in front of a crowd. What does this mean? And more importantly, why do I feel so compelled to understand it?*

Felicia's phone buzzes. It's Charles.

How was tonight?

Weird. LOL.

Come over tomorrow for breakfast? I want to hear all about it. Around 10? I'll cook bacon :)

Can't wait! See you then! :*

Goodnight <3

Goodnight <3

Felicia feels herself inwardly smiling, a warmth growing from her core flooding her entire body. She doesn't know why she was allowing herself to get all wrapped up in whatever happened tonight. Her life is fantastic. She's not going to dwell on weird unexplainable compulsions. She gets out of her car with a sense of overwhelming gratitude for the life she is living and enters the magical cottage she gets to call home.

CHAPTER TWENTY-FOUR

"GOOD MORNING!" PATRICIA IS bright on this dreary and rainy Monday.

"Good morning, Patricia. I can't thank you enough for pulling the extra weight around here while I was with my dad in the hospital."

"No worries at all! I'm glad to help. How is your father?"

"He's back to his old self already. His old complaining self." Charles shrugs. "I take him to his doctor early this afternoon. I'll be leaving at 2:00pm."

"That's good...I guess. He's like, a tough man. It's going to take more than a little thing like a stroke to dampen his spirits."

Patricia smiles and then shuffles around some papers on her desk. She looks up at Charles, "Mr. Baker is coming in today at like, 10 for his interview." She shuffles around some more things. Her organization style seems haphazard, but she always seems to find what she's looking for. She picks up a few pieces of paper and hands them to Charles. "His first name is Harvey. Here's his resume."

"Thanks."

This past week has made Charles realize he needs

more help around the funeral home. He needs more time to look after his father. However, deep down he knows this is a lie. In reality, he just wants to spend more time with Felicia.

"I'll be in my office if you need me. Otherwise, just let me know when Harvey gets here."

Charles scans over Harvey's resume for the third time as he walks towards his office. Mr. Harvey Baker has over 30 years experience in the life celebration business. He is one of the most coveted in the industry. He is fiercely loyal. The only reason he is on the market at all is because his current employer decided to retire and sold their business to a corporation; he'd rather work for a family business. Charles hopes he will make a good impression and can convince Harvey to work for him. He sits down at his desk to silently rehearse the things he plans to say.

With the interview over and Harvey successfully signed on as a new employee, Charles feels the tension release from his body. He has no idea how long he's been in a state of agitation, but he is pleased to feel it slip away.

His father's stroke did not do anything to increase his worries. If anything, it showed that his fear was not unwarranted. Even though it will continue to be an uphill battle, he is happy to have the support of the doctors in his efforts to rehabilitate his father. Because that's what this will be; a rehabilitation.

Ron was a healthy man while his wife was alive. She would make sure he ate right and got the appropriate amount of sleep. He was working and exercising because he was in good spirits, in love with his wife and his family—and simply with life itself. Ron had always been someone that Charles could look up to.

Watching his father deteriorate over the past two years has been heart wrenching. Charles could not understand how someone could go from one extreme to the other so quickly. He always thought being raised surrounded by this business had helped him have a strong understanding of loss. His family was met with it every day. They catered to the grieved and assisted them in their time of need. Yet nothing could have prepared him for his father's reaction to the loss of his wife. Even while witnessing his own grief for his personal loss of his mother, it never made any sense to him. Though it does now.

Charles bore witness to grief time and time again. Not only from living at the funeral parlor, but from his own personal losses of grandparents and great aunts and uncles in such a big family. What he's realized is the thing he did not experience until now was the fullness of true love. This is what has now caused him to be capable of making sense of what his father is going through. Not the witnessing of grief, but love. Sure, Charles has often felt the love of his family, but it's just not the same as the power of true romantic love for someone you choose—who also chooses you. The well of warmth, comfort, connection, peace, and sheer joy that he feels inside his body since he met Felicia is overwhelming. He cannot imagine what would happen to him if this feeling was suddenly stripped away. On cue, his phone buzzes.

How'd the interview go?

Fantastic. I hired him!

Yay!!! :) I'm so happy for you!!! Celebrate later? ;)

Charles takes a moment before he replies. A winky face after 'celebrate later'? He is unsure what this means. Charles and Felicia have been spending almost all their free time together, but they have yet to explicitly pronounce their love for one another. Not with the words—or the action. Could this be what the winky face is implying, or is Charles overthinking it? It doesn't matter how long it takes to profess their love, he knows it's real, and that's all that really matters to him.

Sounds like a plan. What did you have in mind?

How about I cook for you for once? My place at 7?

I'll be looking forward to it all day

:)

Charles starts getting things buttoned up for his early departure from work. He spends the next hour placing orders for supplies and returning emails and phone calls. He collects his things and heads for the door of his office. Before he turns off the lights and closes down for the day, he takes a moment to smile at how everything is finally going right in his life. He's hired a new employee, he is in love, and now his father will be getting the help he needs. Life is fantastic.

"Good afternoon Ron, how did your weekend go?"

Ron is sitting on crinkly paper, wearing a hospital gown—and a sneer. He wonders if doctors just make people wear these things so they can feel superior. How is he supposed to feel like an equal talking to a fully clothed man while his ass is hanging out?

"It sure was better than being in the hospital, I'll tell you that. The food's no good there, doc. I thought you said my diet was important. And sleep. You said sleep is important too. How is anyone supposed to sleep with all those machines buzzin' and beepin'? Not to mention—"

"Dad," Charles interrupts, "I think he is asking how you felt over the weekend—physically."

His father would have gone on for an hour if no one stopped him.

"Isn't that right Dr. Morgan?" Charles shoots an apologetic look to the doctor.

"Yes. That's what I meant Ron. How do you physically feel?" Dr. Morgan returns Charles' look with one that says thank you.

"With my hands." Ron smirks and displays his hands. No one laughs. Ron gives up with these people. "I'm fine doc. If it's my time, it's my time. No need to waste money and energy fixing up someone who don't want to be fixed." He shrugs. "And I'm sure as hell not gonna spend my last days on this earth forcin' cardboard foods down my throat and shapin' up my body like I was in the navy again."

"Ron, by today's standards you're a young man. You have a lifetime ahead of you if you just make a few simple changes to your diet and lifestyle."

Ron understands what the doctor is trying to say. The issue lies in the fact that the doctor does not understand him. No one seems to. Ron has lived a happy life full of love and pleasant memories that some never become fortunate enough to get a chance to experience. He's had his fill. He just doesn't want to do it anymore. It's that simple. He doesn't want to continue to experience life alone while putting any burdens on the family he's got left. He misses his wife, and it does make him sad and lonely. He is not, however, sad about wanting to die. He's grateful for the life he got to live. He'd like to go out on a high note. He doesn't want to add another 20-30 years to his story. What if the remaining years end up tainting all the other ones? It all makes perfect sense to Ron. He'd never kill himself. He believes in an almighty and powerful vengeful God. Heaven and Hell. He knows he'll never see his wife again if he goes the cowardly route. Therefore, he is not actively trying to die, but he will passively continue to live his life in a way that does not prolong it.

"I 'preciate what you're trying to do, doc. But I'm goin' to just keep doin' what I'm doin'. And since I fought for this country's freedom, I'd say that's my right."

Dr. Morgan has seen this before. He knows pushing is not the solution.

"Okay, Ron. You're right. It's your life and you have the freedom to do as you choose." He pauses to let out an exhale. "You also have the freedom to change your mind. I'm going to have one of the girls up front print you out a packet in case you do. And don't hesitate to call me if you have any questions. You can go on and get dressed."

Dr. Morgan leaves the room and Charles follows out behind him.

"Don't worry, I'll make sure he follows your instructions." Charles says to the doctor.

"You're a good son. But just make sure you remember that's what you are—his son—not his father." Dr. Morgan puts a hand on Charles' shoulder.

"Thanks."

CHAPTER TWENTY-FIVE

FELICIA'S COTTAGE IS FILLED with the mouth watering aroma of garlic. Luckily, it is doing wonders to cover up the previous scent of burnt food.

Felicia wanted to do something special for Charles. And don't they say the way to a man's heart is through his stomach? Felicia never cooked an entire meal before in her life. She always had someone else around to do it for her. People who love to cook rarely want to share the responsibility. Her ex loved it and so did Sean. She never felt the need to learn. While living on her own, she deferred to take-out or things that only needed to be microwaved. But she figured it couldn't be that hard, she might as well try it.

Forty minutes later, Felicia was at Betty's door with a look of defeat to go along with her food covered clothing. Betty took one look at her and started laughing. She immediately knew what had happened. Betty used to love cooking for her Barney. She was happy to oblige in preparing a meal for Charles.

"Alright, sweetie. I better get out of here so you can get ready."

Betty is packing up all of her cooking utensils. No wonder Felicia didn't manage to make a meal. She doesn't have any of the essentials. Betty makes a mental note to drop off another care package.

"Have a nice night." She winks at Felicia.

Before Betty gets a chance to walk out the door, Felicia embraces her in a dramatic hug that would make Sean proud.

"Thank you so much Betty! You're a lifesaver!"

"Anytime darling."

Felicia walks Betty to her car and thanks her a second time. She comes back inside and gets dressed for the evening. She already has her outfit picked out. She picked it out even before she sent Charles the text this afternoon. She is jittery with excitement.

Charles and Felicia have been seeing each other for several weeks now. As much as she loves the courtesy and respect he has shown her through all this time, she wishes he'd make his move already. He says such incredibly sensual things and she always expects something physical to happen, but it never does.

Tonight, she decided she will do her best to make him understand she is ready and willing. This outfit is the first trick she has up her sleeve. Although, the sleeves are see-through, so she won't be able to hide anything there. Charles seemed to have loved that simple black dress she wore on their first date. Black is the color she chooses for this evening as well. A low cut black cami under a see-through black lace sweater—with even more of a plunging neckline—paired with a black knee length lace skirt with a slit up the thigh. With her hair down in loose waves, she awaits his arrival.

There is a knock on the door at precisely 7:00pm.

The vision Felicia sees when she opens the door encourages her to believe Charles has the same kind of night in mind. He is holding a bouquet of flowers—red roses—one of her favorites. He is wearing a fitted black tee that shows off every curve of his muscles. Felicia starts to move her eyes down to inspect the rest of his ensemble, but has to instead look away and steady herself. Dinner first. *Then* dessert.

"You look stunning as always," Charles says as he hands Felicia the flowers and kisses her on the cheek. He steps past the threshold.

"It smells amazing in here."

Tonight, the radiance from Felicia is the most vibrant he's ever seen. He thought it would start to fade with their time spent together—the familiarity of it—but it has only continued to grow.

"Doesn't it? I hope it tastes as good as it smells. I tried something new."

Felicia convinces herself that this is not quite a lie, as she did try something new. It doesn't matter that they won't be eating her new creation because it's lying outside in the trash can. She still technically *did* try something new.

"Let's get to it. I want to hear all about your day," Felicia says, as she leads Charles into the kitchen.

Charles takes a seat at the dinner table. It is covered with a black tablecloth and matching cloth napkins. A bowl of fresh flowers with a burning candle is placed as a centerpiece. Felicia brings the meal to the table and has a seat across from Charles.

"*Buon appetito,*" Felicia says, just as Charles did during their picnic.

Throughout the meal, the conversation flows easily. Felicia talks of her job and how she still manages to find a new thing each day that inspires her. Charles talks of his new employee, Harvey. He hasn't even started yet and is already Charles' favorite. They talk of Ron's trips to the doctor's offices and how he's still the stubborn man that everyone knows and loves.

Mid-laughter, Charles suddenly blurts out, "Felicia, I am truly, madly, deeply in love with everything that is you." He doesn't know why he felt compelled to say this, he just did.

Felicia nearly chokes on the wine she is sipping. She clears her throat.

"Charles," she begins, then realizes she doesn't know how to go on.

"It's okay. You don't have to say anything." He places his hand over hers. "I just wanted to say it. Needed to say it." He smiles.

During the ensuing awkward silence, Felicia is trying to figure out what exactly is happening. As soon as she heard the words, she felt the same short lived terror that invaded her at the end of sound therapy. Just as then, it was gone in an instant, but it was absolutely there. She doesn't understand it. She feels so completely safe and warmed by Charles, so incredibly at home. Yet these words do not quantify how she is feeling. There are no words to explain what is going on inside of her. There is a struggle pulling her in two different directions.

"Anything for dessert?" Charles breaks the silence. He too was trying to figure out what went wrong. He knows Felicia has strong feelings for him. He believes she must be hurting inside. He believes he saw her light wink out—for just a moment—after the words passed by his lips. He doesn't want the evening to become awkward, so he tries to shift it back to casual. Felicia seems to appreciate this.

"Of course."

Felicia does in fact appreciate the change of mood.

"I picked up some cannolis at the bakery. I'll clear the table and grab them."

Felicia stands up to remove their dinner but she first places her hand on Charles' and smiles, mimicking the kind gesture he showed her. She wants him to know that all is well.

The cannolis shifted the atmosphere back to laughter and lightness. Delicious Italian desserts have a way of doing that. Felicia tells Charles a story about Sean's new sound therapy and how he believes the baby will be born in perfect health so long as he keeps playing tuning forks daily. She tells Charles that Nicole believes even though the baby will be in perfect health, he or she will not have a father around if Sean doesn't stop. Charles asks when he will get to meet Nicole and Sean. Felicia likes the fact that he is interested. She assures him it will be soon.

Tonight does not end up being the night that Felicia and Charles physically display their love for one another, yet it is a good night all the same.

CHAPTER TWENTY-SIX

THE SUN IS SHINING. Birds are chirping. It's a beautiful day.

Nicole and Sean are getting ready for their Memorial Day picnic. As much as they both abhor war, they understand the sacrifices that are made for their freedom and always spend the day honoring those who have lost their lives serving others. Their way of honoring consists of candlelit vigils and moments of silence and gratitude. This year—at Felicia's request—they've gone a bit more commercial. She explained to them that their methods, as wonderfully as respectful as they are, may not be understood by others. And today is the day they finally get to meet Charles.

"Are you sure we have enough decorations?"

Sean is nervous. Today they are meeting not only Charles, but his father as well. Sean learned Ron was in the military and he wants to make a good impression. He spent the last week painting mason jars red, white, and blue to place around the yard. He went around collecting red, white, and blue paper from all the local recycling bins to make paper chains. He planted an American flag in the yard using impatiens of the appropriate colors. He spent countless hours on Pinterest gathering ideas ensuring that all the food would be patriotic.

"Of course. Everything is perfect!" Nicole embraces her husband. Her hormones have leveled out and she is finally enjoying her pregnancy.

She loves the effort Sean has put into this day. He has the tendency to go overboard, but he only does it in order to make everyone's life a bit brighter. She looks up at him and imagines the wonderful father he will be. She leans up and kisses his cheek.

"Don't worry. Today will be amazing."

The gate creaks open as Felicia walks into the yard.

"What in the world?" Felicia says as takes in all the work Sean has done. "No time to make a miniature statue of liberty?" She smirks.

"Oh my Gods and Goddesses! What a wonderful idea! I wonder if there's time." The smoke forming around Sean's head is almost visible as his wheels turn trying to come up with a quick plan.

"I'm just messing with you Sean. Everything looks wonderful." Felicia embraces her brother-in-law. She turns to Nicole. "And you look wonderful as well." Felicia embraces her sister.

"Thanks. It's great to see you."

Nicole is happy to see her sister. She is not as happy to meet Charles. She still does not approve of this relationship. It's just a feeling, but she always trusts her gut.

"Charles and his father should be here shortly. I'm so excited for you guys to finally meet them!"

Felicia knows her sister is not fond of Charles, but she feels it's more the idea of him than anything else. She knows once she meets him—and sees him as an actual person instead of the idea—she'll change her mind.

"I'm glad you're happy." Nicole says, trying not to

disappoint her sister, but also not wanting to lie. "Come inside. Help me bring out the food."

Felicia and Nicole go inside while Sean continues making last minute adjustments to the yard. As usual, there is enough food to feed an army.

Felicia is piling up trays on her arms. Working as a waitress comes in handy. She leans towards her sister. "You're gonna love him, ya know."

Nicole is doing a not-so-well job of handling trays herself. "If he makes you happy, I'm happy."

"Hey! You sound like me!" Felicia laughs as her sister shakes her head and maneuvers her way back outside. Felicia follows behind, wondering if this maybe wasn't the best idea after all. Nicole's hormones may have leveled out, but she still doesn't quite seem herself.

Outside—as the table is set and Sean finally seems to be satisfied with the decor—the gate opens and Charles and Ron enter.

"Happy Memorial Day!" Sean shouts. "You must be Charles. It's wonderful to finally meet you." Sean embraces Charles—who has previously been warned by Felicia about all the hugging that goes on here. Charles hugs Sean back and even manages to lift him off the ground. Sean is beaming.

"And this must be the infamous Ron." Sean winks. "Pleasure to meet you as well."

Surprisingly, Sean sticks out a hand and offers a traditional masculine shake. Ron takes it with a look of relief.

"It's nice to finally meet you, too." Charles responds as Sean guides him and his father further into the yard. "Felicia talks about you guys all the time."

He looks around. "This is a nice place you've got

here."

"Thanks! We love it."

"Happy Memorial Day!" Felicia says, as she and Charles kiss hello. "Happy Memorial Day, Ron. I'm glad you came. It's a beautiful day for you to get outside. I know you don't like it when it's chilly."

"My boy promised me that if I came, he'd let me eat whatever I wanted. So I'm just here for the treats." Ron winks at Felicia. He eagerly looks towards the table with the food on it. He smiles. "So if you don't mind."

Ron walks to the food, grabs a plate, fills it with cookies, and sits down at the table.

Nicole finally makes her introduction. "Hi. I'm Nicole." She eyes Charles. No one says anything. Felicia notices Charles is eyeing Nicole with a reciprocal hard stare. The tension can be cut with a knife.

In his usual fashion, Sean's childlike enthusiasm saves the moment.

"Oh look! A hummingbird!"

Felicia and Ron both turn their heads in excitement to see. Nicole and Charles remain locked on one another.

"How magical!" Sean beams. "Hummingbirds are good luck, you know! They mean troubling times are over."

Sean muses for a moment.

"I don't know who's been having troubling times, it's definitely not me, but hooray for whichever one of you it is!" Sean's statement breaks the staredown—but not before Nicole gives Charles a quick raise of the eyebrows.

"Ron looks like he's having a glorious time! Aren't you Ron? What do you say we *all* grab something to eat."

Everyone grabs a plate and fills it to their liking. Ron

has gone back for another plate of cookies. Charles sits next to his father and Felicia sits next to Charles. Nicole and Sean both take a seat across from them.

"So Ron, Felicia tells us you were in the army?" Sean asks.

"Navy." Ron replies between bites. "Where's the can?"

"You mean the bathroom?" Sean questions.

"Yeah. It's time to drain the lizard."

"Dad—" Charles starts but doesn't finish because he is distracted by Sean's laughter.

"Oh, I like you Ron!" Sean says with a smile from ear to ear. "You say exactly what you're thinking! How liberating! Come on, I'll show you where it is." The two of them head inside.

"So, Charles," Nicole abruptly says as soon as her husband is inside. She once again resumes her hard stare. "What exactly are your intentions with my sister?"

Charles swallows down the bit of food suddenly caught in his throat. "I'm sorry, what?"

Nicole smiles politely. "I'm asking what exactly are your intentions with my sister." She glances at Felicia whose face has turned red. "What? I'm liberating myself. Taking a cue from Ron and saying what I'm thinking." She shrugs her shoulders.

Felicia is embarrassed and tries to make light of the situation.

"You don't have to answer her, Charles. Her pregnancy must be making her overprotective of her loved ones."

"It's fine," Charles says. He places his hand on Felicia's thigh and smiles warmly. "She's just looking out for her family. I get it." He turns to Nicole. "My intentions are to make sure your sister has the happiest and healthiest life possible. To shower her with love and warmth at every possible opportunity."

Charles is relieved his father is not here to hear him talk like this.

"I've never met a woman so incredibly deserving of the best life possible. Felicia is simply the most amazing woman that has ever existed."

Nicole rolls her eyes. "And what makes you think you're the man for the job?"

Charles is taken aback and feels a sense of anger wash over him. He does not mind being questioned about his feelings for Felicia, but for someone to assume he is not good enough for her triggers his rage. He takes a moment to collect himself.

"How dare—" he stops himself and takes another moment, breathing as deeply as possible. He thought he was calm until he opened his mouth.

Felicia is feeling her own sense of rage. Why is her sister acting like this? Charles told her it was fine, but he doesn't look fine. To be completely honest, she's never seen him like this before. He looks as though he is about to burst. That increasingly familiar wave of terror passes over her again—for only an instant. She speaks up.

"Nicole, what's with you?"

"Nothing is with me." Nicole gives Felicia a confused look. "I'm just asking him questions. Isn't this how we get to know one another?"

"I mean, yeah, questions are fine, but aren't you being a bit rude?"

"I'm just messing around. Charles seems like the type who can handle it." Nicole looks to Charles who she realizes does not appear to be handling it. She decides to back off.

"I'm sorry. I didn't mean to upset anyone. Charles, you seem to make my sister happy and that's what I care about. Maybe these hormones are still taking over more than I thought."

Charles has regained his composure.

"No, it's fine. Maybe I'm just still more stressed out than I thought." He lets out a deep sigh. "My father's health still worries me. I can't believe I agreed to let him eat whatever he wants today. How many cookies do you think he's had so far? It's like living with a toddler."

The door opens and Sean is laughing so hard he can barely remain upright.

"If you ruin my bread, I'll ruin your head!" He says through his tears of laughter, clearly mimicking Ron. He arrives back at the table. "That father of yours is hilarious!"

"You may think he's funny—only seeing him in small doses," Charles says to Sean. "Maybe you guys should take him for a week as a test run for having a child."

Charles grins and laughs.

"Oh come on," Nicole says, "he's a grown man and was in the military. He can't be *that* bad. I think you're being a bit dramatic." She has not only stolen Felicia's line but adopted her eye roll as well.

"Don't get me wrong, I love him to death. It's just a lot of stress dealing with him since my mother died. He doesn't want to live anymore. He has better days than others, but its like he's intentionally trying to live as unhealthily as possible. I thought the stroke would have scared him straight, but it seemed to have the opposite effect. It's like his plan is working."

"I don't know. The man seems full of life if you ask me." Sean puts in. "He seems to be enjoying himself. He lights up when he talks about your mother."

"That's just it though. Mom's gone." Charles leans back in his chair, defeated.

"She's not gone. She's still alive in your memories and his. She's just crossed over. Her energy still exists," Sean says, like it's the most obvious thing in the world.

The door opens as Ron comes back from using the bathroom. He must have went looking through their refrigerator because he has a cannoli in his hands.

"Hiding the good stuff are you?" He is smiling. Sean is right, Ron is enjoying himself.

"Dad, where did you get that?" Charles is embarrassed and turns to the others to apologize.

Felicia places her hand on Charles' thigh before he can get the apology out. She quietly says, "He's fine. Try not to worry so much." She kisses him on the cheek. She turns to Sean. "Why don't we get grilling before everyone fills up on dessert. You start up the grill, I'll grab the food." She rises from the table.

"Great idea!" Sean bounces up and prances towards the grill. "Wanna help me with this? Show me how it's done?" Sean asks Ron, who lights up at the opportunity.

"I'd be happy to. Where's the lighter fluid?"

"Not that kind of grill Dad." Charles yells over his shoulder.

"Not that kind of grill? You kids and you're fancy technology. Let me tell you, in my day, you had to do everything by hand." Sean leads Ron to the grill as he continues his story about how much better things used to be back in his day.

Nicole and Charles find themselves alone at the table. Charles seizes the opportunity.

"Why don't you like me, Nicole?"

"Who says I don't like you?" She has a challenging look on her face.

"It's fairly obvious that you take issue with me dating your sister. What have I done wrong?"

"It's nothing you did—I just get a bad vibe." She leans in, challenging him further, " So—what are you hiding?"

"Hiding?" Charles makes a face. "I'm not hiding anything."

Felicia comes back outside with a tray full of various sliced up vegetables, cobs of corn, and something that resembles burgers—although she knows it can't be real meat. Charles rises to help her, although what he's really doing is trying to get away from this conversation.

"Let me help you with that."

"Thanks." In a lower tone, Felicia says, "was my sister interrogating you again?"

"Oh no, she's fine. It's fine. I just figured you needed a hand." Charles gives her a sheepish grin.

They both know he's lying, but Felicia appreciates it. She gives him a look and another kiss on the cheek.

"Thanks." Felicia says again, knowing that Charles understands what she means.

They take the food to the grill.

There is no further interrogation from Nicole as the day carries on. Ron is the center of attention for most of the afternoon. Sean and Felicia truly enjoy his stories and take every opportunity to spur him on. Nicole doesn't say much—nor does Charles. At least three of them are enjoying their Memorial Day.

CHAPTER TWENTY-SEVEN

BETTY ARRIVES AT FELICIA'S cottage bright and early. The plan is for the two women to go over the property together to see about hiring contractors to take on some of the structural work with the buildings. Felicia has been more of a help than Betty could have ever dreamed. She is empowered by Felicia's excitement at bringing more beauty to the property. They have discussed opening the grounds to the public. They want to start having walking tours once everything is in order. They decided on both free tours, and paid guided tours—this way they can spread the beauty to others even if they do not have the money to spend.

Betty gets out of her golf cart and raises a hand to knock on the cottage door. Before she's managed to make contact with the wood, the door swings open.

"Good morning Betty!" Felicia is the only person Betty has ever met who is as much of a morning person as her. "Another beautiful day in paradise!" Felicia gestures her inside.

"Good morning! And it is! Shall we sit on the veranda?"

She means the back porch; Betty always has a way of making everything sound fancy. Felicia loves it.

"Of course!" Felicia gathers up some papers and they proceed through the house and into the backyard. Felicia spreads a hand drawn map on the table and weighs it down against the wind with some river jack from the nearby rock garden.

"This is incredible, Felicia. Absolutely incredible," Betty says, looking down at the map as wonder and awe spread across her face. "This was a fabulous idea! It will come in so handy, I can't believe I've never had a map drawn up before—although I guess I never really had the need. How did you do this?"

"It was easy. I just made small sketches while driving around each day. At night I'd come back and add the new places to this master copy. Then I redrew the whole thing once I had all the places marked. It was no big deal, really." Felicia feels herself blushing.

"I think it's fantastic." Betty looks over the drawing a bit more. "And look, you even named places. 'The Starlit Pond'. 'Bed of Roses'. And what's this," she points to the map, "'Eden'?"

"Oh. That's the place I go to feel at peace. This job was a fresh start for me. And that's the first place I felt at home. So I call it Eden." Felicia shrugs as she feels her blush deepen. "Silly, I know."

"It's not silly, sweetheart. As I said, I think it's wonderful."

Betty looks at Felicia with that maternal gaze that comes so naturally to her.

"I know you've had some difficulties in your past. And I'm thrilled to see that it's all fading behind you."

"Thanks, Betty. I really mean it."

And Felicia does mean it. Betty is such a calming

presence in her life. She knows she cares for her. And in the way Felicia needs to be cared for—not in the self guided way Nicole has always shown her.

"You're welcome, dear. If you ever want to talk about your past or anything troubling you, please know I'm here for you. Simply to listen—not to judge."

"Thanks. I—," Felicia wants to open up to Betty, she just doesn't know if she can. She has never allowed herself to be vulnerable before. But with the fiasco the other evening with Charles and dinner, and the weirdness that went on during Memorial Day, she feels she needs to try sooner rather than later. As well as not wanting to repeatedly experience these self perpetuated awkward moments, more importantly, she doesn't want to let the beautiful relationship she's begun with Charles to die. As much as she doesn't want to admit it, she knows her past is interfering with not only her present, but her future. "I do want to release whatever this is I'm holding onto." Felicia looks down at the table. "It's just hard."

"I know." Betty places her hand on top of Felicia's. "I'm going to say something to you that my father used to say to me all the time. 'Do what is easy and your life will be hard. Do what is hard and your life will be easy,'" she pauses to let the words sink in. "I've tried to live my life according to that credo. And I have to admit—it's worked out quite well for me."

"Your father sounds like a smart man. And he raised a wonderful daughter." Felicia looks up at Betty. "I think I can do this."

"That's another thing my father always used to say to me, 'it doesn't matter whether you think you can or think you can't—you're right.'" She smiles.

"Betty, its just, I think my real issue is that I don't believe I've had any trauma. I don't believe that anything is a big deal that's *ever* happened to me. I think to complain about my past would be to be ungrateful."

"Oh sweetie, I may not have known you all that long, but I have already seen you minimize your emotions. Regardless—talking about yourself doesn't need to be complaining—just think of it as sharing."

"I think I'm in love with Charles." Felicia hears someone say, a moment before she realizes it was her. Now that it's out there, she might as well roll with it. "No. I *know* I'm in love with him. It's just that whenever I think it to myself—let alone try to say it to him—this wave of terror passes through me."

"That's completely normal. Love is a scary thing."

"That may be true—but it doesn't feel like love is the thing that terrifies me. It's like. It's just. I dunno. I used to have panic attacks like crazy. I would get flooded with adrenaline with no rhyme or reason behind it. It would just happen and take over. That hasn't been happening to me anymore. Truly, it's been a bit weird. Never in my life have I gone without a panic attack occurring at least once a week, and I haven't had one in months. Not since I started dating Charles—or maybe since I started here. I don't remember exactly when. It's not like there was a flashing light that said 'congratulations, this is your last panic attack.' I wish I could figure out why they stopped. Because everytime I get this flood of terror, I'm waiting for a panic attack to hit me. Then, it never does. I try not to let it bother me because—like I said about complaining—it feels ungrateful. How can I possibly worry about figuring out why I have these tiny bursts of terror when at least it isn't a panic attack?"

Felicia takes a break, she feels as though she's been rambling. She's not sure what point she is trying to make. Or if she even is trying to make one at all. Maybe she just needs to vent.

"I dunno—don't get me wrong—I'm light years better than I ever have been before. I'm finally living my life and enjoying it. I appreciate all this beauty with the flowers and landscape that I'm surrounded by. I'm living in the moment and I feel like I'm creating beauty for everyone to be able to appreciate. I met this amazing man and breathe him in every chance I get. But something is off—something inside me. Something doesn't feel right and I'll be damned if I know what it is—or if it matters."

"I'm not sure it does, sweetheart. If you're happy—I say let it be. Things have a way of working themselves out. Plus, I'm sure Charles knows you love him—even if you don't say the words. *Acta Non Verba*." Betty shrugs her shoulders.

"What's that mean?" Felicia cocks her head to the side.

"Actions, not words." She smiles. "He knows how you feel. Men can be dense at times, but not Charles—and not with this. But then again, I've always thought highly of him."

Felicia is so thankful for Betty. She feels a sense of gratitude wash over her.

"You know what Betty? This was great. You're right. I feel better already. I don't need to figure out why I became better or why I still feel off. I'm going to continue focusing on the present." She grins from ear to ear and raises her eyebrows up and down a few times.

"Now what do you think about a water fountain on the pond coming in—on 'Swan Lake'? Oh! And a gazebo in the middle that looks like it's floating, with a wooden path out to it over the water?" Her grin gets even bigger. Felicia sometimes forgets that the reason she took this job—aside from the obvious—is because she wanted a purpose in life. And spreading joy through beauty is her way of doing just that.

"What a marvelous idea!" Betty claps her hands together in a very Sean-like manner.

The two continue discussing plans. Felicia proposing most ideas and Betty encouraging her with her own excitement. As the day grows on, they take a break for lunch and Betty then leaves to make some phone calls to contractors. Felicia decides to head over to 'Eden' and work on some things around there.

As she drives the golf cart to the northeast corner of the property, Felicia reflects on how much she has going for her. Gratitude once again floods her system—still having difficulty believing that this is what she gets paid to do for a living. It is a beautiful day and she is headed to her peaceful place.

CHAPTER TWENTY-EIGHT

THE RADIO TURNS ON. *Friday I'm In Love* by The Cure starts playing.

Another amazing song to set the mood. I do a couple laps around the room, utilizing my best Robert Smith swagger—I have to say, it's improved drastically over the years.

It may not be Friday, but I definitely am in love! Not only with this music—but with my new life purpose. I think I've finally perfected it. Not that it wasn't close to perfect before because let's be honest— I'm incredible. Alas, the bag over the head idea is just genius! I feel it prepares my guests for what's to come—and I'm nothing if not a gracious host.

I take the bag off Rebecca's head.

"Good morning sunshine!"

She doesn't say anything. I take a few floating steps backward to assess her demeanor. Oh—she looks angry. But then again, she's always angry. I shrug my shoulders while still dancing, not missing a beat.

Enjoying life is the only thing that matters. We get one life. One. The suffering going on in the world today astounds me. No one should have to suffer. I'm doing my part. I just wish other people would do theirs. This is the burden I carry that I am selflessly trying to lighten as best I can.

"How are we feeling today?"

"I'm feeling like I'm going to rip your fucking head off you psychopath!" Rebecca struggles in her bindings. "You're fucking crazy!"

So angry!

I slap her across the face. This behavior, I do not deserve. I'm helping people. Why can't she see that? I really had high hopes for this one too, but she will never learn. I prance across the room ignoring her potty mouth and instead tuning in to the music. She's not even worth my time—I know my value. Let's get this one over with. *Chop Chop*, I think to myself and laugh at my accidental pun. God I love my life.

CHAPTER TWENTY-NINE

DART IS SITTING AT his desk, reviewing all of his personal notes from the homicide investigation. He's been working some angles on his own without the county guys—nothing official. His gut is telling him they are missing something obvious.

He's spent some of his time conducting more interviews of those who know Tim well. He didn't go through the hassle of getting any subpoenas—nothing on the record. He is not the lead on this case. So he instead just had some friendly conversations with the interested parties. After so many years on the job, Dart has a knack for talking to people and getting them to casually reveal what he needs to know.

After having these conversations, he no longer likes Tim as the suspect. Something doesn't sit right about him, but he doesn't believe he set up his wife's murder to save himself the divorce money. He wouldn't have even had the resources to do such a thing.

Dart's been going in circles with this. He needs a break.

He leans back and stretches his arms overhead. He decides to get up to get himself another coffee. As he's walking to the coffee station, he is intercepted by Hibbs.

"Great! I was just coming to get you. I'm on my way to see Dumb and Dumber— I could use your help." Hibbs is shaking with excitement.

"What have I been telling you about tact, Hibbs?" Dart says in a low volume voice. "You can't walk around here shouting inappropriate nicknames for your superiors."

"Sorry—I'm wound up. You're not going to believe this." Shifting from foot to foot, he opens the folder he is carrying and puts it in Dart's hands. "Another missing person."

Dart reads over the paperwork.

"Okay, and what does this have to do with the homicide investigation? Why do you want to bring it to the County guys?"

"That's the insane part. This chick—she was reported missing by her girlfriend, Roselia. They're lesbos—if you can believe it. Anyway, this Roselia chick says she runs some kind of support group. Some weirdo shit held down the street at that witch store. They got all types of crazy going on down there."

Hibbs pauses to catch his breath. He is definitely excited. Dart wishes he would stop making offensive comments and get to his point. He's going to have to have a heart to heart with him before he lands in HR.

"So get this, the dude whose wife died—Tim—he goes to Roselia's group. She knows him well. But here's the extra kicker. That other dude—the missing army guy—she knows him too, he goes to one of their things. So this crazy witch chick has ties to all 3 missing people. That can't be a coincidence—right? I'm onto something?" Hibbs smiles with eyebrows raised, anxiously awaiting a reply.

"I'm not sure I like what you're implying. We have one missing person who turned into a homicide. And now two other missing persons. You mean to say that you think we're going to end up finding the bodies of the other two?"

"Of course! Its just too fucked to think anything else! We've got a serial killer in Newtown!" He leans closer to Dart, "and it's probably a witch!"

Dart abruptly—albeit gently—grabs Hibbs by the arm.

"I'm not going to tell you again, keep your voice down and show some respect. You can't walk around here screaming 'serial killer' and talking about witches. You've been watching too much TV. Stuff like that doesn't happen. You're not going to embarrass me by taking this to the County guys. I'm taking this file and you're taking a walk. Get outside, calm down, and then come back in and we can calmly talk this through."

Hibbs does as he's told and takes a walk. Dart does not enjoy reprimanding his guys, but sometimes it has to be done. He may have let his own emotions take over there for a minute. The thought that more people have been killed triggered him.

He lets out a breath, grabs a coffee, and heads back to his desk with the file. Dart needs to stop letting his emotions get to him and think this through like a detective. He flips his yellow legal pad open to a fresh sheet. He never even considered the missing person could be connected to the murder victim. He's going to have to sketch this down like his idol *Poirot*.

What do we know? He writes this down at the top of his blank page and underlines it three times. Crystal is reported missing by her husband in the middle of March. Three days later, her body is found. Mike is reported missing by his mother about a month later, in the middle of April. Nothing turned up during that investigation. Dart figures he just skipped town. Now—a little over a month later—Rebecca is reported missing by her girlfriend. He writes down each name and date. He tries to find anything that implies these three victims are related.

He taps his pen on the paper. Two women and one man. One straight married woman in her 30s, one straight single man in his 20s, one gay woman in her 30s. Crystal didn't have a job and neither did Mike—but Rebecca was the breadwinner with a great career. They all lived in the borough—but that's it—no pattern at all. Crystal's body was carelessly dumped in plain sight shortly after being reported missing. If Mike was murdered, they should have found his body by now.

Dart leans back in his chair. He stretches and then takes a sip of his coffee. He thinks. His gut is trying to tell him something—but he's had this feeling all day—even before Hibbs' news. He does not see how these missing persons have anything to do with his murder victim. He decides Hibbs is grabbing at straws. For now, he has to treat this new missing person as an unrelated incident. He will talk to the girlfriend Roselia and go from there.

There is a knock on his door.

"Come in." Dart yells through the metal.

Hibbs opens the door and sticks his head in.

"Hey. I think I'm good now." He abashedly mutters.

"Do you *think* you're good? Or are you good?"

"I'm good. I'm good."

"That's what I want to hear." Dart smiles. "Wanna go visit Roselia with me?"

"Sure thing."

Dart and Hibbs are on their way to the interview. They decided not to take the cruiser and instead go on foot. Roselia is at work—just a block from the precinct—and it's a beautiful day. The one thing Dart misses most about his time in Philly, is walking a beat on nice days.

They shortly arrive at Roselia's work and she escorts them out back for privacy from customers.

"I hope you don't mind—I asked Lisa to join us." Roselia motions to a young woman dressed in jeans, combat boots, and a musical band tee. Her face is soft—offsetting the hard style of her clothing. "She is a good friend of ours and also works here at the store."

"That's quite fine. The more information we can gather, the better."

Dart offers a friendly smile as the ladies take a seat on the garden bench. He begins, "I know you already filed a report with Officer Hibbs here, but I'd like to go over it again—see if there is anything else you can remember."

Dart flips open his notepad.

"You said Rebecca went missing on Tuesday night; she went for a walk and never came back?"

"Yes. It was the Full Strawberry Moon. Rebecca went for an evening walk to soak in its beauty and its power."

"Does she take walks in the evening often?"

"Every full moon. Rebecca was more in tune with the planets than anyone I've ever met. She liked to keep up on her healthy relationship by doing a walking meditation each cycle."

Dart glances to Hibbs to make sure he remembers the conversation they had about keeping his judgments to himself. He seems to be restraining himself well, but Dart knows he must be bursting at the seams.

"Does anyone know she engages in these routine walking meditations?"

"Well, sure. Just about all of our regular customers—not to mention all of the subscribers to our vlog."

Roselia sees that Dart looks confused. "We have a website, 'Raising your vibration with Rebecca and Roselia'. We upload videos of advice and tips on expanding your spiritual practices. Just last month we made one on moon phases."

Dart is scribbling in his notepad. The list of people with the opportunity to confront Rebecca is going to be large. Why do people post their lives on the internet?—a question for another time. With the lack of physical evidence, motive is the only thing that may help shine some light on whatever happened.

"I know Officer Hibbs asked you this before, but can you—or you Lisa—think of anyone who would want to harm Rebecca?"

"Of course not. Rebecca was loved by all." Roselia clasps her hands at her heart, closes her eyes, and bows her head.

"Well," Lisa says, "there are a few people I can think of who may feel less than fondly of her."

She looks over at Roselia with an apologetic shrug. She looks back to Dart.

"Rebecca has so much to offer, but she also can be a bit of a hot head. I know for a fact that a couple customers refuse to come into the store while she's working. Her vibe interferes with their peace."

"Do you know the names of these customers?"

"Well—sure—but they wouldn't harm her. They'd never harm anyone. They're pacifists. That's why her vibe bothers them so much. I just meant that she does rub certain people the wrong way."

"I'd like their contact information anyway if you don't mind. Maybe I could reach out to them just to talk."

"Their names are Sean and Mandy Eckles—but they don't really have contact information—they don't use cell phones and live in an RV. There are a couple places they spend more time in than others, but they have no fixed address."

"Alrighty then."

Dart starts to write down their names and then crosses them out. *How can someone living today not have a cellphone?* He feels a headache coming on. This line of questioning is not working. He turns to Roselia.

"Is it possible that she just kept on walking? Went on an extended meditation of some kind? A retreat if you will."

Dart has heard of people withdrawing from society—like the Eckles seem to have done. He wouldn't be surprised to find out that's what has happened here. Rebecca'll probably show up in a couple weeks claiming to have met God.

"No. She just got back from one last month. Plus, she'd never leave without telling me. We're soul mates." Roselia straightens. "That's the other thing. We have a connection. I can feel her energy, even when she is not around. And I know something horrible happened. Just like what happened to Tim's poor wife. And Mike."

Roselia wipes away the single tear that has fallen down her cheek. Lisa puts a comforting hand on Roselia's shoulder and picks up the conversation.

"It's okay that you gentlemen don't understand the things we do around here—not everyone does—but Roselia has a gift. If she says something horrible happened, something horrible happened. It's as simple as that. I, myself, personally worked with Mike on releasing his victim mentality. As much as I don't *want* to believe it, I also have no choice but to agree that something horrible happened to him as well."

Lisa looks into the eyes of both Dart and Hibbs to make sure she hasn't lost them. Dart is unreadable, but Hibbs is eager to learn more.

"Once Rebecca went missing, I sat with my spirit guides. They helped me to understand that we have an injured spirit in our town. Someone is going around hurting people under the false guise of salvation."

Dart is speechless. Hibbs takes over.

"I cannot comment on an ongoing investigation, but are you—"

Dart finds his voice and interrupts, he knows what Hibbs was just about to say.

"Officer Hibbs is correct. We cannot comment on ongoing investigations—which is good since we are not here about any existing cases." He glances at Hibbs. "So please—forget what he was just trying to say and instead answer this completely unrelated question." Dart is going to put Hibbs on parking ticket duty when they return to the station.

"Do you have any idea who this 'injured spirit' is? Did

your guides happen to give you a name?"

He cannot believe he's asking this, but this woman could be using 'spirit guides' as a cover because she actually knows more than she's saying and doesn't want to incriminate herself.

"Just an injured spirit. I can meditate more deeply on it and gather more information." Lisa has her eyes closed and is nodding to herself.

"Well— don't worry about doing that just yet," Dart closes his notebook and peers at Hibbs who looks—once again—like he is about to burst.

He turns back and addresses the woman. "Thank you for your time ladies. We will be in touch if and when we find anything out. Please do not hesitate to reach out to myself or Officer Hibbs should you feel the need."

"They don't believe us." Roselia says to Lisa—not caring that she said it loud enough to be heard by Dart and Hibbs.

Surprisingly, it is Hibbs who steps forward. He kneels down to bring himself level with Roselia.

"We are genuinely sorry for your loss and I assure you we will do everything to bring the person who harmed your soulmate to justice. Please just try to understand that we truly cannot discuss certain things with you. It's all politics—surely you can see that—but, rest assured, I hear you and believe you." He offers a warm smile.

He stands up hoping Dart will be proud of the tactfulness he just displayed—or at least wait until they are back to the station to ream him out.

"Have a good day ladies."

Dart now understands why all the ladies think Hibbs is a heartthrob—apparently he knows how to talk to women when he wants to. Maybe he won't put him on parking ticket duty after all.

CHAPTER THIRTY

"GOOD MORNING HUN, I made your favorite!" Sean is standing in the kitchen with a broad grin on his face. He loves doing nice things for his wife and the future mother of his child, "Belgium waffles with fresh berries!"

Nicole wanders to the table in a daze. The combination of her sensitive nose and never-ending ravenous hunger caused her to get up and come downstairs while still half asleep.

"Thanks babe," she manages in her stupor.

Sean places a plate down in front of her and she digs in.

"Anything you want to do today before I head over to the shelter?" Sean asks.

The food has fully awakened Nicole.

"I'd like to stop by the health food store if you wanna join me. I ran out of my herbs for the feet swelling yesterday—I already think I'm going to have to switch to flip flops—but I need to get more."

"Wonderful! I mean, not that your feet are swelling again, I just mean that I used the last of the buckwheat flour in these waffles, so I can pick up more. Afterwards, could we stop in across the street at Feeling & Healing? They're having a sale."

"Sure. I'm out of peppermint oil as well."

"Great!" Sean kisses his wife on the forehead and sits down across from her to eat his waffles.

"How are you feeling? I mean, aside from your feet."

"I'm just tired. Maybe I can pick up something today for that too. I dunno if anything will work though." Nicole takes another mouthful of food. Sean is a really great cook; she can't imagine being pregnant without him around to satiate her never ending appetite. "I've been having trouble falling asleep. Do I seem irritable to you?"

Together they made it through the mood swings at the beginning of this journey creating life—but just barely. Nicole has not been quite herself as of late. Sean has just been sending her healing light and otherwise not mentioning it; he's been afraid to. Now that she opened the door he feels he has no choice but to be honest with her.

"Now that you mention it—maybe a little?" Flashbacks of her earlier aggression sends a chill down Sean's spine. "But it's not a big deal."

"I guess not. I just feel like I was acting like a B word at the picnic. I feel bad. Like I should apologize to Felicia."

"Oh babe, if you were acting rude—which it didn't seem like to me—I'm sure Felicia understands. She knows you've been having some issues. I wouldn't worry about it now. If you still feel bad next time you see her, mention it then."

"You're right. I guess I'm overreacting." She pauses to consider. "What did you think of Charles?"

"Charles? Well—he didn't really say much—but I love his father! That man cracks me up! Such a free spirit!" Sean chuckles to himself remembering some of the things Ron had said and done.

"I know that you love Ron—we all know you love Ron. But with Charles, did you get any vibes that seemed off?"

"No."

Sean knows that Nicole has been overthinking everything lately. It started with the vision she can't seem to decipher. He doesn't like the fact that she's starting to not trust herself—which is all overthinking really is—but he can honestly say that he gets no bad vibes from Charles. Maybe she just needs to relax a bit.

"How about you go get ready for the day, take a nice long shower, and I'll get all this cleaned up and prepare you a special lunch for while I'm at the shelter."

"I guess I could do that. But what about Charles? What should we do?"

"Nothing, hun. We're going to try to let that go."

Nicole is not happy about this but she is excited about the special lunch. Sean is so good to her.

"Okay." She finishes her waffles and heads back upstairs to shower.

The health food store is walking distance from their home—much like everything in the borough. There are colorful flower pots lining the sidewalk and baskets hanging from the storefront with bright cheery blooms spilling over their sides. It always looks so beautiful this time of year.

The bells on the door chime as Nicole and Sean enter.

"Good morning!" Buck pops his head out from the back room when he hears the door. "Nicole, how's the pregnancy going?"

"It's going Buck...it's going. I need more herbs for swelling."

"Aw, sorry to hear. I'll grab them for you. Anything else?"

Buck is in his late 60s with the classic look of a hippie—from the actual hippie era.

"Sean needs buckwheat flour."

She glances over her shoulder and notices Sean is gone. "But I think he went off to grab it himself. Do you have anything that I can take to fall asleep at night?"

"Melatonin. Tried and true. I'll grab that as well. Anything else?"

"I think that's it, thanks. How's Nancy doing?"

"She's great. The grandkids have off from school so she gets to spend the day babysitting. She's in her own personal heaven."

"That's great. Excuse me while I go to try and find my husband. I'll meet you at the counter."

Nicole spins around and bumps directly into Sean. She looks up at him, "find it?"

"Yup!"

Sean has not only the buckwheat flower, but also several other things in his hands. He is like a kid in a candy store.

"How about you?"

"Buck's getting everything for me."

They browse a bit—Sean has to make two stops at the counter to unload, his arms were full from all the goodies he collected—and Buck is soon there with Nicole's items to ring them up. They pay, say goodbye to Buck—he wishes Nicole luck with her pregnancy—and proceed across the street to Feeling & Healing.

There is a somber feel in the store today. The ever present positive vibe seems to have left the building. Sean approaches the counter as Nicole roams to the back of the store to browse.

"Hey Willow," Sean says, "what's going on around here? I thought you guys were having a sale."

"We postponed it. With everything going on, it just isn't the right time." Willow has a bleak look on her face. "Did you hear about Rebecca?"

"No," Sean cocks his head to the side, "what about her?" A look of concern blossoms on his face.

"She's missing." Willow looks down as she shakes her head, "Roselia's a mess. She's not even here today. It's the first time she's ever taken off." She looks back to Sean. "Her and Lisa are preparing a vigil."

"A vigil? I thought you said she was missing."

"Roselia believes she has passed on."

Sean doesn't even question the accuracy of this, he knows Roselia is gifted.

"Oh my Gods and Goddesses. I am so sorry to hear."

"Sorry to hear what?" Nicole approaches behind him.

"Rebecca is missing and believed to have passed on." Sean states gently.

"That's terrible. What happened?"

Willow explains the events that took place and Roselia and Lisa's belief about a killer in Newtown. Nicole is shocked and worried at the same time. If there really is a killer, and they are hurting people associated with the store, should her and Sean be afraid?

"What do the police say?"

"Officially, they say these disappearances are unrelated to Tim's wife. Unofficially though—Roselia feels they are linking the missing persons with the murder and doing everything they can."

Sean has remained silent during Willow's explanation. He suddenly chimes in with a determined voice.

"We're going to need several selenite wands and a slew of black tourmaline." He winks at Nicole, "don't worry babe, I got this."

Nicole can't help but smile.

CHAPTER THIRTY-ONE

FELICIA IS STANDING OUTSIDE of her former job—Tony's—waiting for Charles; he and her are going out for dinner this evening. Felicia looks down at her phone. He's only three minutes late, but this is totally uncharacteristic for Charles. He is always not just on time, but early. She hasn't seen him since the picnic and she worries that his encounter with Nicole has scared him away a bit.

While Felicia is lost in thought, Charles appears.

She is simply stunning. Charles creeps up behind her and places his hands around her waist. Felicia startles for only a moment, before she realizes it's him and proceeds to snuggle into his embrace.

"For a moment there, I thought maybe I was getting stood up." Felicia offers playfully. She reaches up to give him a peck on his cheek. She breathes him in. "You smell good."

He squeezes her a little tighter.

"Thanks. Sorry I'm a bit late. My dad decided to choose this evening to tell me he wants to sell the business."

Felicia spins around to face Charles.

"Sell the business? What in the world for?"

"Oh, I have no idea. We really didn't get into it, I didn't want to keep you waiting."

"You're sweet, but I would have understood," She smirks, "after I worried myself sick thinking you were breaking up with me of course." Her smirk turns into a smile. "Let's go inside, I'm starving."

As they enter the restaurant, Felicia is pleasantly greeted by the familiar sights, sounds, and smells of her old job. She doesn't miss working at this place, but she is grateful for the time she spent here. They are seated at a table and the hostess tells them Kendall will be with them shortly.

"Great." Felicia says under her breath.

"What is it?" Charles asks, truly interested.

"Nothing. Our server—Kendall. We never really got along. Just petty girl stuff, I think. She always just seemed to have it out for me. It's no big deal, really."

On cue, Kendall appears across the room. Her attempt to hide her eye-roll was not a very good one—she is rarely aware that her face is speaking her emotions more loudly than her words. But her customer service smile is back on her face by the time she arrives at the table.

"Good evening Felicia. It's nice to see you." She turns to Charles. "And who's this stud muffin?"

Felicia does an internal eye-roll—she is good at hiding her emotions when necessary.

"It's good to see you too, Kendall. This is my boyfriend Charles." Charles smiles warmly and offers Kendall a greeting.

"It's nice to meet you." Kendall gives Charles a long once-over. She turns back to Felicia as if her ogle never happened.

"How have you been? You liking your new job?" She quickly glances at Charles once again and then looks back, "You seem happy."

"I am loving it, thank you. And I am happy."

"We both are," Charles cuts in.

Kendall's less than subtle flirtations do not sit well with Charles. He places his hand over Felicia's.

"Ready to order, Love?"

They place their orders and Kendall begrudgingly leaves the table. Even though it was short, Felicia is grateful to be done with the small-talk.

"Thanks," says Felicia, "some people just rub me the wrong way."

"You're preaching to the choir." Charles chortles. "Speaking of—what did your sister and Sean have to say about me? I somehow managed to rub Nicole the wrong way."

"Ignore her. You're fine. She's just her. Always trying to protect me, whether I need it—or want it—or not. She holds my safety in higher regard than my happiness. She's always been that way. What can you do? She's family." Felicia shrugs.

"Yeah. Family." Charles purses his lips. "My father is starting to get on my last nerve. I love him dearly—obviously that goes without saying—but he's driving me insane. And now with this idea to sell the business?" Charles leaves the statement unfinished and blows out a breath. "I think I need a vacation."

"A vacation—what's that?" Felicia chuckles. "I haven't been on a vacation in years."

Charles appears to have gotten lost in thought.

"What?" Felicia asks him.

"Well, I was just thinking."

He pauses and nods his head up and down a few times.

"Yes. Let's do it. Let's go on a vacation," he pauses again, "This weekend."

"We can't just go on a vacation. That's not how things work."

"Why not? Harvey is more than capable of running the business while I'm away. I'm sure Betty will give you some time off—she loves you, ya know. Just something easy, a few days. We could buzz down the shore. A long weekend. My treat."

Felicia only has to think for a short moment.

"You know what, yeah. Let's do it." Felicia smiles. "I'll talk to Betty tomorrow."

Kendall comes back with their drink orders and informs them dinner will be out shortly. She lifts her eyebrows at Charles—more than likely not even realizing she keeps making these types of gestures.

"Can you believe her?" Felicia remarks.

"She's just trying to get under your skin. She can give me eyes all she wants. Any woman could," he leans in, "you're the only one for me."

"Oh, Charles. I cannot get enough of you. I'm so excited to be going on this trip! This was a fabulous idea!"

"I'm excited too. I just wish I didn't feel like I *needed* this break. I wish things would work themselves out a bit."

"They will. They always do." Felicia pauses a moment when she realizes that the statement she just made is true. Things have been working themselves out for her.

Some things just take a little longer than others.

"So!" Felicia smiles showing her teeth while raising and lowering her eyebrows. "Which shore do you want to go to?"

"I've always been partial to Cape May."

Charles and Felicia spend the next hour over dinner planning their trip.

Chapter Thirty-Two

Tonight's weather is perfect for Bridge Club. It is early enough in the day—and far enough along in the year—for the sun to still be shining when the ladies arrive at Joanne's.

This month Gladys has made cookies—four different varieties. Her husband not only did not retire as planned, but has been taking on extra hours with all the recent happenings. She therefore has a lot of extra time on her hands. She had to force herself to stop at four different kinds.

The wine has already been opened and the cards have been dealt.

"Sue, your hair looks wonderful!" Joanne says. The other ladies are a chorus of agreement. Sue now has purple streaks throughout her blonde hair.

"I thought I'd do something fun for the cruise." Sue shakes her head, showing off her tresses. "We leave this weekend." She smiles from ear to ear.

"I was going to plan a trip, but—as you all probably have surmised—my Dan did not end up retiring. He isn't even talking about doing it anymore. All he talks about is his work. Murder this. Missing person that. And that's only if he's even home," Gladys gripes.

"Oh sweetie, I'm sorry." Says Betty.

The group once again are a chorus of agreement.

"I still can't believe they haven't figured out who hurt Tim's wife. He's such a sweet man. I wish there was something we could do," Joanne says.

Gladys laughs to herself. "If you can believe it, I've been trying to solve these cases from home. I have a lot of free time. Not to mention a lot of experience."

"Experience?" Joanne & Sue say at the same time.

"Obviously," Gladys says as she pauses for effect. "I've read every Agatha Christie novel ever written. Some of them twice." She raises her eyebrows while smiling with all of her teeth. This statement causes a round of laughter.

"Oh I know! We should start our own amateur detective agency," Joanne adds between chuckles. She suddenly bursts out with an even louder laugh. "We could call ourselves 'Betty's Bitties'." She has tears in her eyes. So do the rest of the women.

"WWHD?" Sue awaits to see if anyone understands the reference. They all just look at her like she's nuts. Sue isn't a reader, but she owns every episode of Criminal Minds on DVD. A Christmas gift from her daughter who realized her mother will never keep up with electronic advancements and decided to embrace it instead of fighting it.

"What would Hotch do?" Sue finally offers when no one else says anything.

More laughter ensues.

"Let's get these cards out of the way. I'll get us some more wine," Joanne says while standing up to rearrange the table.

"You ladies are serious about this? I was just having a bit of fun in my spare time," remarks Gladys.

"Of course!" Betty states proudly. "Plus, do any of us really enjoy playing Bridge?" She looks around the room both fearful and expectant.

"Thank God somebody finally said it! I've just been coming all this time for the sweet treats, good wine, and great company." Sue exclaims, relieved.

"Amen!" The other three women shout in unison as they raise their glasses in the air. They somehow already managed to polish off their first bottle.

The table is quickly cleared and Betty is sitting with a pencil in her hand and pad of paper in front of her. The sun is starting to set and the room becomes filled with a red glow of light.

"Alright Gladys, tell us what you know."

Betty's Bitties spend the next two hours running through everything they know, coming up with possible ideas and connections. Laughter and playfulness take part in the evening just as much as actual work.

Betty has suggested a paranormal presence at least 3 separate times. Her idea of aliens was not shot down quite as quickly as that of a vampire or clown being the top suspect—but it was shot down nonetheless. This is not Derry and she needs to stop using Stephen King books as a guide.

Gladys tells them about the missing people who—even though Dan does not necessarily agree—may also have been abducted and murdered. She tells them about Roselia and the victim's connections to the store.

The conversation keeps jumping around the table.

After the comment about the store, Betty bluntly says, "Okay. So obviously it's a witch."

"Come on Betty." Joanne rolls her eyes. "You really need to stop with all the nonsense. No more Stephen King. Some of us are actually trying to solve this."

"First of all, my Stephen has never written a book about witches. Second of all, I apologize. I misspoke. I think wiccan is the accepted term."

"She actually might be onto something. It could be a devil worshiper or something like that. God only knows what goes on in that store," says Sue.

"No, I've been in there with my Julie. Those women are all really sweet."

Joanne gets stares from the other women. She has been known to think everyone is sweet. Even the man who was taking pictures of women undressing in the dermatologist's office and got arrested for it a few years back. She still couldn't believe it was true even after seeing his face on the front page of the paper. Not her sweet Bobby. She looks at the faces around her and sees she is not being believed.

"No, really. I asked Julie about it specifically because I was scared of voodoo. She assured me that no one there dabbles in the dark arts. That's the term you know—dark arts." Joanne says proudly.

"Dark arts or not, that store is definitely the key." Gladys brings a more serious note to the conversation. "Betty, write that down. I know we live in a tight knit community—and a lot of people know each other—but not many people visit that place. It's too much of a coincidence to mean nothing."

"Sorry, Joanne, I'm with Betty and Gladys on this one.

The store is definitely the key." Sue's words come out slurred. She is enjoying her wine a bit too much tonight. Joanne takes notice.

"Well gals, I think that's enough investigating for one night." Joanne stretches her back which makes an audible crack. "This was fun."

The ladies agree. They stand up from their seats and begin helping Joanne clean up.

After the cleaning is done, Joanne walks them all to the door as they say their goodbyes.

Betty arrives home and gazes out across her landscape and takes a moment to reflect on the evening. They all had a wonderful time, herself included; that in an inarguable fact. But the thought that this night is even possible due to the odd happenings in her area truly scares her. She's never felt unsafe in her home before; she makes sure to lock the deadbolt tonight as she closes the door.

Betty's thoughts then turn to Felicia. She knows Felicia doesn't watch the news or keep up on current events—bless her soul for being able to detach—but she probably has no idea that people are going missing around town. Betty searches for her phone and finds that it's dead. She doesn't understand that you can plug a dead phone into its charger, turn it back on, and make a call or send a text while it's plugged in. This night really has her worried, so she decides it's not too invasive to swing by. It's 10pm. Betty herself may be tired—but it's not late for someone of Felicia's age.

She drives down to the cottage and happens to arrive at the exact time that Felicia is arriving home. Felicia hurries out of her car.

"Betty, hi, is everything okay?" She asks with concern. She is well aware that Betty is usually in bed by now.

"Everything is fine sweetheart, I didn't mean to startle you. We just finished Bridge Club and I wanted to swing by and make sure you were okay."

"Of course I'm okay. I'm just getting back from dinner with Charles." Felicia closes the door to her vehicle and approaches Betty's. "How was Bridge Club?"

"It turned into more of a detective club. Mind if I come in for a moment?"

"Not at all." Felicia walks to the cottage, opens the door, and steps inside. Betty notices she didn't need to unlock it—which makes her glad she decided to stop over here.

"I'm sorry—did you say detective club?"

Betty manages a small laugh.

"Yes. Gladys' husband is a police officer in Newtown Borough. We were discussing him not being able to retire and got a bit carried away."

"Oh, okay."

Felicia has no idea what Betty is talking about but decides it's better not to question what these ladies do during their one 'night out'. Plus, it's late.

"That's why I came down here. I'm probably just being a worrier, but I wanted to make sure you started locking your doors. A couple people have gone missing and I wanted to make sure you took some extra precautions. A beautiful young woman like you can't ever be too careful."

"Thanks, Betty. You're sweet." Felicia is warmed by Betty's concern about her. "I've felt so safe since I started living here. It never even crossed my mind that something bad could happen. I'll make sure to keep the doors locked."

"Great." Betty smiles. "I feel better already. How was your dinner? How's Charles?"

"Dinner was great. Charles is such a dream."

Felicia might as well ask Betty about the time off now, since she's here.

"He wants to take me to the shore for a long weekend. I hate to even ask—I haven't been here that long—but do you think it's possible I could take Friday off? Charles has been a bit stressed lately. He needs a break and wants me to join him."

"Of course you can. I know that man has his hands full with his father."

"Thank you, Betty. You're the best!"

Felicia leans over to give Betty a hug.

"It's my pleasure." Betty hugs her back. "When I heard Charles hired someone to run things, I was unsure whether he would actually start taking some time for himself. I'm glad to hear he is. Ron has never been the easiest man to be around—even while his wife was alive. I can't imagine how hard the past couple years have been on Charles."

"I never knew him before, so I can't really comment on that."

Felicia wishes she could have met Charles' mother, she seems like she was a great woman. Felicia continues on, "we didn't really discuss this much—Charles himself just found out a bit before our dinner—but Ron's decided he wants to sell the business."

"Oh poor Charles. Hopefully this is just a passing idea

Ron is having and he won't actually go through with it. He gets these ideas sometimes. Dot used to reign him in. One time, I remember, he thought it would be a good idea to hire entertainers for their funerals."

Felicia gives Betty a perplexed look.

"Yes, entertainers—as in clowns." Betty chuckles at the memory. "Ron hired a clown without telling anyone. A clown! For a funeral! His argument was that he thought it would cheer people up."

Betty looks down and shakes her head. "He meant well, that's for sure—he almost always does. Luckily, Dot saw him sneaking a clown in the back door and quickly sent him right back out before any of the mourners had a chance to see."

"That Ron does have a kind heart. He just doesn't quite understand what is appropriate at times."

"That's basically the gist of it. Dot used to keep him in line. They were such a great couple. A pot and a lid if there ever was one."

"That's what I've heard. He misses her so much."

"He does. He is still hurting. I just hope he doesn't hurt Charles by selling the business. What will Charles even do? He doesn't know anything else." Betty considers. She looks down and notices her watch. "Oh, would you look at the time? Way past my bedtime." She looks back to Felicia. "Charles will be fine. I'm glad you had a nice dinner and I am excited for you two to get away. I'm off to bed."

"Have a nice night, Betty. Thanks for stopping by."

Betty heads to the door and pauses at the threshold. She turns back to Felicia.

"Don't forget to lock this behind me."

"I won't. Goodnight, Betty."
"Goodnight."

CHAPTER THIRTY-THREE

"WELL ISN'T THIS A bitch?" Dart says to Hibbs as they stand behind the local wine and spirits. Two corpses lay in the same location in which Crystal's body was found. The trash men are going to want a raise if they have to keep calling in discovered bodies.

Two vehicles pull up as Hibbs is roping off the area with crime scene tape. A man and woman step out of a black Ford Explorer and open the hatch to gather their supplies for collecting evidence. They duck under the crime scene tape and quickly get to work.

Lewis and Bell exit their vehicle as well and head over towards Dart.

"What do we have here?" Lewis asks Dart, but Hibbs is the one who answers.

"These are our missing persons. Michael and Rebecca."

"This what the other body looked like when it was found? All covered in dirt and shit?" Bell asks.

"No," Dart responds, ignoring the fact that Bell should know the previous crime scene photos inside and out.

Bell was never really one for the finer details of things. Everyone always said the only reason he got this job was because of who he was related to. Dart never believed the rumor before—but he's starting to see why others did.

"She was not dirty, not like this."

"But it's obviously the same guy—right? I mean, same cuts across their throats, same dump site, it's gotta be." Hibbs says. "Man, I told you," he adds, under his breath.

Dart heard the comment and ignores it. It is not so much that he is feeling lenient today, it's simply the fact that he is mad at himself for not believing Hibbs' theory—or Roselia's—sooner. Now he feels like he has to play catch-up.

"I would have to agree with you. Hopefully the crime scene guys will find some evidence this time. There sure does seem to be more of it."

"Why do you think they're so dirty?" Lewis asks.

Dart looks to Hibbs, the answer seems obvious.

"You wanna take this one?"

"Yeah." He turns to Lewis and is about to start speaking as though to a three year old. Then, he hears Dart's voice in his head and decides to try a different approach.

"Well, I could be wrong, but—" *Tact*. "Since the first missing person was reported over a month ago, and judging by the state of decomp that can be smelled from here, I'd surmise they were previously buried and then dug up." He looks to Dart, "that what you were thinking?"

"That is exactly what I was thinking."

"Yikes," says Bell. "Why'd anyone wanna go and do something like that? Seems like a lot of work to me."

Dart can't believe these guys are the experts that were brought in to help.

"That's part of what we're here to figure out. My

first instinct says the smell was starting to get to him. Depending on how deep they were buried—or shallow rather—the smell has a good chance of seeping through the soil. I'm surprised it took this long, but we'll have to wait for the coroner's report to let us know the exact days of death. I'll see if I can get them to put a rush on it."

"Speaking of smell, I've had enough. I'm going back to the office," says Lewis.

"I'm with you on that," agrees Bell. "Call us when you hear anything."

Lewis and Bell hustle back to their vehicle and exit the area.

Hibbs sidles up next to Dart.

"Can you believe those guys? I mean, what exactly do they do?"

"Not our problem," Dart turns to the scene in front of them, "this is. If anyone is going to solve this, it's going to be us. Sure, those guys'll get the credit—life lesson—it's the nature of the beast. But we don't do it for the credit, Hibbs. Or the thanks; we do it for justice."

"Speak for yourself. I do it so I can intimidate people with a gun." Hibbs shrugs, "plus—chicks dig cops." He's smiling.

"Don't sell yourself short Hibbsy, I know you better than that. I know you're here because deep down you're a good guy and you want to make a difference. One day, maybe when you're older—or find yourself a nice woman to set you straight—you'll realize it and drop the facade."

Now Dart is smiling as well. He puts his hand on the back of Hibbs' neck and gives him a fatherly shake.

Back at the station, Dart and Hibbs are going over a new approach to the investigation now that it has, in fact, turned into a multiple homicide. Dart is still angry at himself for not pursuing this sooner. He tries not to let that get to him.

They stopped to see Michael's mother and Roselia on the way in—to advise them of their loved ones' deaths. Dart is normally good with these types of conversations and was proud of himself for not letting his personal anger interfere with his ability to console.

In case nothing turns up in regards to physical evidence, they decide to see if there is any solid link between the victims. Known associates—something more than just the store. They don't have much information to go on. It'll take some time to get the autopsy and evidence reports, so they might as well keep the fire burning while it's hot. They have no choice but to call this what it is—serial killings.

They decide to bring Tim in to talk at the station. Dart still has the nagging feeling that he is missing something obvious. In these types of situations, the first victim usually provides the most valuable information. Formal procedure is more important at this point as well. They don't want to find the perp and not be able to nail him due to some bureaucratic technicality. Dart knows that what a criminal does means nothing if they can't legally prove it. And lawyers seem to be getting more and more clever with each passing year.

"Not available until after five," Hibbs informs Dart after making the phone call to Tim. "But he agreed without a subpoena—so that's good. I didn't even need to tactfully threaten him," Hibbs grins, "he simply agreed to come in—just not until after work."

"That's good at least," Dart pauses, "and I'm sorry I gave you such a hard time about your serial killer theory when you first brought it up."

"No sweat. I've been working on it in my spare time anyway. Nothing could have prevented Rebecca's death. I haven't come up with anything that woulda helped—I believed that witch when she said she was already dead. This is just crazy, right?"

"Yeah. I've seen plenty of murders during my time in Philly, but never a serial."

"No experience with building a profile? That's what they do on TV shows. Is that what we should be doing?"

"Real life is not like TV. We don't just call in the FBI and let them take over. I mean, you see how helpful the county guys have been."

Dart closes his eyes and rubs his hands over his face. What is he missing?

"The 'why' is always the most important thing—motive. That's one thing that always holds up in both television and real life. And that's what we should be focusing on. Why were these victims murdered?"

The two officers sit in silence for awhile. Both of them are trying to get into the mind of a serial killer. Dart is using what he's learned from reading people and interacting with them over the years. Hibbs is using what he's learned from watching TV.

Their thoughts are interrupted by a knock on the door. Brianne pops her head in.

"A woman is here to see you— says her name is Lisa and she has information about the case. She asked for you specifically," she signals towards Hibbs.

Hibbs looks to Dart. "Go ahead," Darts says, "I should do some rounds. The worst thing would be to lessen our presence in the area right now. There are still plenty of living residents around here that need to be protected."

Hibbs follows Brianne out the door.

"Officer Hibbs, I'm so glad you're in. Can we talk somewhere?"

Lisa is cheery today. Hibbs' notices she is a good-looking woman. And she's much more attractive when she smiles.

"Sure. This way."

He leads her to the back of the station. They sit down in a secluded area.

"So what can you tell me?"

"I made a list," Lisa says, as she hands him a piece of paper. "I'm not sure what it is—I used automatic writing led by my spirit guides."

Hibbs looks down at the paper that is now in his hands. He scans it to see a list of people's names, including Tim's.

"Automatic writing?"

"It's a way to communicate with higher beings. I do it often, and when I noticed Tim's name on this particular list, I realized it may be important to the case. A list of victims past and future perhaps?"

"But Tim wasn't a victim." Hibbs looks at her, confused.

"Wasn't he? He lost his wife and has to live with that. In my opinion that makes me more of a victim than Crystal. She is in a better place—one where pain doesn't exist. Tim is the one who was left to suffer."

She's not entirely wrong. Hibbs scans the list again and notices a few names he recognizes. He notices something else.

"Why are they all men?"

"That, I cannot answer with certainty. I would imagine it could just be that my guides are naturally more in tune with masculine energy."

Hibbs considers the weirdness of the conversation he's having right now. He knows other departments have used psychics before, so he justifies to himself that this isn't all that strange.

"Could this be a list of people involved in the...the wrongdoings?"

"Anything is possible. The guides simply provide us with the messages. It is our job—on this side of the veil—to decipher their meanings."

Hibbs thanks Lisa for her time—not without offering a flirtatious smile—and also for bringing him this list. He is going to get an earful when he brings it up to Dart, but maybe since he didn't believe these ladies before and they turned out to be right, he may go easy on him.

CHAPTER THIRTY-FOUR

FELICIA AND CHARLES HAD a wonderful weekend getaway. They ended up going to Cape May. It was a magical time spent watching and listening to the waves of the ocean, soaking up the warmth of the sun dappled by the coolness of the passing clouds, and dining at the most exquisite restaurants the beach town has to offer. The long weekend flew by with a sense of ease and importance.

Monday morning at the nursery does nothing to remove the peace and wonder that has overtaken Felicia this past weekend. She hopes she never loses this sense of childlike awe when peering across the landscape that she gets to call home.

As she roams to the far corner of the property—known to her as Eden—she passes by a construction crew. Betty told her that today is the day they would be starting. She stops to make sure they know what they're doing and don't have any questions. She often has to remind herself that this is her job, to keep things running smoothly; it's not just to soak in the beauty of the nature that surrounds her.

"Good morning fellas!" She greets the workers as they turn to look at her. She sees a familiar face.

"Tim, Hi!"

"Good morning. Betty told me to expect check-ins from a young woman named Felicia. I had no idea it was you. How have you been?"

"I've been fantastic," Felicia thinks better than to ask Tim how he's been—she doesn't want to start an awkward conversation. Instead she says, "I didn't know you worked construction."

"Yup. More of a hybrid company really. Landscape construction. I built this company from the ground up. I used to mow lawns for the neighbors to make money as a kid. It just seemed like a no brainer to start my own landscaping business. I started off just mowing lawns, but then bought some heavy equipment. I noticed people not only wanted their lawns mowed, but ponds and pergolas built in their yards. I'm the only one stop shop in the area."

Felicia had no idea that Tim had his own company. Now it makes sense as to why Crystal didn't have to work.

"I'm glad to hear it. I apologize for being under informed, but I haven't had a chance to see Betty yet this morning. Where did she tell you to begin? We have so many ideas for the place, I'm not sure which ones Betty decided to do first."

"We're going to start with the floating walkway and sitting area in the pond. And the fountain, of course. Since it's a focal point when driving in, Betty thought it should take priority. But then we'll move onto the far northeast corner and methodically work our way down."

"Great!" Felicia looks around, "This is all so great! I'm excited that it's already starting."

"Hey, boss! The trencher is hitting rocks. We need you over here," one of the workers yells over the sound of heavy machinery.

Tim signals that he's heard with a nod.

"Duty calls. It was nice talking to you, Felicia. I'll see you around."

"Of course. Let me know if you need anything."

"Thanks."

Felicia resumes her journey to Eden. She arrives and takes in her surroundings. Finishing up the formal bed out front is on her agenda for today. She wants to have everything properly rooted in the ground before the heat of the summer kicks in. The days have been warming quickly and the dog days of summer will be here before she knows it. She makes some final additions to her notepad and heads over to the garden center portion of the property to pick up her list of plantings. She is loading up the golf cart as Betty comes around the corner.

"Felicia! Good morning!" she chimes.

"Good morning, Betty. I just spoke to Tim. I'm so excited that they are starting. I can't wait to see all the magic we're going to create."

"I am too! So incredibly excited!" Betty looks around and her eyes land on Felicia, "And look at your beautiful tan! How was your trip?"

"Amazing. I simply cannot believe that this is my life. I've never felt this way before and I love it."

"I'm so glad to hear it. You deserve it."

"Thanks. You know–I obviously have told you about my panic before—but I don't recall if I ever mentioned getting lost in my thoughts. It used to happen to me all the time. Like—seriously—*all* the time. Anymore, I feel like I'm getting lost living life instead. I can't thank you enough for all you have done for me."

"Oh Felicia, sweetie, all I did was give you a job that you are more than suited for." Betty offers a smile and a quick pinch of Felicia's arm. "What are you working on today?"

"I'm finishing up the formal garden in Eden. How about you?"

"Gerald is coming by so we can discuss getting the necessary permits for walking tours. He's been so excited about all of this as well. He says we should file with the historic district. I don't really understand all of it, but Gerald does, thank God. He gets excited about the most boring things." Betty chuckles.

"To each their own." Felicia shrugs.

"I'll let you get back to work."

"Thanks Betty."

Felicia resumes loading the cart and heads back over to Eden. After a few hours of sweat filled joy, Felicia's grumbling stomach tells her it's time for lunch.

She arrives back at her cottage and makes herself a sandwich. She's proud that she has graduated from eating pop tarts for breakfast and Cheetos for lunch. She hasn't yet figured out this whole cooking thing, but she has at least discovered how to make herself a somewhat proper meal.

She sends a quick text to Charles before resuming her work, just to say she's thinking about him, before she heads back out the door.

Felicia is driving the grounds and stops to check on

Tim and his crew. She finds Tim talking on his phone. He sees her and signals that he will only be a moment. She closes her eyes and soaks in some of the sunshine.

"Hey. Sorry about that; I was just confirming the lumber delivery," Tim says.

"No worries. How's everything going?"

"We had a few snags this morning but it's been smooth sailing since then. We'll have the footers down and the uprights set by the end of the day. Tomorrow you should be able to walk over the water." Tim smiles.

"Wow. You guys are efficient. I like that."

"We try," Tim says modestly. He pauses for a moment before continuing on, "and hey—I'm glad you stopped back. I was thinking, maybe you and I could grab dinner some time?"

Felicia is a bit taken back by this comment. She tries to hide her surprise.

"I'm sorry Tim. I'm seeing someone."

"Oh, okay." He has a dejected look on his face, but only for a short moment. He quickly recovers, "I guess I should get back to it. Enjoy your day!"

"Thanks, Tim. You too." Felicia continues driving on. *That was weird.*

Under normal circumstances, Felicia would not have been surprised to have been asked out. Afterall, she is a young and attractive woman. But this man's wife just was murdered. And as far as she knows, the killer has not even been found yet. Tim creeps her out. She gives a little shake. Her phone rings, it's Sean.

"Hello?"

"Felicia! I'm on my way to the hospital right now. Meet me there," Sean says in a frantic tone, "hurry!"

"What's going on?"

"I don't know. Nicole fainted at the store. They called to tell me an ambulance took her to the hospital. Just get there! Please!"

"I'm on my way."

CHAPTER THIRTY-FIVE

FELICIA CALLED BETTY ON her way to the hospital to let her know she was leaving. Betty completely understood; she told Felicia not to worry and to just go.

Felicia rushes through the maze of hallways and corridors in search of her sister. She turns a corner and spies Sean talking to a man in a white coat, presumably Nicole's doctor. She hurries to his side.

"Dr. Ashworth, this is my sister-in-law, Nicole's sister, Felicia."

"Nice to meet you."

Dr. Ashworth is a dark haired handsome man with a full head of hair—impressive for someone his age.

"I was explaining Nicole's situation with Sean. She's going to be fine, both her and the baby, but she will need to take extra care over the coming months. Sean will fill you in on the rest."

Dr. Ashworth nods to both Felicia and Sean and makes his exit.

"She's in here," Sean nods to the nearby room, "but since she's resting, we were speaking outside the room. We can go in, but just make sure to keep your voice down."

Felicia has never seen Sean so calm in all the time

she's known him. Apparently he does have an off switch.

"I'll behave." Felicia winks at Sean. The doctor's words have settled her down. He said her sister and unborn niece or nephew will be fine.

Seeing this side of Sean makes her love for him grow. She understands what her sister sees in him a bit better now.

They enter the room to see Nicole lazing peacefully on the bed. If not for the hospital setting, one would not think anything wrong. Sean takes a seat in the chair next to the bed.

"Hey guys," Nicole says with a peaceful smile on her face.

"Hey sis, how are you feeling?" Felicia pulls up another chair.

"The baby is fine, so I'm fine. The doctor says I just need to take it easy. Apparently, I've been stressed. Stress is not good for the baby. So I'm going to think calming thoughts."

"What have you been stressed about?" Felicia asks and she is interrupted by Sean; he gives Felicia a glare.

"We don't need to talk about that now," he says, "the important thing is, everyone is okay and will continue to be okay," Sean looks to his wife, "right?"

"Right."

Nicole closes her eyes and settles further into the bed.

Felicia doesn't know what to say. Sean called her to be here. But they seem to be doing fine without her. They're constantly telling her not to hide her feelings yet that seems to be exactly what is going on right now.

What could possibly have Nicole so stressed that she won't even talk about it? It doesn't matter. Nicole and the baby are fine, and that's what matters.

"Okay, well now that I see you're okay, I think I'm going to head back to work if you don't mind." Felicia stands.

"Thanks for coming to check on me. Sorry if I got everyone worried." Nicole stretches her arms forward to receive a hug from her sister.

"No worries. I'm glad you and the baby are both okay. Let me know if you need anything."

"I will. Thanks."

Sean walks Felicia to the door of the hospital room.

"Sorry I took you away from work. I got that phone call and panicked. I'd never been so scared in my life. I didn't know what to do."

"As I just said to Nicole, no worries. Really. I appreciate you calling."

Felicia embraces Sean and makes her way towards the exit. She wanted to ask him what has Nicole so stressed but thinks better of it. She honestly would rather be at work.

Felicia calls Betty again from her car to let her know Nicole and the baby are fine and she will be arriving back soon. During the short ride from the hospital, Felicia begins to ponder some things. It's interesting how different people all react so differently to negative situations. She saw Tim this morning, who recently lost his wife to a horrific crime, yet his world seems untouched; he even had the courage to ask her on a date. Sean simply received a phone call about his wife fainting and his world crumbled down in that moment. Yet, only a short time later, his life seems peaceful again. Nicole has been stressed enough to lose consciousness, yet lying in a hospital bed, she seems completely fine. Felicia wonders what goes on inside of people. Do we ever really know how others are feeling? Do we know what's going on behind the scenes? Is the person experiencing their own life even consciously aware?

She pulls up to her cottage and shuts off the car. A few short months ago, these questions in her internal dialog would have sent her spiraling. They would have taken control of her. Now, she simply opens the door, gets out of the car, and continues living her life. She is comforted by how much she's grown. She exits the vehicle—and her chain of thoughts—and jumps in the golf cart to head back out into the wondrous beauty of her surroundings.

Nicole is discharged from the hospital once all of her test results come back negative. The medical term for what she experienced is vasovagal syncope. It was simply a loss of oxygenated blood due to a drop in blood pressure from a stressful situation.

Nicole is settled comfortably on the couch at home with a warm cup of herbal tea. Since Nicole was in Feeling & Healing when the episode occurred, Sean feels he should head over there and let them know her and the baby are okay. Yet he is torn because he does not want to leave Nicole alone.

Nicole assures him that he cannot be with her one hundred percent of the time, and now is as good a time as any to leave. The chances of her having another episode this close to the last is slim to none. He agrees with this logic and also realizes he can ask the ladies down at the store if they wouldn't mind keeping an eye on her when he can't be home. It's right down the street and they always seem willing to help people in need. He kisses his wife and her belly—he's been doing this more and more lately, no matter how much Nicole protests—and heads out to Feeling & Healing.

Lisa is arriving on the porch entrance to the store at the same time as Sean.

"Oh my Goddess, Sean! How is Nicole? How is the baby?"

"They're both fine. She's home already. Relaxing. That's why I'm here. To let everyone know they're both okay. And to thank you all for coming to her rescue."

Lisa visibly relaxes.

"You're welcome! But we only did what anyone would have done in our position. One of us called nine-one-one while the rest joined hands and sent healing light."

"I'm so thankful you did," Sean hesitates, "But there is another reason I stopped by. Nicole needs to take it easy for the next few months. Stress is what the doctors say caused the episode. Frankly, I'm worried about leaving her alone. Do you think maybe you could rally up the troops and take turns checking in on her when I can't be around?"

"Of course! Willow has your number. We'll work out a schedule."

Lisa places her hand on Sean's arm. "You're not alone in this. We will be there when needed and sending light even when we are not around."

It's Sean's turn to visibly relax.

"Thank you so much."

He suddenly feels his old self again.

"Oh! Let me go in and grab some salt bath packets for Nicole!" He claps his hands and scuttles into the store.

Chapter Thirty-Six

"Hi Patricia, how are things going?" Charles has been out all day running errands for the parlor. This being after he already overslept. He hardly had time to say more than two words to his father before he left this morning.

"Just great Mr. Y!"

Charles accepts at this point that Patricia will never be able to adapt to calling him by his first name.

"Mr Baker is fantastic!"

Or calling anyone older than she by their first name.

As if on cue, Harvey walks in from the back.

"Hey Charles," Harvey pulls Charles into a bro-hug. This man is always in a pleasant mood, "how was your trip?"

"Great! Thanks for asking."

"I'm glad you enjoyed yourself. Did you get the supplies from the list I left on your desk?"

"Yes, thank you for that. You didn't have to do inventory while I was gone—it was only a couple days. It could have waited."

"Don't mention it boss; it's what I'm here for."

"I had to get some things myself. I had to go hand pick some specific selections for our client, Mrs. Lucas.

You know how picky she can be, so I went down to the distributor in person. The stuff from your list is still in my trunk."

"Great! I'll go get it."

Before Charles can tell Harvey he doesn't have to, he's whistling and strolling out the door.

Charles looks to Patricia.

"That guy really is fantastic, isn't he?"

"Yup!"

Charles starts down the hall—then something tugs at his instincts to pause.

"Anything happen that I should know about while I was gone?" he casually asks Patricia with one foot still hovering in the air, facing down the hall.

"Well," Patricia hesitates, not sure if he knows or not already. "Have you like, talked to your father yet?"

She has an apprehensive look on her face.

"Not really," Charles brings his lead foot back and walks towards her desk, "why?"

"Well," she hesitates again.

"What did he do? You can tell me."

Charles can feel his ears starting to flush from an increase in blood pressure. He cannot imagine what his father got into while he was gone.

"I mean, like, nothing happened per se. But he brought a few different people through here to look at the place this past weekend."

Patricia physically shrinks back. She perks up a bit, albeit apprehensively.

"But don't worry. Harvey and I scared them off."

"What exactly does 'scare them off' mean?"

Charles now feels the blood rushing to his face as

well. He thought his father was up to his antics again. He guesses he was wrong. He is sure that these two meant well, but he is terrified of what Patricia is capable of doing when she feels her job—and someone she cares about—is being threatened.

"Nothing too bad. The important thing is that it worked!" She smiles like a child then shrinks back again. "I just don't think your father was too happy."

The door opens and Harvey walks inside with his hands full—still whistling. He reads both Charles and Patricia's body language. He abruptly stops whistling and looks to Patricia.

"Did you tell him?"

"Maybe?"

Harvey turns towards Charles.

"It's no big deal. Trust me. Nobody was injured and the stains will eventually wash out."

He gives Patricia a wink, resumes his whistling, and continues strolling into the back without a care in the world.

Charles looks to Patricia for further explanation as the desk phone rings. She answers it, relieved to not have to explain what the stains were.

"Good afternoon, Yaniero Life Celebrations, how may I help you?" She offers a palms up shrug to Charles. He heads to his office.

Charles has been avoiding the conversation with his father about selling the business. They only spoke of it the one time prior to his date with Felicia last week. He thought if he just ignored it, it would go away; that his father wasn't serious about it anyway. Now that he hears his father is in fact serious about it, he cannot put off the conversation any longer.

Charles finishes up a few things around the office and looks at his phone. Somehow he lost track of time; it's already 7:00pm. This probably happened because as much as he knows he needs to have this conversation, he's dreading it. He may actively feel that it needs to be done, but subconsciously he is still putting it off. He shuts off all the lights and heads out the door.

The house is quiet. Charles expected to see his father in his usual spot on his recliner watching whatever garbage TV is on at this time of night. He's not here and the TV is off. Maybe he called it an early night. Charles walks down the short hall to his bedroom. The door is open. He peers in.

"Dad?" Not in here either. He heads back out to the kitchen. He pauses at the table and looks around. The dirty bowl from breakfast is still in the sink as well as a few used glasses.

He pulls out his cell and calls his father. He can hear the phone ringing down the hall. He walks towards the sound and sees his father's cell sitting on the nightstand, plugged into its charger at 100% battery life. Charles can feel his heart in his chest increasing in speed. *Settle down. He probably just went for a walk.* Ron is supposed to be getting exercise daily and it is a warm evening. Charles just wishes he would have taken his phone. His father rarely remembers it. Modern technology is not something Ron has ever embraced.

Charles makes himself dinner and sits at the table, expecting to see his father walk through the door at any moment. Moments turn into minutes and Charles has finished eating; still no sign of his father.

He looks at his phone. It's after 8:00pm. He begins to worry again. He doesn't want to overreact, but this is unlike his father. He may be an adult, and can come and go as he pleases, but he never has before.

Charles takes a few deep breaths to gather himself. Maybe Charles going away for a few days has changed his dad. Maybe he liked being on his own and is just gallivanting around town; or maybe he's mad at Charles for leaving, and this is his way of getting back at him. Either way, nothing to worry about.

Although, it couldn't hurt to take a ride around town and look for him.

No. It's nothing. He's a grown man.

Charles shakes off his worry as much as possible and tries to distract himself by watching television. He settles onto the couch and turns on the TV. The Phillies game is on. He didn't realize the season had started up again. *This explains it.* His father is probably down the street watching the game at one of the local sports bars. Charles puts down the remote and decides all is well. He'll watch the game too. This way, he and his father will have something to talk about when he gets home. Anything to avoid the needed conversation about selling the business.

Charles awakens to a light shining in his eyes. He takes in his surroundings and realizes he is still on the couch. He must've fallen asleep during the game. The light that woke him was that of the sun. He looks at his phone, 5:38am. He guesses his father must've seen him sleeping and not wanted to disturb him. *He could have at least turned off the television*. It's got the score ticker scrolling across the bottom of the screen. Phillies won, 5 to 2.

Charles shuts the television off, stretches—sleeping on the couch is never a good idea—and walks down the hall to the bathroom. His father's door is still ajar. He peers in and sees that no one has slept in the bed. Panic sets in.

Get a hold of yourself, Charles. Deep breaths. Charles calms down just enough so that he can think straight. He decides he is not overreacting. Maybe last night he was, but he isn't now.

He should notify the police. He doesn't think he should call nine-one-one to report his adult father missing—but he doesn't know what else to do. He grabs his phone sees it is at 3%. He never plugged it in last night. He rubs his temples. *I'll just walk down to the station. It's right down the street. Feels like a better option than calling nine-one-one anyway.* Charles does not even have to get dressed as he's still in his clothes from yesterday.

He walks outside and down the block and quickly arrives at the police department. It is not open; they don't get in until 7:00am. He had no idea police stations closed. There is, however, a non-emergency number listed on the door. Even though his phone's dying, he did bring it. It has enough of a charge to at least save the number. He enters it and heads back home.

He plugs his phone in and dials the non-emergency number. It rings and goes to voicemail. He leaves a message explaining what happened and hangs up.

He stares around the room. What is he supposed to do now? He takes some more much needed deep breaths.

He supposes he should put some fresh clothes on. There is no way he will shower and risk missing the return phone call from the police. He considers breakfast but his appetite is non-existent. It's barely 6:00am; he decides to head to the office to keep himself distracted until the police call.

At precisely seven on the mark, Charles' phone rings. "Hello?"

"Hello, Mr. Yaniero? This is Officer Dart from Newtown police department returning your call. I'd like to come speak to you in person, are you home?"

"No, but I can be in about 90 seconds, I'm at work."

"You're at the funeral home, correct?"

"Yes, I can meet you outside."

"I'll be there in less than five minutes."

"Thank you."

Charles shuts off the lights, locks up, and goes outside to meet officer Dart. A cruiser pulls in the lot before he steps a foot on the blacktop.

"Mr. Yaniero. Pleas tell me what happened," Dart says.

"Please, call me Charles," he takes a breath, "well, I got home from work and my father wasn't there." He points behind himself at the home he and his father share together. "Then I fell asleep on the couch and he still wasn't home when I woke up this morning. I understand that he's an adult, but this isn't like him. Something is wrong."

"I agree with your choice to call and I'm thankful you did it so soon."

As soon as Dart heard the message when he got in this morning he became worried. He can't help but think he's speaking to the son of victim number four. He

does not want to scare this man—just come right out
and tell him that his father could have potentially been
kidnapped by a serial killer—but he does want him to
know this could be a serious situation.

"Are you aware of the recent disappearances of a
couple folks from around here?"

"I heard something a while back. Did the missing
people ever turn up?" Charles shakes the cobwebs from
his head, he still isn't thinking clearly. "Sorry, I don't
understand what this has to do with my father."

"Maybe nothing. I do not want to worry you more
than you already are, but figuring out where your father
could be is extremely important. Time sensitive."

The timeline is not exact, but based on the time last
seen and the autopsy reports, all the victims appear to
have been held for a short period of time prior to their
death. Only a day or two.

"Perhaps we should go inside and sit down."

"I'm fine right here. What do the missing people have
to do with my father?"

Time sensitive? The blood tries to rush from Charles'
head with this thought, but his anger is keeping him
upright.

"Do you suspect the missing people were kidnapped?"
he doesn't even allow enough time for officer Dart to
answer as he nearly growls, "tell me!"

Dart was worried this might happen. He has never
had a conversation with Charles Yaniero personally, but
he's been known around town to have a bit of a temper.
Dart was so concerned about worrying him, that he
didn't even consider the fact that he could anger him. He
decides to lay it all out. Angry people do not like being

coddled.

"Yes. The people were kidnapped. We do not just *suspect* this, we *know* this. I cannot discuss private information on an ongoing investigation, but some information has gone public. Their bodies were discovered yesterday, the families have been notified and it's been on the news. They were abducted and then murdered. And the body count is up to three. And I'd like to see it stop at three, but I need your help. If, in fact, your father was taken by the same man, he has 48 hours to be found before being killed."

Charles wobbles, but once again remains upright.

Dart places his hand on Charles' elbow to steady him.

"I apologize for being so direct. But as I said, this is time sensitive. Perhaps we can go inside now. And sit down?"

Charles leads Dart into his home and their conversation resumes from the couch.

"Run me through what happened yesterday." Charles does. Dart follows up with the usual questions about who would want to harm his father and whether or not the door was locked or if anything was out of place.

There has never been a sign of any struggle, nor had any of the victims had their phones with them. This implies the victims not only left voluntarily, but in a hurry; a ruse of needed help is the working theory.

"Your father is much older and in less than ideal physical health than any of the previous victims. I don't mean any offense, but would he be capable of—or willing to—help someone if they asked for it?"

"Definitely not a stranger. I mean, he'll help Mrs. Swarz take packages inside; she's one of the neighbors who recently lost her husband. Or Mrs. Betsch, another widow, if she needs weeds pulled or her lawn mowed. But he's not the type to help just anybody out. Not to be crass, but he only helps those women because—and I quote—they have nice gams."

This is the same response Dart received about the other victims—well, not the nice gams part—but the general consensus was the victims would have helped people they knew, but it was questionable as to whether or not they'd help strangers. Two of the victims being women was the logic behind them not helping just anyone. Even trusting people know not to trust too much, especially not in the evening when you're a young woman alone. The working theory of needed help also consisted of a known party; someone the victims would have trusted. Not necessarily a friend that they'd invite into their home, but someone they knew enough to let their guard down.

"Okay. What I want you to do is make a list of anyone that your father would have trusted enough to go off with. List everybody. And I mean everybody. If he's friendly with the UPS guy, put him down."

"You can't possibly think it's Wayne. He's the nicest guy ever." Charles interrupts.

"I didn't mean to imply anything about Wayne. I just meant, be thorough. We have lists from the other victims' loved ones."

Dart does not mention the list from Lisa, even though the names match.

"Believe it or not, there are quite a few names that are on all the lists, so at this point we'd like your list to help us narrow it down more." Dart shrugs. "Living in a small friendly town means most people know each other."

"I guess it's not so friendly anymore," Charles says under his breath. Louder now, "sure, I'll get right on it."

"Thank you. In the meantime, I'll send out some extra guys to canvas the area. My partner and I have several interviews with persons of interest lined up for today. If you could just buzz by the station and drop that off when you're done, it would be a big help."

"Of course."

"We also expect more evidence off the latest victims. The County is supposed to send it over later today. We're definitely working hard. We're gonna get this guy."

"Thanks."

CHAPTER THIRTY-SEVEN

THE RADIO TURNS ON. *Broken Wings* by Mr. Mister starts playing.

Oh this is a good one. I twirl around the room feeling the power of the music coming alive inside me. I smile at Ron as I realize he isn't getting a chance to witness the profoundness of my movements with that bag over his head.

I gracefully prance over on my tiptoes to remove it—doing a couple of twirls along the way.

"Nice to see you, Ron. I hope you aren't too uncomfortable darling."

I'm not used to dealing with someone so fragile and I truly hope I am not making this too unpleasant for him. That's one of the reasons I chose this slower beat.

I sway my head and shoulders back and forth.

"I'm not uncomfortable," Ron smiles, "and I also ain't no dummy. I watch the news. I know what's about to happen. And I want to preemptively thank you for reuniting me with my wife."

"You're welcome, of course." *This guy gets it. Maybe wisdom truly does come with age.* "You understand that a life without joy is not one worth living."

I wink, "I knew I liked you, Ron."

"Not only that but think of the burden I'm imposing on my loved ones that are still here." Ron's smile turns wistful. "Let's get on with it, shall we?"

Something about what he just said isn't sitting right with me and I feel a twinge of anger.

"Is that what you think? You think you're a burden to your loved ones?"

"Well, yeah. I assumed that's mostly why you're doing this." Ron looks at me like it's obvious, "for Charles."

I feel the anger welling up inside of me. I try to focus back into the rhythm of the music to calm my nerves. I cannot do this if I'm angry. If I do it when I'm angry, it would make me a killer. I am not a killer. I am a savior. Ron notices the change in my demeanor.

"Was it something I said?" he asks, "or do you have to fart?" Ron chuckles.

His comment set off something else inside me besides anger. I allow this new sensation to come over me. I feel so stupid for not realizing it before. *Stupid. Stupid. Stupid.* I have to face it, I screwed up. This man is not unhappy. He knows how to live life and have fun. I somehow confused misery for selflessness. He is worried about his loved ones, not himself.

"Seriously now, what's going on?" Ron seems both confused and disappointed.

"Nothing, Ron. Nothing." I will not take this shining light from the world. "I guess we need to have a talk."

The radio turns off.

CHAPTER THIRTY-EIGHT

FELICIA PULLS INTO YANIERO'S with a flower delivery. She hasn't done a run since the seasonal employees came in, but she chooses to do it today. Yesterday had her out of sorts—with seeing Tim, and Nicole going to the hospital—so she wants to see Charles to help get her peace back; her usual stress relief tactics are not working.

She would have like to have seen Charles last night, but she was tired from the hectic day back to work. She hasn't even heard from him in over 24 hours. This doesn't worry her though. He probably also had a lot of work to catch up on. She gets out of the van and heads to the front of the parlor.

"Hi, Miss Gerhard. He hasn't been in today. Did he know you were stopping by? Want me to like, ring his cell for you?"

"Um, nah. That's okay, thanks."

Felicia is surprised to hear he's not at work. It confuses her for a moment, but she quickly regains her bearings.

"I'm here with a delivery. Can you meet me around back?"

"I'll send Harvey out to help you with it."

"Thanks."

Felicia doesn't even make it out the door before she texts Charles.

I'm at your place doing a delivery. Are you home? :)

I'm here. Need to see you. Come up when you're done

Felicia is interrupted by the rear door opening. Out walks Harvey.

"The infamous Felicia! Charles talks about you all the time. I feel like I know you already. How nice to actually meet you!"

Harvey wastes no time scooping Felicia up in a bear hug.

Felicia is laughing.

"I've heard wonderful things about you, as well. It is certainly my pleasure."

"How was your vacation? I know Charles had a great time, but what about you?"

How sweet is this guy? "I had a wonderful time as well; it was truly relaxing. A weekend in paradise," Felicia smiles, "thanks for asking."

"Don't mention it! Flowers in the back?"

"Yup!" Harvey's energetic personality is rubbing off on Felicia. He reminds her a bit of Sean. "You grab the flowers and I'll grab the packing slip out of the front for your signature!"

"Sounds like a plan, man!"

Harvey actually puts his hand up for a high five. Felicia enthusiastically slaps his palm. He brings the flowers inside and signs the paperwork.

"It was nice to meet you, Harvey. I'm going to go over and see Charles—just so you don't think anything is wrong if you see the van still parked out here."

"Thanks for the heads up. Enjoy the rest of your day!"

"You too!"

Felicia feels a bounce in her step as she heads to Charles' place. The door is cracked open, so she walks in and announces herself.

Charles is sitting at the kitchen table, writing. He gets up as soon as Felicia enters and is across the living room in what seems like a single stride. He embraces her and buries his face in the hair on the top of her head. She can feel him starting to shake as sobs are released. Felicia buries her face in his chest and holds him tighter. She has no idea what is happening and is thankful the sudden mood shift from her elation to this, doesn't knock her out of sorts.

Felicia knows this is not the time for questions, it is a time for solace. She gently rubs his back.

"It's okay. Whatever it is, it's okay." Charles' sobbing eases with each stroke of her hand until it has all but stopped. He leans back but does not loosen his arms from around her body.

"I'm so glad you're here," Charles exhales a breath that he feels as if he's been holding since last night. He looks Felicia directly in the eyes and gathers the courage that being in her presence gives him, "my father is missing."

"Oh my God, Charles," is all Felicia can manage.

"It gets worse. Let's sit down."

He leads her over to the couch without letting go of her.

"The police were here earlier. They believe he has been taken by a serial killer."

"Oh my God," Felicia says again. "Charles, I just...oh my God."

"The cop said they're getting a whole slew of new evidence today, that they're onto something, and that if the killer sticks to routine, there is at least 48 hours to find him."

"Oh my God, Charles," Felicia says for what will probably not be the last time today. "You seem so calm considering."

"No choice. I gotta stay positive. I was going to call you, but I've been making a list for the police since this morning. I just finished. I'm heading over to the station now."

"Let me get the van back to Betty so someone else can finish the deliveries. I'll come right back."

"It's okay." He kisses her. "I'm going to see if the police say I should be doing anything specific. If not, I'll drive around doing my own searching. There still is a chance that he's playing a prank on me to punish me for leaving him for the weekend."

"Well— still—do you want me to come?"

"It's really okay. I'm okay. I'll see what the police say. And if I do drive around and find him, I really don't think you'll want to be around for that." He smirks.

Felicia looks disappointed.

"Listen babe—you've already helped me like no one else can. I needed that cry and could not have done it without you here. You fill me with the courage I need to be vulnerable," he smiles, "so thank you.

"But now that I've gotten that release, it's done. Vulnerability is not what I need right now." He embraces Felicia and then pulls back for another kiss. "Plus I don't want to put any stress on you. That's not what people do to the ones they love and I love you more than I've ever loved anything or anyone."

Felicia is calmed by this. She always complains that people aren't there for her in the way she wants them to be. They do what they want and call it caring.

She will be there for Charles the way he wants her to be—even if she feels his needs don't match his wants. It's not for her to decide.

"I love you too, Charles." As she says this, she realizes she truly and fully does. And it doesn't scare her anymore.

CHAPTER THIRTY-NINE

THUNDERSTORMS SOUND IN THE distance. This evening is going to be a wet one.

Felicia decides to do a bit of cleaning around her cottage in order to keep herself occupied. She doesn't want to think about Charles or his father.

She's carrying a pile of dirty clothes to the washing machine and suddenly trips.

"Damnit!" she yells as she stumbles and drops the pile of clothes on the floor.

She lets out a sigh and looks over to see what she's tripped on. There is a box sticking out from under her bed. It must be something left over from her move—although she doesn't think she's missing anything and doesn't recall putting a box there.

She crawls over to the culprit, avoiding putting weight on her toe that is already turning black and blue. Felicia opens the box and peers inside.

What in the world is this? There are some items in the box in individual baggies. She picks up each item; a wristwatch, a wedding ring, a dog tag, and a pair of earrings.

Whose are these?

She starts to inspect each item. The wedding ring has

initials inscribed on the inside of the band: TS to CH 6-9-07. She expects the dog tag to have a name to match the initials, but it does not: Michael T Holt. Felicia then picks up the watch and the earrings but there's nothing remarkable about them.

Suddenly, there is a resounding boom and a bright flash, then silence.

The power goes out.

Felicia sits a minute waiting for it to go back on.

After a few moments and several thunderclaps later, she decides the power may be out for the night. *Just my luck. I guess I won't be doing any laundry tonight.* She rolls her eyes. She haphazardly shoves the items back in the box and begins crawling towards where she thinks she left her phone in order to use the flashlight.

At the exact moment she manages to get her phone in her hands, she hears a beep coming from the microwave as the power is restored. *Well, I guess I will be doing laundry after all.*

Felicia hates housework. She would rather be outside in the dirt instead of inside cleaning it up. She decides to listen to some music. Maybe that'll help lift her spirits and make these tasks less dreadful. She goes into her bedroom, plugs her phone in to make sure it doesn't die mid-song, and connects it to a portable Bluetooth speaker that she can slip into her pocket.

Felicia walks back into the living room and lets out a sigh. She is removing each item from the mantle in order to dust it thoroughly. This place needs a deep cleaning. She picks up a porcelain figurine that Nicole gave her as a housewarming gift when she moved out west. She flips it over and back again in her hand. *Huh, that's odd.*

This whole time I thought this was a rabbit, but now that I'm looking at it, I actually think it's a cat. Yeah, look at this tail. She rubs her finger over the back of the figure. *This isn't a fluffy ball, it's a long tail curled up into a ball shape. All these years, what was I thinking? This isn't a rabbit.*

A sudden wave comes over her. She feels her heartbeat in her ears. She feels as though she can't take in enough air. *Not this again. I can't be having a panic attack. I don't get these anymore. I'm in love, I'm happy. I'm cured. What is wrong with me?* She forces herself to do some breathing exercises.

It's not working.

She decides to try focusing on the music. She's heavily tapping her foot and thumping her hand on her thigh to the beat of Katy Perry's *Roar*. She's trying to focus on the beat to calm her body and her thoughts. The song ends and she has realized she is slightly calmer. The next song begins and she recognizes it as *Never Gonna Give You Up* by Rick Astley.

What the hell is this? I don't have any 80s music on my playlist. She goes into the bedroom to grab her phone and change the song.

Felicia rounds the bed to get her phone off the nightstand and stops dead in her tracks.

"Hello, Felicia. It's nice to see you again. Hmmm, how long has it been?"

Charles returns home from the police station. He closes the door, leans his forehead against it, and lets out a breath in an attempt to clear his head enough to figure out what to do next.

"Rough day?" Ron is sitting on the couch in the living room. He's munching on a bag of pretzels. "I bet it was nothing compared to mine. In fact, let's put a hundo on it." Ron grins and puts out his hand for a shake.

Charles runs over to his father, swats his outstretched hand away, and embraces him with all his strength.

"Dad, thank God you're okay."

Ron struggles to get out of the embrace.

"Okay. Okay. That's enough. I don't need to turn gay," he chuckles.

"Dad! I'm sorry. We thought you were kidnapped by the serial killer. I'm just coming home from the police station." Charles reaches into his pocket and pulls out his phone. "I better call the police and tell them you weren't."

"Uh. I'd wait on making that call. Just let me talk first."

"What, why?"

"Because I was."

"Was what?"

"Kidnapped by the serial killer. But I need to tell you something. It's time sensitive. Unfortunately, I can finally admit I'm not my young self anymore. It took me a hell of a lot longer than I would have liked to get back home."

Charles sits on the couch next to his father, ignoring the sound of pretzel crumbs being ground into the cushions.

"What do you mean you were kidnapped by the serial killer? And then what? What? I'm confused. You mean to tell me you escaped?"

"No. They let me go."

"They let you go? What does that mean?"

"Just shut up a minute, I've got more important things

to say."

Felicia gasps and holds in the breath. She opens her mouth to speak, but no words come.

"I never thought we'd be able to go this long without one another. I'm truly impressed." The intruder starts bobbing their head to the music.

This gesture allows Felicia to exhale and find her voice.

"How did you get here?"

"Wrong question, Felicia! Dance with me darling, celebrate the epiphany we had!"

"No. Stop. What do you want from me? I thought I was rid of you!"

"Oh Felicia, Felicia, Felicia. You know that was never going to be possible."

Felicia crumbles into herself. She truly believed she was rid of this. She had been healed. She starts sobbing.

"Stop crying!" The intruder screams. "You know I've always hated it when you cry! This is why I'm here. This is why I *have* to be here. You think you want to be rid of me? *Me*? It is *I* who will never be rid of *you*! You're weak and pathetic. You don't know how to enjoy life. Always moaning and complaining—*woe is me*. Look at you! Go ahead and look. Really look! All it takes is a stubbed toe or a thunderstorm and you crumble!"

"That's not true!" Felicia screams back through tears. "You have no idea what I've gone through! On the inside! No one does! The terror and pain that consumes me."

Felicia shakes her head as if she can shake away not only the thoughts in her head but the image before her. "Consumed me. Consumed, past tense. I'm better now.

Better! I don't need you anymore." She is panting heavily. "I just needed to find a peaceful job and someone to love me. I'm better now. I've just been confused a bit lately, but that's all. I'm better." She says this, trying to convince herself more than anyone else. "I don't need your help."

Laughter erupts in the room.

"Oh darling, I know you better than you know yourself. You think those things saved you? You think it was your new job and precious boyfriend?"

A pause.

"That's what you think *healed* you?"

More laughter.

"I am the one who healed you. I am the only one that can save you. Just like I did before with that pathetic ex of yours. Think about it!"

"No!"

The intruder advances and grabs Felicia by the throat so that their eyes are level with one another.

"Look at me!" There is a smirk to go along with these eyes. "Think." The hand lets her go.

Ron explains everything that happened over the past day. Charles sits on the couch next to his father, taking in all of this information. It's not hard for him to 'shut up' as his father requested, simply because he is in a state of shock. Shock eventually turns to understanding and then fear.

Charles rises from the couch. "Dad, I'm sorry, but I gotta go!"

"I know you do, son. Drive like you stole it," Ron winks.

The dancing resumes while Felicia collapses to the floor.

She thinks. She thinks about her new life. Her new job. Her new home. Her new boyfriend. She thinks about her ability to be present in the beauty of nature and truly enjoy her life. She thinks of the peace and joy that floods her whenever she is around Charles, her love. She thinks about how she no longer gets lost in her thoughts, losing precious time from her precious life. She thinks of the disappearance of her panic attacks and the additional loss of time that was consumed by them. With all of these thoughts, she is flooded with gratitude for who she has become. Suddenly a flash of terror flicks by.

Realization dawns. To whom or what does she owe her new sense of self? Her breath catches in her throat as the realization spreads. It's been too easy. She should have known. She'll never really be healed.

"Oh! Ding, ding, ding! I think she's got it. Yay, Felicia! Go ahead, you can say it."

"I will not."

"Why?"

"Because saying it out loud makes it real. Makes it true."

"Oh darling, stop being so dramatic. Denying things never makes them go away. The things we resist, persist. You haven't learned that by now?"

A sparkle catches Felicia's eyes. Tears of hope form in them. The sparkle seems to be calling her through her watery vision. She slowly advances on her knees to the sparkling glint. All in one motion, she picks up the knife.

Felicia has risen from her knees and is standing mere inches from the intruder. She now has strength behind her voice.

"I won't let you do this anymore. I won't let you hurt me or anyone else."

"You won't let me? Let me?"

Wild laughter fills the room as the intruder takes a step back.

"You think you have any say in this? Darling, I thought I told you to stop being dramatic. Come on, dance with me."

"No. You don't get to tell me what to do anymore."

Felicia smiles sweetly. "I used to actually think I could control you, be rid of you. I truly thought love would heal me. But now that I have it, I know it's not true," Felicia shrugs her shoulders, "and I realize there's only one thing left to do." She takes a step forward.

Charles opens his door before he even manages to shift into park. He's out of the car and doesn't even bother to knock as he bursts into Felicia's cottage.

"Felicia!" he screams when he doesn't see her in the living room. He pushes open the bedroom door and finds something blocking its movement. He looks down in horror and picks up his phone.

"911. Where is your emergency?"

EPILOGUE

THE VIEWING TAKES PLACE on a cloudy day at Yaniero's funeral parlor. Most of the town is present. There are a lot of people murmuring about it being wrong to have the funeral here— but neither Ron nor Charles are bothered by the utterances. The small room is packed. Police are present.

It is not often that a serial killer comes to town and is put on display for all to see.

Dart is here. He put in his resignation as soon as the killer was discovered—Gladys is already planning a cruise. Betty is here. She is sitting with Betty's Bitties, who have all come to pay their respects. Rosella, Lisa, and a few others from the store are here as well; linking hands to send healing light. Tim is also present—mostly to support his friends—Nicole and Sean; he volunteered to help them through Nicole's pregnancy. Their friendship is blossoming, he and Sean are thinking of forming a sound healing band. Nicole and Sean are sitting up front, next to Felicia.

Felicia is the only one not dressed in black.

She looks beautiful laid out in her coffin.

Consumed by peace.